HEAVEN ON EARTHA

DAISY M. JENKINS

Heaven on Eartha

Published by Wheatmark®
2030 East Speedway Boulevard, Suite 106
Tucson, Arizona 85719 USA
www.wheatmark.com

ISBN: 978-1-62787-861-6 (paperback)
ISBN: 978-1-62787-862-3 (ebook)
LCCN: 2020924285

Bulk ordering discounts are available through Wheatmark, Inc. For more information, email orders@wheatmark.com or call 1-888-934-0888.

This is a work of fiction. Names, characters, businesses, places, events and incidents are either the products of the author's imagination or used in a fictitious manner. Any resemblance to actual persons, living or dead, or actual events is purely coincidental.

Dedication

This book is dedicated to the wonderful women who have touched my life in so many meaningful ways. First of all, I pay tribute to my mother, Mrs. Daisy Strickland Bell, and my mother-in-law, Mrs. Jimmie Gipson Loftis. These amazing women worked as maids, cleaning white women's homes and helping raise white children, in addition to their own. They were highly intelligent and exuded dignity and incredible strength in very challenging times.

My dear sisters, the best in the whole wide world, have always been some of my strongest cheerleaders and supporters: Laura Peppetta, Edith Kelsey, Catherine Fisher, and Lucy Bell.

My wonderful nieces always bring joy to my life: Yvette Shields, Linda White, Gwendolyn Haley, Hillary White-Nash, Tesha Bell, Bekiwe Zabane, Stephanie Bell, Twynette Gordon, Adrienne Dickens, Tamara Kirk, Gayle Bell, Robin Fisher, April Jean, and Lanisha Jean. I won't name my host of great-nieces, but they know they're loved.

My sisters-in-law, Cynthia Bell and Dorothy Buster Bell, and my special daughters, Ferol Barnes and Cristina Roman Jenkins, are very dear to me.

My sister-friends are the women whom I chose as sisters: Vivian Montgomery, Rosetta Bullock, Sally Murray, June Smith, Carmen Marriott, Gail Dunlap, Lillian Brantley-Thompson, Ernestine Butcher, Bernice Harmon, Felicia Jackson, Wyllstyne "Styne" Hill, and Sherry Cook.

These are women who love life, family, and friends and have the faith and tenacity to go the extra mile, and then some, when they see a need. They are multigenerational and multitalented leaders, educators, entrepreneurs, innovators, social activists, advocates, and warriors. They are simply amazing!

Contents

1 The Planet Eartha

A rare display of triple rainbows colors the sky with arches of red, orange, yellow, green, blue, and violet once the sun kisses the droplets of water that linger after sheets of rain have fallen from dark skies. These brilliant rays replace the chill from the storm and wrap the planet Eartha in a warm hug. The air is fresh and washed of impurities, and an energizing blanket of dew drapes over the lush green terrain. Mountain bluebirds with gorgeous plumage flap their wings to shake off droplets and fly from their perches to the ground below as they search for insects and other delicacies.

As far as the eye can see, field after field of brightly colored, blooming flowers provides a visual feast, coupled with the intoxicating scents of roses, jasmine, lavender, and gardenias. The aromas complement each other, as if to say, *Our fragrances are even better together than separately.* A herd of fallow deer with dark chestnut coats and white spots race through the fields, playing hide-and-seek with each other. Some chase exotic butterflies with large, iridescent wings whose rows of orange, yellow, and black pigment look like hand-painted works of art with the most intricate designs. Their flight patterns tease the animals in a game that tall, stately trees observe, waving their branches with delight. The trees represent every species known to humankind. Banyan trees are dominant, with their huge size and rich brown bark. They join the magnificent queen palm, elegant aspen, deep mahogany, hardy oak, red maple, flowering dogwood, yellow birch, and other beautiful varietals that offer shelter from the sun's powerful rays and help maintain ecological balance.

Raging rivers filled with sky-blue waters plunge into deep ravines, creating thundering waterfalls that spread for miles. Turquoise streams meander along beds and banks, as colorful fish chase each other and hide from would-be predators. The larger fish, six feet long, form a barrier around the smaller ones, protecting their own.

Majestic mountains rise above the clouds to heights not visible to the eye. Some have white snowcaps that accentuate their beauty. In one range, a line of peaks of different heights resembles stairsteps into the sky. When the sun sets over the mountains, their dark brown hues change to a brilliant crimson. Scattered orange cumulus clouds float lazily in the atmosphere like puffy cotton as the day begins its journey to night. The mountain ranges create a protective boundary around a valley teeming with activity from all forms of life in Eartha's populated metropolis called Ecstasy.

For centuries, the Planet Eartha was one of the best-kept secrets of the universe, maintaining its isolation from other life forms in the galaxy. This secret was turned on its head when a spacecraft from Planet Earth carrying a team of five American women astronauts veered off course during an international mission into a different solar system. The legendary story the astronauts tell is that when their shuttle landed on Eartha, they were fearful about what they would find. As they used telescopic lenses to scan the landscape of a planet that looked much like Earth, they wondered if life existed out there. Was there a mixture of toxic gases in the atmosphere or enough oxygen to sustain human life? And if there were living beings on this planet, would they be hostile or welcoming?

As their oxygen supply ran extremely low, with about twenty hours remaining in their tanks, the women decided to take a chance and venture outside their spacecraft. Whether they'd die inside or outside it, they were sure that death was imminent. Just as they suited up to exit the vehicle and explore the terrain, they detected a barely audible sound: *thump, thump-thump, thump-thump-thump.* The hypnotic, rhythmic noise grew louder and louder, like iron fists banging against empty metal pots—*clang, clang-clang, CLANG-CLANG-CLANG*—until it sounded like a thousand sledgehammers hitting metal walls, again and again: *BANG, BANG-BANG, BANG-BANG-BANG; BANG, BANG-BANG, BANG-BANG-BANG.* The banging was so loud that pressure built up in the astronauts' ears and they began to feel faint. Just as they were losing consciousness from the unbearable noise, they reached out for each other's hands so they would be joined as one when their approaching death arrived. Fortunately for them, death took a detour.

They awaken several hours later, lying next to each other on five hospital beds, alone in a large room that resembles a laboratory with glass walls. A thick, foglike substance outside the walls hides from view whatever is out there. The astronauts are restrained in their beds with thick straps at their waists and feet, with gowns that cover their bodies. As each slowly wakes from her deep sleep, their captain, Bekiwe, best known as Beki, a South African immigrant to the United States, calls out to the other four women, "Are you okay?"

Lillian, from Ohio, says, "Yes, thank God, I'm okay."

Vivian, from California, answers, "Yes, I have a headache, but I'm fine."

Cristina, from Arizona, says, "Yes, I think I'm all right."

Gwen, from Massachusetts, says, "Yes, I'm okay, but I feel strange."

Lillian calls out, "What are these awful, puke-colored gowns we're wearing?"

Cristina, with slightly slurred speech, answers, "They look like hospital gowns. Where are we?"

Beki says, "I don't know, but I have a feeling we'll soon find out. I believe we're being watched. Someone or something is behind these glass walls. It may be premature to thank God, until we find out what's out there."

Suddenly, the glass walls begin to slowly rise, like the curtains before the first act of a Broadway play. Lillian immediately begins praying, "Lord, you said you'd never leave me or forsake me. I'm one of your children; please don't leave me now."

Beki turns toward Lillian and puts her finger to her lips to silence her. As fear permeates the room, each woman's heartbeat races in anticipation of the something or someone that could bring them unknown harm in an unknown world.

Then a voice coming from the ceiling begins speaking in perfect English, and the sound engulfs the room. "Greetings, beautiful sisters from another universe. We're so happy to see you. Please don't be afraid, for we wish you no harm. You are guests on Planet Eartha. After waiting for centuries for your arrival, we decided we could wait no longer, so we steered your vessel to our great planet. Welcome!"

Beki answers, "Thank you for welcoming us, but why are we restrained in these beds, and are you the ones who were making that awful noise in our spacecraft?"

The voice answers, "Ah, the beautiful sounds. They were part of our greeting. Our apologies for any problems they caused you. You would have perished if you had stepped out of your vessel without the proper preparation, and those sounds are part of the Eartha access ritual. It appears that you're fine now. We've monitored your vitals, and you're all in perfect shape. You were quite tired and dehydrated, but we took care of that."

Beki lifts her body as far as she can in her restraints and looks over at the other astronauts. She asks the voice, "Do you mind telling us what happens next? How long will we be confined to this room and these beds? We have no idea who you are and what will happen to us here. Even with your assurances, we have every reason to fear for our lives."

The voice responds, "We totally understand, and you will meet us shortly. In the meantime, you've been through a lot over the past few days, and your bodies need more rest. I assure you, once more, that we have no desire to harm you. We've had ample opportunity to do so over the past several months while you were orbiting the galaxy, but that has never been our intention. You're our guests, and we look forward to your getting to know us. We already know everything there is to know about each of you, which is why we brought you here. Now, we'll dim the lights and allow you to rest."

Beki begins to speak, but before she can utter a word, she suddenly feels very tired and wants only to sleep. She looks around and sees bobbing heads and heavy eyelids as the other astronauts succumb to the same urge. They almost simultaneously fall into a deep slumber.

They awake several hours later, feeling much more refreshed, and discover that they are now free of the restraints. The glass room is still fully enclosed, but they can now get out of their beds. They stand and stretch their bodies and reach out to hug each other. They immediately notice that they are wearing different clothing, not the green gowns they had on earlier. The new outfits are pale blue two-piece pajamas with drawstrings at the waist. The fabric is so soft that it feels like a warm hug all over their bodies. Vivian comments, "What is this material? I've never worn anything so comfortable."

Beki responds, "'Comfortable' is not the word I'd use right now. I worry that we were in such a deep sleep that we never felt anyone changing our clothes. It had to involve several people or other beings. Why did they bring us here? I certainly don't want to be used like a lab rat."

At that point, the walls begin to slowly rise again.

2 The Welcome

The rising glass walls stop halfway up, and the thick white haze slowly fades away to reveal twenty bare legs and feet that look the same as the astronauts' human legs and feet. They have varying shapes and colors, from long and slender and rich chocolate to short and muscular and the color of vanilla ice cream. The legs and feet stand in a perfectly straight line, pointed toward the rising walls. They don't move as the wall stops rising, and not a sound is audible besides the frightened astronauts' breathing. Their hearts pound in their ears, and each of them is paralyzed with fear about what awaits them from the legs and feet beyond the wall. Are there ten women, or could it be one beast with twenty legs and feet? Is someone or something playing with their imagination, and the legs and feet aren't even real?

The glass wall begins to slowly rise again and stops at the upper waists of ten beings clothed in matching, midlength, unbelted black dresses that look like Hawaiian muumuus. Their arms are now visible, too, and also look 100 percent human, whether they're slender, muscular, flabby, toned, or wrinkled with age. The arms hang loosely and unmoving beside each body, hands pointing downward.

The glass wall continues to rise and stops just above the heads of the ten women, revealing their faces. Each woman has an unreadable smile and physical features like those of the astronauts or any other woman from Planet Earth. They have hair of different colors and textures: brown French braids; one blond ponytail; one shaved head; one black Afro with reddish highlights; one shoulder-length brunette bob; one neat gray bun; salt-and-pepper dreadlocks; one waist-length, tousled red head; one black-and-blond pixie cut; and one long black ponytail. They wear no makeup or jewelry. Each woman has a natural beauty that is based not on physical appearance but on a palpable energy that arises from her inner self and radiates warmth and peacefulness.

The astronauts' anxiety begins to dissipate as they take in the aura of the ten women. While they notice the women's diverse and distinct physical features, they don't really think about their race—an omission that is unusual for humans from Planet Earth. Of the ten Eartha women, the astronauts later determine that two are Caucasian, two are of African descent, two are Asian, one is Native American, two are Hispanic, and one is mixed race. They would soon learn that race has nowhere the emphasis on Eartha as it does on Earth. As for gender . . . well, that's another story.

The glass wall begins to rise again and comes to a stop as it connects with the top of its upper frame. At this point, the thick haze behind the women begins to evaporate, revealing the skyline of what appears to be a sprawling metropolis. Its innovative architectural designs include sleek circular buildings in harmony with winding waterways. One bright red circular building rests on its side with a large center hole. Its multishaped windows are suspended from invisible steel wires, creating the illusion of floating panes.

The ten women walk over to a shelf lined with ten pairs of shoes and select the pair that belongs to each of them. The astronauts are still too afraid to move or speak as they watch the women putting on their shoes. Once the last of them is ready, the woman with the neat gray bun steps forward and begins to speak. As she does, the astronauts realize that hers is the voice they heard coming from the ceiling. "My dear sisters," she begins, "we hope you're well rested. I assured you earlier that we mean no harm to you. We've waited so long to see you and have studied you ever since we selected you for this voyage."

Beki can wait no longer and says, "You know us? You've studied us, and you said you steered our spaceship here? But how did this happen? Of all the beings in the galaxy, why did you choose the five of us?"

The women look at each other, and the one with the dreadlocks steps up to speak. "Beki, you're quite a leader, and we're honored to have you, Cristina, Lillian, Vivian, and Gwen as our guests. Each of you has accomplished so much, and we're especially pleased that you were selected to be part of the first all-female space crew in the United States. We know the work you put in and your commitment to a successful space mission."

Lillian raises her hand but doesn't wait for permission to speak. "If you know so much about us and the sacrifices we made for this mission, why did you steer us off course? It just doesn't make sense."

Dreadlocks and Gray Bun glance at each other, as if deciding who will respond to Lillian's question. The gray bun says, "Lillian, I'm sure nothing makes sense to you right now, but very soon you will have absolute clarity on why you're here. For now, we just ask for your patience and that you give us a chance to tell you about who we are. Until then, you must be famished. We'd like you to join us for dinner."

Gwen frowns as she says, "I'm relieved that you ladies don't look like the space aliens I had conjured up in my head, but we still don't know you, and we have no idea what kind of food you eat here on this planet. We may not even be able to eat it."

The women exchange glances again and start chuckling as Dreadlocks says, "Oh, don't worry, we know that a couple of you are vegans and the rest of you love steak, shrimp, chicken, roasted potatoes, and other food items that we enjoy here. We have important work for you to do, so we certainly didn't bring you here to poison you."

Blond Ponytail walks over to one of the large walls, with ten drawers embedded in it. She pulls open a couple of drawers, removes five sets of clothing for the astronauts, and issues the correct one to each. The astronauts look at each other with wide eyes as they receive their outfits. Cristina examines her black capris and tiger-print sleeveless top and asks, "How in the world do they know my size and that I love animal prints?"

Vivian looks down at the deep-purple midi dress hugging her hips and beams as she comments, "This is crazy. I don't think even my mother knows that my favorite color is deep purple. I love this dress, and it fits perfectly."

Beki asks, "How did you know that these outfits are

ones that we would have picked out for ourselves? How exactly do you know us so well?"

Gray Bun says, "I told you that we know each of you ladies very well. This is not the first time we've met you. But before we go any further, please get dressed, and we'll come back for you for dinner in one hour." Gray Bun points to the clock on the wall behind the beds and says, "The clock shows four forty-five p.m., so please be ready at five forty-five." She nods at the other nine women as a sign to exit, and they turn in unison and walk out of the room. As they step beyond the raised glass wall, it slowly begins to lower, until it meets the floor gently, once again enclosing the astronauts.

Gwen whispers, in case someone is listening, "What the hell just happened? They know the clothes we like and our sizes, and she said they've actually met us. This is downright creepy. Do you think the human appearance is a disguise by aliens to trick us? As hungry as I am, I'm not eating with them—absolutely no way!"

Beki shushes Gwen: "Shh, they can hear you. We need to be careful; I'm sure these walls have ears. Remember the top-secret sign language they taught us at the space academy? Let's use that for our communication from now on."

Cristina nods her head in agreement. "Great idea, Beki." She proceeds to sign the words "I'm so scared. There's something sinister about these women. They're putting on a friendly front, but, hell, we could be their dinner."

Beki signs, "Okay, let's not get carried away. We've survived this whole ordeal because we're strong women. Let's see what they want from us. And, Cristina, I don't think we're dinner tonight."

Lillian then signs, "I'm with Cristina. They can welcome us all they want, but I'm not eating a thing with those broads. Hell, the sister with the dreads reminds me of one of my homies from Ohio. No, I won't eat even if they have fried catfish and hush puppies." Lillian and Cristina then high-five each other.

Vivian joins in the conversation and signs, "I agree with Beki that we should wait and see what they want from us. I actually feel much better now that I've seen the women. They appear pretty harmless."

Gwen signs, "It's just like Vivian to side with Beki. Always the good soldier. Harmless? Really? Humph! You and Beki can eat with them while we watch you turn into a frog or, better yet, grow two heads."

They all laugh, and then Beki speaks out loud: "Okay, ladies, let's get dressed so we're ready for dinner when they come to get us."

Cristina signs, "I still think Gwen is right about them being aliens in disguise. You're walking in first, Captain Beki!"

Beki just shrugs her shoulders and smiles at Cristina.

They proceed to change into their issued clothing, shedding their blue pajamas. As she finishes dressing, Gwen signs, "I can't believe this outfit fits me so perfectly. It's as if they measured my body while I was asleep. And it's my favorite color. This is beyond scary!"

3 The Grand Buffet

The front glass wall rises slowly at exactly 5:45 p.m., and in walk Brown French Braids and Blond Ponytail. Ponytail has a lukewarm smile on her face, and Braids forces the same as she asks, "Ready, ladies? Dinner is ready, so let's not keep the others waiting." She turns toward Ponytail and begins walking out. Ponytail stands to the side and remains in the room as the astronauts walk past her.

Beki hesitates before stepping beyond the wall and exchanges looks with the other astronauts, whose wide, unblinking eyes are all directed at her. Without speaking a word, they convey a strong message that they trust her to lead the group into this new phase of their journey.

As if reading Beki's mind, Braids stops walking down the long hallway, turns to Beki, and says, "Please don't be afraid. No one is going to harm you."

She then turns and walks at a slightly faster pace, with Beki behind her, then Vivian. Cristina and Lillian walk almost shoulder to shoulder behind Vivian, and Gwen brings up the rear, followed by Ponytail. Gwen keeps looking back at her, but Ponytail never changes her facial expression and looks straight ahead.

As the astronauts walk through the long hallway, there is no haze and they are mesmerized by their unobstructed view of the city lights from the floor-to-ceiling windows that line the outer walls. The night sky is filled with twinkling stars dancing in a highly choreographed light show. Shining brightly nearby is a blue moon with a ring of silver around it. It looks similar to a round turquoise stone like those found in the Southwest on Earth, mounted in a polished sterling silver ring. Cristina has to grab Lillian's arm to steady herself when she almost loses her balance while caught up in the allure of the spectacle. Lillian helps to steady her and then gives her one of those *Girl, don't you dare fall and take me down with you* looks.

French Braids makes a right turn as they come to the end of the hallway, and they step into an elegant room with dark hardwood floors and one wall covered with embroidered images of diverse women walking in a lush garden. The astronauts gape at a giant glass wall that provides a 360-degree view of the city skyline. The wall is perfectly clear, with no sign of a smudge or even the tiniest fingerprint, and there is no reflection in it from the room's lights. The five women have an incredible feeling of openness, as if they can literally step out into the sky and dance with the twinkling stars.

The other eight women are seated in bright orange and teal upholstered armchairs around a large, U-shaped table made of a material resembling dark mahogany. Around the table's midsection are five place settings reserved for the astronauts. Gray Bun, seated at one end of the table, opposite Dreadlocks at the other end, stands and greets the astronauts warmly at the entrance to the room. The other women follow suit. Then Gray Bun says, "Please come in and take your seats." She points at the astronauts' designated places, and they take their seats along with the ten women.

Gray Bun speaks in a manner with which one would call a meeting to order: "First of all, thank you for joining us for dinner. We have prepared a feast that we hope you will enjoy."

Lillian and Cristina steal quick, furtive glances at each other to confirm that there's no way they are partaking in this meal.

Gray Bun continues, "Of course, we have lots to share with you tonight, but first, we owe you the courtesy of sharing our names, since we already know yours. We'll go around the table and introduce ourselves. I'll start: I'm Edith."

Salt-and-Pepper Dreadlocks follows with, "Welcome, all of you. I'm Brooke."

Brown French Braids says, "Hello, ladies. I'm Robin."

Blond Ponytail says, "Hi, I'm Gail."

Shaved Head says, "Hey, ladies, I'm April."

Red-Highlighted Black Afro nods and says, "Greetings. I'm Felicia."

Waist-Length, Tousled Red Head says, "Hello, I'm Carmen."

Black-and-Blond Pixie Cut says, "Welcome to Eartha. I'm Lucy."

Shoulder-Length Brunette says, "Hello, I'm Laura."

Long Black Ponytail says, "Greetings, astronauts. I'm Catherine."

Beki nods at the ten women and says, "It's great to meet you all. We were talking earlier about how we were looking forward to dinner tonight. Weren't we, ladies?" The astronauts look at each other as if to conjure up the right response among them and then rapidly nod their heads in agreement.

What happens next leaves the astronauts with open mouths and wide eyes. Edith calls out, "Catherine, please share a special greeting with our guests."

Catherine turns to Laura and begins signing, in the astronauts' top-secret language, "I promise we're not going to poison you, and for sure you won't turn into a frog or become a two-headed monster if you dine with us."

The astronauts are speechless. Brooke chuckles while looking at Lillian as she signs, "We even have the best catfish and hush puppies. I'm not sure if anyone likes them, though—unless she has homies from Ohio."

Lillian looks down at her hands, and her face flushes.

At this point, Beki leans forward, tightly grabbing her chair arms with both hands, and her voice becomes high-pitched as she squeals, "You've welcomed us, yet you have us under a microscope and you're monitoring our every move. I'm sorry, but that doesn't feel right. Actually, I'm not sorry. What do you want from us, and how long are you going to hold us captive? This is downright humiliating."

Edith shifts in her seat and says, "Beki, you're right, and I apologize for the close surveillance, but it was necessary to continue learning about you—"

Cristina interrupts her, saying, "But you said you already know everything about us. If that's the case, why do you need to keep spying on us?"

Edith continues, "We have lots of information on all of you, but there are still things we're trying to sort out. For example, how do you act physically and emotionally under pressure? Are you still a close-knit team under stress? Who is most capable of helping us with our mission?"

Brooke joins in, adding, "Why don't we have dinner, and then we can further explain our mission and the help we need from you?"

Edith nods and looks off to one side, as if sending a signal to an invisible party.

The rear wall opens up to reveal a magnificent buffet with aromas that tempt even the die-hard astronauts who were adamant that they wouldn't eat the food. All of the Eartha women get up from their chairs, walk over to the buffet areas, and begin making their food selections. Beki and Vivian exchange glances as they get up and take in the most amazing culinary display they've ever seen. After helping themselves to delicate china plates, they first walk toward an array of fruit featuring bright yellow pineapple florets; red, black, and green seedless grapes; red and yellow seedless watermelon slices; pale orange and yellow mangoes; green honeydew melon slices; rich orange papaya halves; and other tropical fruit selections. They decide to sample some of the fruit before trying any of the other food, and make their selections from these luscious delicacies.

After walking back to her seat, closely observed by Cristina, Gwen, and Lillian, Beki takes a bite of the pineapple. The look of pure pleasure on her face speaks volumes. She says, "Oh my God, this is the sweetest pineapple I've ever tasted." She then samples the mangoes and is equally pleased. "I've never had mangoes this delicious."

Vivian samples the red watermelon and papaya, then joins Beki's audible, nonverbal displays of enjoyment: "Um, um, I don't even have words to describe how good this fruit tastes." Looking at Cristina, Gwen, and Lillian, she says, "You sure you don't want to eat something? This fruit is amazing."

Having watched Beki's and Vivian's reactions, the Eartha women, their eyes moving back and forth from their plates of food to Lillian, Gwen, and Cristina, seem to be waiting to see if the other three astronauts will decide to sample the buffet. Gwen keeps looking at the beautiful fruit and finally says, "You know what, I really don't want to offend our hosts, because who knows—they may become angry if we don't eat something. I think I'll grab a bite, just to be sociable. We can't let Beki and Vivian get all the brownie points. You guys want to go with me?"

Cristina and Lillian respond, "Oh, what the heck. We might as well."

Edith and Brooke are paying close attention but show no outward expression of interest.

Lillian grabs a delicate plate and runs her fingers around the decorative edge of the fine china. The next thing that catches her attention is in the meat-and-seafood section of the massive buffet. There sits a large platter of perfectly fried catfish surrounded by delectable-looking hush puppies.

As if drawn by a very strong magnet, Lillian bypasses the fruit and heads straight to the catfish and hush puppies. The aroma reminds her of her mother frying catfish in the kitchen and rolling balls of hush puppies with cornmeal and onions that she cooked in the fat with the fish so their flavors could marry. Lillian adds fish and hush puppies to her plate, as well as several spears of perfectly steamed asparagus. She can't wait to get back to the table, and when she sees that all of the women are engaged in conversation, she decides to discreetly sample a hush puppy.

She quickly pops one into her mouth, feeling assured that no one is looking. All of a sudden, her knees buckle and she has to grab the table to steady herself. The taste is so incredibly delicious that it literally brings tears to her eyes. Before she knows it, she has grabbed another one, and then another. Cristina looks over at Lillian, sees what is happening, and quickly walks over and whispers, "Are you really going to eat the platter of hush puppies while you're standing here? Why don't you take the food on your plate—what's left of it—and eat it at the table, instead of standing here eating like a heathen? These women are watching you, probably waiting for you to turn into a hush puppy. It's so embarrassing."

Lillian looks over at the table, and heads quickly turn away, but she catches a smile on every face, except for Beki's and Vivian's; they are as embarrassed as Cristina. Cristina, glancing over at Lillian's and Gwen's plates, is all smiles when she catches a whiff of her favorite Cornish hens with garlic butter sauce. She adds two of the delicacies to her plate, along with sautéed butternut squash, wild rice, and a warm, buttered roll. She quickly looks around to see who's watching, then grabs one more roll.

Lillian adds a few more hush puppies to her plate, and then she and Cristina join the others at the table. Beki and Vivian glare at Lillian as she takes her seat, but she's too preoccupied with her meal to let it bother her. Cristina, despite her claims that she wasn't going to eat any of the food, savors and devours every morsel. Her favorite dish, garlic butter shrimp scampi, is one of the items on the buffet. Gwen, although she demonstrates more finesse than Lillian, also has a heaping plate of scampi and, to her fellow astronauts' surprise, goes back for seconds. When she pulls out her chair next to Lillian, Lillian looks at her and says, "I guess you and I might turn into something weird tonight, but we'll be able to say that we enjoyed our last meal. Girl, you are killing that scampi."

Gwen leans in to Lillian and whispers, "You should talk! At least I brought my food to the table."

Beki gets their attention and gives them a *You need to stop talking right now look,* as she presses a forefinger to her lips.

After everyone has eaten to their satisfaction, Edith stands up again and speaks to the group. "Special guests, I hope you enjoyed the buffet. I believe we had a food selection that you found most delightful; our aim was certainly to please. Now, if you would be kind enough to join me in the conference room, we can share information about why you were invited here. We have a mission that we think you'll be interested in supporting."

Beki exchanges looks with her sister astronauts and signals, by slowly rising from her chair, that they should join Edith. As she stands, she responds, "The buffet was absolutely delicious, and I think our enjoyment was obvious. We're anxious to know why you brought us here and what supporting your mission means for us."

4 THEY KNOW US

The astronauts follow Edith and the other Eartha women into a large, glass-walled conference room that affords yet another mesmerizing view of the turquoise moon and twinkling stars. As they watch the stars dancing around the moon, Brooke walks up to a keypad with several buttons. As she presses one of them, beige and brown panels slowly and silently come down from the ceiling and cover the glass walls. The astronauts' attention then diverts to an oblong, high-tech table with embedded interactive touchscreens. Each person in the room has an assigned seat with her name scrolling across an electronic banner. As Cristina walks over to her seat, her initial reaction is to reach out and touch her screen. She jumps back when her chair turns around and greets her: "Hello, Cristina, and welcome! Please be seated and let me know how I might adjust to make you most comfortable."

Beki and the others receive the same greetings as they approach their own chairs. Cristina reluctantly takes her seat, and the chair senses her anxiety and begins massaging her neck and back. She looks around to see if the others are having the same experience and sees Gwen smiling with similar delight.

Brooke walks up to the keypad and presses another button, and one wall becomes a massive projection screen. Edith begins the meeting by further introducing the Eartha women. "Ladies, we gave you our names, but I'd like to tell you more about the ten of us. We are Eartha's Supreme Highnesses and were elected by the women of our planet to lead our government. I am the Supreme Leader elected by the nine women seated with you. Eartha is a planet governed by women. Here, unlike in your nation, we hold fair elections and would never tolerate voter suppression or any unscrupulous means, including wealth, to determine who will govern. Every woman gets to vote here, and the ten women who get the majority of votes are elected to govern for a ten-year term. You'll learn much more about us in the days ahead, but I will now turn the meeting over to Lucy and April, who, along with some of the other women in the room, have spent considerable time on Planet Earth and, for the past two years in Earth time, in the United States. Oh, and one more important thing to share: We don't allow photographic equipment from other planets. It's useless anyway, because of our scrambling devices. We just want to make sure you're aware of this restriction."

Edith takes her seat, and April begins speaking. "Lucy and I were deployed to Earth—specifically, the United States—to learn about the women in your country. Women from Eartha have already visited other continents on Earth to learn about their treatment of women."

Cristina raises her hand and asks, "But why did you choose the United States?"

April responds, "We were most intrigued by how women were treated in the United States, and we learned so much during our visit. We saw women in power and what it took for them to assume power. The men in national leadership positions were some of the biggest cowards we've ever encountered."

Beki shifts in her seat and looks around, noticing that the other astronauts are nodding their heads in agreement as they listen to April.

April continues, "They throw around the document you call the Constitution as the basis for government by the people and for the people, but what we saw was a government ruled by a very small, unelected, wealthy segment of the population. We saw the very rich living in opulent mansions, and we also saw poverty in the form of people living in boxes on the streets. We saw scantily clad women, some in uncomfortably tight-fitting skirts and dresses, using their bodies and gyrating to win attention, money, and fame, literally prostituting their character."

Lillian squirms in her chair and, barely moving her lips, whispers softly to herself, "What's wrong with tight-fitting skirts?"

April doesn't appear to notice Lillian as she says, "We were appalled at the large numbers of women who were unhappy in their own skin, getting breast enlargements, face lifts, and injections in their rear ends—and some dare to suggest these are their natural bodies. People become multimillionaires and even billionaires feeding off the insecurities of women on your planet.

"We saw incredible injustice in your legal system toward poor people and people of color, especially Black people. It made us weep to see the number of Black males hauled off to jail and prison for minor crimes or no crimes at all, while the rich or friends of politicians with high-powered lawyers typically receive a light prison sentence or probation, even for a serious crime. Your highest courts pander to their wealthy and political allies, instead of being committed to being purveyors of true, equitable justice. Shame, shame!"

Gwen shakes her head in silent agreement and clasps her hands beneath her chin.

April takes a deep breath and continues, "Another one of the biggest concerns we had was about how your nation treats its children. The number of them living in poverty is unfathomable. Your nation is one of the richest on Earth, and we had a hard time comprehending how you could almost dehumanize your children. We heard so much about the "right to life," but once the children are born, some of the ones who yell the loudest about that right are eager to let them starve, become homeless, or be wards of your states. We also paid attention to the ongoing efforts by politicians to destroy public education, which has a devastating effect on the poor and on children of color. It appears to be one more tactic to fill your privatized prisons, which benefit wealthy shareholders."

Vivian's shoulders tighten, and she lowers her head as if she has to personally bear the shame.

Lucy jumps in and says, "We lived on the streets, we went into jails and prisons, and we went to your churches, which were equally appalling among everything else that we saw. We saw men and women who said they were called to preach the Gospel leading small and megachurches that preyed on their congregations to finance their extravagant lifestyles. It was disheartening to see poor people and elderly people on fixed incomes being told that it was God's will for them to contribute to the coffers of these men and women. Your nation is also supposed to be a Christian nation, but many of your religious leaders support politicians who lead lives that are totally counter to biblical teachings. They support leaders who mistreat the poor and people who don't look like them or speak the same language. They look the other way when they separate immigrant children from their parents and put them in cages. Some of those same religious leaders live ungodly lives and are guilty of the sexual sins they preach against from their holier-than-thou pulpits."

Gwen raises her hand and asks, "You know about our Bible?"

"Yes," Lucy says, "we've studied the Bible from cover to cover and concluded that these Christian leaders have no fear of your God. During our travels around your country, we also saw young girls and women, even boys, being rounded up as sex slaves and used by evil men and women to fulfill their sexual fantasies. We saw people living in squalor and exploited by wealthy slumlords. We also saw many good people who were dedicated to fighting injustice and committed to doing what's right, including helping others in need. We're not being judgmental, because you have a great nation. It's just that we abhor injustice, unkindness, and especially ill treatment of those who are powerless and experiencing life's struggles. We just don't have such negativity here, and the magnitude of its existence in your nation cut to the core of who we are as Earthans.

"Anyway," she continues, "you're probably wondering why we went on this mission to Planet Earth."

Beki smiles as she says, "Now I *know* you're mind readers, because that's exactly what I was thinking."

Lucy nods at Beki and replies, "April and I were sent to your country because part of our overall mission was to see if Eartha could help right some of the wrongs we've seen and studied about for several years in the United States and in other nations on your planet. The work that the five of you were doing and the struggles you endured to get funding for your mission really caught our attention. We especially liked the diversity of your crew, and as we got to know your hearts, we selected you to support our mission on Earth. To be truthful, we found it hard to believe that in your twenty-first century, some of your men were still questioning the ability of an all-female crew to travel into the galaxy. So we decided to fund your space mission, and that's why you're here with us."

The astronauts eye each other in disbelief and Beki quickly stands from her seat and literally shouts, "Hold on, now. Wait a minute! Our mission was funded by a wealthy businessman who had his sights set on joining a future space mission with our crew if this mission is successful. I'm not sure of your connection, but there's definitely a mix-up here. We spoke with the guy who funded our mission, and he was definitely not a woman."

At this point, Brooke touches her screen and brings up a video of what appears to be a busy beauty salon. She asks Beki, "Did that guy resemble anyone in this room?"

Beki pauses for a moment as she closely studies the screen and then responds, "Absolutely not, and please don't play games with us."

Brooke continues playing the video, which shows Gail

entering the salon. She first walks to the workstation of a woman in a navy-blue smock, who begins applying all over Gail's face a thin substance that transforms her from a woman with a blond ponytail into a handsome, middle-aged gentleman with a light brown mustache and beard.

Next, Gail next walks over to another woman, in a forest-green smock, and removes her clothes. The woman applies a white, creamy substance all over Gail's body, and it instantly begins turning her from a tall, willowy female into a short, muscular male. The woman then gives her a set of male clothing that fits her new body perfectly.

Gail's next stop is with a woman in a bright red smock, who sprays a yellow substance into her mouth, changing her voice from that of a soft-spoken female to a deep baritone.

Beki's mouth hangs open as the video ends with a full-body shot of Gail's transformation into the rich businessman who the astronauts were sure funded their space voyage.

5 Introduction to the Mission

Edith stands as April and Lucy take their seats, and speaks in a gentle tone to the astronauts. "We have the power to make positive change in people's lives, and you can help us do this on Earth, in your nation. We promise that we have no intention of harming anyone. We would like people from Earth to visit our planet and learn about how we have successfully eliminated sexism, racism, misogyny, and a host of other isms that April and Lucy shared with you from their visit on Earth. Of course, they didn't tell you anything that you didn't already know. Rest assured, your help with this mission will bring goodwill to millions of people in your nation. Would you like to hear more?"

Beki glances around at her fellow astronauts and takes in their raised eyebrows and eager facial expressions, as they lean forward in their chairs with anticipation. She then responds to Edith, "Yes, we'd like to hear more about the mission and what it means for us to help."

Edith claps her hands and says, "Wonderful! Felicia will share the details with you."

Felicia stands and walks to the front of the U-shaped table. She nods at Edith and then focuses directly on the astronauts as she says, "Ladies, this is one of the most important missions we've initiated in the past century. Your nation provides so many opportunities for Eartha to promote positive change, change that greatly improves the quality of—or even saves—lives. Our mission has basic decency and humanity at its core. It enables people from America to visit a planet that they know nothing about at this point. To support our mission's success, you will return to Earth and your nation and tell them about this beautiful planet, which so closely resembles your own. You will enthusiastically share with national media the details of your amazing visit and will let people know how much they will enjoy visiting Eartha, even more than any place they've ever visited on Earth. You will become Eartha's key ambassadors in America and globally. Additionally, you will provide the transportation for the first visitors to come to Eartha, with our help. We will coordinate future trips with your space program because the interest in coming here will be so great after the first visitors return home and share their experiences."

Gwen raises her hand and asks, "How are we going to do all this? For heaven's sake, we don't even know how we're going to get back to Earth. And now you want us to come back here after we leave? No way—that's out of the question. These space missions require enormous funding, and we have no remaining money. Do you plan to bankroll the entire program? Does Eartha have gold mines or endless amounts of wealth?"

As the other astronauts vigorously nod their heads

in agreement, Felicia walks closer to them and responds, "Money is not something we ever worry about on our planet, so you don't have to spend time worrying about funding. Look, I'm sure you want to go home. And, frankly, this is the only way you'll get to do that. Afterward, you'll make one more trip back to Eartha, and just as we got you here this time, we'll get you safely back home, too."

Beki says, "We don't know enough about Eartha to share much detail with people when we return home. What if they don't buy our stories?"

Brooke says, "We'll prepare you to speak, so you don't have to worry about that. We'll make sure you have access to every form of media known to humankind on Earth to spread the word about our great planet. You'll be very famous. Everyone will love you, and you'll be the darlings of not only your country but the world. People will hang on every work you speak. We'll make sure that you prosper in every way."

Gwen's not finished, though, and asks, with outstretched hands and a shoulder shrug, "How will we know who to bring back to Eartha? We can fit only a few people into a spaceship, and there are more than 330 million people in the United States."

Felicia nods her head and says, "Don't worry about that. We'll select the first visitors for the trip; we're talking about no more than five people. We'll provide very specific details and assist you in every way, including preparing your communication. We selected you to help with our mission because we know your capabilities and your strengths. You will never be alone on this journey."

Beki chimes in, "I'm sure I speak for all of us when I

say that this is totally new to us and that we're still in a bit of a fog about the Planet Eartha and, truthfully, about you ladies. We've heard about your visit to Earth and to our country, and we know we wouldn't be here without your intervention. But frankly, I'm downright scared about what might happen to us if we fail or make any misstep in support of your mission."

Edith stands and says, "We understand your concerns, but we assure you that if you follow our instructions, you won't fail. Think about it: We financed your space mission so we could bring you here. We know every detail about you, including your clothing preferences. We even know your secret sign language. Have you received any indication so far that you should doubt our ability to succeed with this mission? You must understand that 'failure' isn't a word in our language because we don't believe in it. We've actually never experienced it. And you will execute to perfection because we will be with you every step of the way."

Lillian raises her hand and asks, "What do you mean, you'll be with us every step of the way? Are you going back to Earth with us on our spaceship?"

Edith and the others exchange glances and smile as she answers Lillian, "We already have a presence on Earth, and, yes, some of us will always be with you. You won't know who or where we are, though. As we've said before, you are not alone in this effort. We will fully equip you for your roles upon your return to Earth. Remember, you will all greatly benefit from your support of this mission. But now it's getting late, so why don't we let you get some rest, and we'll start our preparations tomorrow? Ladies, we need to get you back to your quarters."

With slumped shoulders and downcast eyes, the astronauts are now too fearful to speak. A dark cloud of sadness hovers over them as they finally grasp the reality that they will return home but will no longer have control over their thoughts, their actions, or, basically, their lives. Brooke observes their grim demeanor and turns to them to offer some final words of encouragement: "Don't look so bewildered; you ladies have sad faces like the people I saw on Earth attending the funerals of their loved ones. I'll take you back to your room, and you'll soon see that everything will work out just fine."

The astronauts don't respond to Brooke's efforts to calm their fears. Their faces reflect the anguish over their assignment as they slowly walk back with her to their glass room. As they stop in front of the front wall, it rises, welcoming them back. With smiling eyes, Brooke pats Beki lightly on her right shoulder with long, slender fingers.

Beki glances up at Brooke with narrowed eyes and raises her hand, as if to brush Brooke's away, but suddenly changes her mind, for fear of Brooke's reaction. Instead, without looking back, she turns and leads her fellow astronauts into the glass room. Brooke pauses for a moment to watch the astronauts' get settled and then turns and hurries back down the long hallway.

6 FINALIZING THE PLAN

Brooke enters the massive mahogany conference room, where the other Supreme Highnesses are awaiting her return, and the wall lowers. Edith asks, "How are they? I know they don't trust us, and in spite of our best efforts at reassurance, they're not convinced that we mean them no harm. We could use our powers to impact their thoughts, their speech, and even their hearts, but I hope we can gain their confidence without having to do that."

Brooke answers, "I don't think so. I believe they're terrified of not getting back home and then even more concerned that if they do get home, they have to come back here. No, we'll have to use all of our powers to control this mission."

Carmen rises from her seat and responds, "As with other missions, this one will be successful because we will have total control. I don't mean to sound crass, but their feelings don't really matter. They will do exactly as we program them to do. That's the bottom line."

April frowns a little as she says, "I agree that we will

have total control, but let's not be too callous about the astronauts' feelings. You may not care about what other women are feeling, even if they're not from our planet, but I do."

Carmen rubs her chin in silence as she absorbs April's comments, and then says, "You're so right, my sister. Thank you for calling me out on that flippant remark. I stand corrected."

Brooke announces, "It's time to select our five guests from America. Carmen, you have our full attention." She then takes her seat. Carmen walks to the front of the room, where she touches a keypad and the large projection screen reappears, followed by a middle-aged man's round face with reddish cheeks. Carmen turns toward the screen, points to the man's face, and says, "Our first candidate is Judge Morcus Bottomy, juvenile court judge of Willow County, Alabama. Judge Bottomy has faithfully served in the juvenile court system for three decades. He's known as a very tough and prejudiced judge when dealing with young men of color. He routinely sentences Black youth to prison for minor crimes or no crimes at all, even if he has enough evidence to clear the charges against them. He's an avid contributor to the school-to-prison pipeline and is most deserving of being among the first group of guests. Other court officials often talk about the injustices he commits. One of his favorite depraved pleasures is to see Black mothers beg for leniency for their sons. He's known to laugh and say, 'You should have been a better parent. Now a detention center will be your son's new parent.' He's evil to the core."

Gail raises her hand to speak and says, "We'll give Judge Bottomy a special welcome. I can't fathom how such a cruel and evil man is actually a judge with the power to inflict harm on the futures of so many young males of color. I'm in total agreement about his being one of our five guests."

Carmen asks, "Are there any objections to Judge Bottomy's selection?" When no hands go up, she says, "Great—our first guest is confirmed. Felicia, why don't you present your candidate?" Carmen points her hand at the screen to advance to the next slide and then walks back to her seat.

Felicia rises and walks to the center of the room. She points at the screen, and a man with bronzed skin, perfectly chiseled facial features, and sky-blue eyes, who looks to be in his early forties, appears. Felicia says, "This is Mr. Wyatt Stone, a major movie producer. He comes across as a nice person but is actually one of the most notorious sex traffickers in America, and maybe even on Planet Earth. He has an international ring of handlers who kidnap young girls or lure young runaways, some as young as five years old, into his dangerous and highly profitable web. He sells most of his victims as sex slaves and saves a small number to be slave laborers. The interesting thing about this guy is that he has four young daughters and is known as an amazing dad who truly loves his girls. It's difficult to comprehend how he can be so protective of his own children and turn a blind eye to the hell he puts his captives through. He is truly the scum of the earth."

Catherine raises her hand and says, "Mr. Stone will be the perfect guest, and we will give him a special welcome."

Felicia asks, "Are there any objections to Mr. Stone's selection?" No hands are raised, and she smiles and says, "Okay, it's a done deal. Gail, it's your turn to speak about your candidate."

Gail walks quickly to the center of the room and waves her hand at the screen to advance to the next slide. A middle-aged woman appears on the screen with perfectly tanned facial features—high, sculpted cheekbones, a chiseled chin, and plump lips. Her face and body look like the results of several rounds of plastic surgery to control any signs of aging. She is wearing a skintight, backless, lace-up leopard dress with openings on the side that reveal a perfectly toned figure with a small waist that accents her full hips.

Gail begins to describe the woman on the wall. "Ladies, this is the most disgusting piece of human flesh that I had the displeasure of meeting during my time on Planet Earth. Her name is Ms. Sweetie Harris, and she is a fashion designer, entrepreneur, and predator. She peddles her brothel-style clothing line and skincare products to teenage girls. She has more than ten million young social media followers and uses body shaming and Photoshopped models to entice them to purchase her skincare products, clown-like makeup, and outlandishly risqué clothing.

"Her websites typically show 'before' photos of overweight teen girls and then 'after' photos of the same or different girls, looking like this doctored photo of perfection after purchasing her products and clothing. Here's an example of how this devious woman operates." Gail advances to the next slide, which shows two side-by-side photos of a teenage girl. She tells the group, "The first 'before' photo shows an obese teenage girl, around fifteen or sixteen years old, wearing a black bikini. As you can see, layers of fat puddle around her waistline, and the bikini bottom accentuates her oversize buttocks in a cartoonish fashion.

The photo caption reads, 'Do you really want to be in this fat, ugly body?' The second 'after' photo shows the face of a teenage girl wearing a tiny black bikini with a sculpted, slim body that makes her look like one of the skinny models we saw at an American fashion show. The photo caption reads, 'This can be your body—Sweetie guarantees it!' Out of curiosity, I tracked one million of her followers and found that ten thousand of those girls were dealing with eating disorders like bulimia nervosa. Five hundred girls had breast implants at ages sixteen and seventeen. Two hundred girls committed suicide in one year because of social media shaming directly connected to Ms. Harris's websites. There's no question that Ms. Harris has posed a clear and present danger to the young girls who flock to her website. Are there any objections to having her as one of our esteemed guests?"

Brooke says, "Wow, I can't wait to meet Ms. Sweetie, and I totally support her selection." The others nod their agreement.

Gail smiles as she points to the woman on the screen and says, "Congratulations, Ms. Sweetie Harris, you're our third guest."

Edith looks over at Robin next, signaling to her to rise from her chair. Robin walks to the front of the room and points to the screen to advance to the next slide. A sharply dressed gentleman appears, wearing a tailored three-piece gray suit, accented with a pale pink cuff-linked shirt; a pink, black, and gray paisley tie; and a matching pocket square. His hairline is receding, and his mouth has the shape of someone who is attempting to smile but doesn't quite know how to. Robin introduces her prospective guest by saying, "Ladies, allow me to introduce Mr. Jorrome Smithy, a wealthy real estate investor and owner of some of the worst slums in America. He lives in an elegant, twelve-thousand-square-foot mansion with eight bedrooms and ten bathrooms. The mansion is surrounded by well-manicured lawns with a water fountain that features a statue of guess who—Mr. Smithy himself. Meanwhile, he also owns more than two thousand units of substandard housing across America. The living conditions are deplorable—rat infestations, collapsed ceilings, and often no running water—yet he still charges rent. He's in bed with some of the authority figures, so he's never been held accountable for these unhealthy, unsafe environments. In fact, a recent community complaint revealed that twenty-five percent of the children under fifteen years old who live in Mr. Smithy's substandard housing have asthma as a result of toxic mold. I believe Mr. Smithy is most deserving of the honor of being the fourth guest. Are there any objections to his journey to our beautiful planet?"

Lucy raises her hand and says, "I think Mr. Smithy is the perfect guest. I absolutely vote yes." She looks around and sees no objections.

Robin gives a thumbs up and says, "I'm excited to announce that Mr. Smithy is our fourth guest."

Edith stands and adds, "Ladies we have four guests, and I'm fine with four—"

April interrupts her and says, "Please, I'd like you to consider a fifth guest."

Edith takes her seat and asks, "April, whom do you have in mind?"

April stands and walks to the front of the room, advances the slides past several faces, and then stops at the photo of a dark-skinned, middle-aged man in a full-length, purple velvet robe. Solid gold tassels flow from a Nehru collar that glistens with settings of white diamonds and rich green emeralds. He is standing in front of a magnificent facility that appears to be a megachurch. April then shows a short video clip of the robed man standing before a crowd of about ten thousand people. He looks over to a man in a wheelchair, who is crying and begging the robed man to touch him. The robed man walks over to the wheelchair and places both his hands on the head of the man in the wheelchair. He looks up toward the ceiling and speaks barely audible words that sound like "Get up and walk!"

The man in the wheelchair slowly rises from his chair and realizes that the feeling and strength have returned to his legs. He lifts one foot and then the other. The crowd cheers wildly, and the man begins sobbing and jumping for joy and yelling, "I'm healed! I can walk! Thank you, Almighty Apostle Henry Bendy! Thank you for healing me!"

The video cuts to a picture of a cross, and a deep baritone voice says, "You can be healed just like Brother Paul. Send a check or money order in the amount of one hundred dollars to this address [the address is shown on the screen], and you will be contacted for a special call with the Almighty Apostle Henry Bendy. Don't miss your blessing—act now!"

April begins her introduction: "This man is one of the sinister beings I spoke about earlier who uses the disguise of religion to prey on the poor, elderly, and sick in his congregations. He has more than two million followers on his online platforms and an international congregation exceeding thirty thousand members. While many members of his congregation live in abject poverty, he owns a sixteen-seater private jet; has five luxury cars; cruises the seas in his fifty-foot yacht; and has three homes, one of which is a lavish, twenty-thousand-square-foot mansion. He uses actors, like the guy in the wheelchair, to con innocent, vulnerable people into believing that he can actually heal their infirmities.

"I did some research on the man in the wheelchair, and he's one of about fifteen actors on the Almighty Apostle Henry Bendy's payroll who are paid handsome wages to participate in his healing charades. He even sells his own brand of overpriced, worthless products, such as a five-ounce bottle of healing water for twenty-five dollars; small white cotton prayer cloths for fifty dollars; four-ounce bottles of anointing oil for seventy dollars; and flannel healing shawls for one hundred fifty dollars. The rascal sells a three-ounce jar of ointment for skin diseases for seventy-five dollars, and it looks and smells like an inexpensive product on Planet Earth that they call Vaseline. I researched his profits last year, and his net earnings were twenty million dollars. He pushes his congregation to give until it hurts, even the elderly members, whose only income is from a program called Social Security, and in some cases, a program called welfare that pays them less than two hundred dollars per month. One of the most egregious acts of this man of the devil is that he has some members of his congregation, who don't have jobs or income, working at his home for no pay. He calls it their opportunity to tithe their time to the Lord, since they don't have money to contribute to the church. I believe the Almighty Apostle Henry Bendy—who ordained himself as an apostle, by the way—is the perfect candidate to be our fifth guest, and I would love your concurrence."

Catherine raises her hand and says, "I agree with April."

April says, "Thank you, Catherine. Is there anyone who disagrees with this fifth guest selection?" No signs of disagreement arise, and April says, "All right—Almighty Apostle Henry Bendy is guest number five." She then returns to her seat at the table.

Edith rises and says, "Thank you all for a job well done. Now that we have confirmed our five guests from America, we can focus on preparing the astronauts for their trip back to Earth. We have work to do in equipping these ladies for their journey and, most importantly, their return to our planet. Brooke and I will decide who will go to Earth with them and who will lead the command station here. I believe the astronauts will be much more suited for this mission than previous guests from other nations on Earth. Get some rest tonight, because we have lots of work ahead as we prepare for perhaps the most important mission of this era. You are all dismissed!"

With that, the ten women stand and walk in silence toward the mahogany wall, which rises to allow their departure.

7 The Return Home—Is It Near?

After Brooke leaves the astronauts, Beki says to them, "Okay, I know there are no secrets here, but I'm not sure what tonight's messages mean for us. We obviously want to return home, and I was hoping that would restore a sense of normalcy. After tonight, I guess that's not going to happen, at least not in the near future. It looks like we have no choice but to help the women with their mission, or God only knows what will happen to us. I'm so sorry; it's my fault that you're here and dealing with this problem. I couldn't get it out of my head that there was something in the galaxy that we needed to see, and this is the result."

Lillian reaches out for Beki's hand and says, "Girl, don't you dare blame yourself for what's happening to us. We wanted this mission just as much as you did, and we definitely weren't coerced into joining you. We'll do what they ask and hope for the best."

Cristina joins Lillian in offering words of encouragement to Beki. "I agree with Lillian. We joined this mission of our own free will. Hell, I was just as eager as you to find out what was beyond our chosen destination. Don't forget, Edith made it clear that you weren't in control of this mission and that nothing you did brought us to this planet. You don't have control now—none of us do. We're in this together and we'll survive together. I don't know about the rest of you, but I kind of like going home as a hero. I can see myself now, making the rounds on the major television networks. I'm sure we'll be invited to the White House, and maybe I'll have lunch or dinner with my favorite basketball star. I have this thing for the King! Maybe we'll have designer outfits and not have to worry about paying for them. New York fashion houses, here I come!"

Gwen can't control her anger at Cristina's comment and raises her voice. "Cristina, you're the last person I expected those words to come from. You're the tough one among us—at least, that's what I thought. Now you'll do anything to get home and go to fashion houses? Unbelievable!"

Cristina is not having Gwen's barbs and faces her as she responds sternly, "Yes, I will do exactly what they ask to get home. And guess what, Miss Holier Than Thou? You will too, because you have no other choice. Or you could always just stay here when we leave."

Beki steps in to end the squabble between Cristina and Gwen, saying, "Come on, my sisters, the last thing we need is fighting among ourselves. Cristina is right in that we have no choice but to do what's being asked of us in order to get back home. Remember that we're in this together. We need each other! Now, let's get some rest, because who knows what's in store for us tomorrow?"

Cristina gives Gwen an icy stare and bites her lower lip

as she refrains from any further comment. Lillian stretches her arms over her head and says, "I'm with Cristina. Right now, I just want to go home, and if doing what they want us to do gets me home and to my family, then I'm all in. I'm glad that they've been pretty nice so far. Maybe they won't ask us to do anything that's harmful to us or anyone else."

Beki tries to lighten the situation further as she says to Cristina, "It's just like you, girl, to think about what you're going to wear when we have yet to get back home. Thank you for making me laugh, though. I really needed that. Also, I have to admit that the food here was out of this world—pardon the pun."

Gwen yawns loudly, cups her chin with both hands, and says, "I don't know about the rest of you, but after that amazing food, I'm jumping in the shower and then I'm going to get deep into my alien bed. My very comfortable designer pajamas are beckoning me. I'll deal with what our dear friends have in store for us after a good night's sleep. I suggest you all do the same." At her suggestion, the other astronauts shower as well and then change into their pale blue pajamas and waste no time falling asleep.

About seven hours later, Brooke's voice, descending from the ceiling, awakens them. She speaks in a warm, pleasant, even chipper tone: "Good morning, ladies. It's time to rise and shine. Today, you have lots of work to do and little time to waste. You'll be going home very soon. Someone will be there to escort you to the conference room in one hour. Breakfast will be waiting for you, my friends. See you soon!"

Beki raises herself up on her elbows and looks over at

the other astronauts, who are now awake and stirring in their beds. "I'm not sure what work we'll be doing today, but keep thinking about going home, and we'll get through this. They got us here, and they apparently know how to get us back home. I'm confident that we'll be there soon, and in the meantime, I can't think of four other people I'd rather be with on this planet."

A good night's sleep has changed Gwen's mood from the prior night, and she joins Beki with renewed optimism. "About last night: I apologize for my outburst and want you all to know that I'm good as long as we're together. You're my sisters! Now, get your butts up so we can have a group hug!"

They all jump out of bed and huddle as their laughter fills the room. They quickly grab clothes from the wall lined with drawers and prepare to join the Supreme Highnesses for breakfast and whatever other activities are in store for them.

At exactly the appointed time, Catherine walks up to the front glass wall as it raises on cue, and gives a cheerful greeting. "Good morning. I hope you slept well last night. A breakfast buffet is waiting for you in the conference room. Please follow me."

Catherine turns toward the long hallway, and Beki joins her, followed by Gwen, Lillian, Cristina, and Vivian. Catherine occasionally looks back and smiles at the astronauts. Gwen returns her smile and asks, "So, tell us, what is it like being a Supreme Highness?"

Catherine stops, turns to the astronauts, and says, "There is tremendous joy in being in the company of women who are wise, kind, and very, very powerful. We use our powers to help others on our planet and throughout the galaxy. You will learn more about us after breakfast, so I'll won't go into any further detail now."

Gwen says, "Thank you, Catherine," and they continue walking down the hallway to the conference room. When they enter, Edith greets them: "Hello, ladies. You look quite refreshed." She points to the buffet area, featuring an assortment of delicacies, exotic fruits, and every imaginable breakfast food item, and says, "Please, help yourselves. A full day awaits you."

Beki walks toward the buffet, still not speaking, and motions for the astronauts to join her. As they follow her, the Supreme Highnesses, who have already served themselves, observe their every move. Catherine walks over and whispers something to Edith, and Edith nods and looks over at the astronauts while Catherine takes her seat.

After a hearty meal, Edith does her usual nod to the next Supreme Highness to speak, and Brooke walks to the center of the room in front of the large, U-shaped table. She makes eye contact with the five astronauts and says, "We know you've been quite anxious about what supporting our mission means for each of you. Well, today we will provide full details about the role you will play, individually and collectively. First of all, you'll be happy to know that your return trip to Earth will take place within two days."

Beki's mouth opens wide, and she yells, "Two days? That's impossible! We need fuel, replenishment of food, some minor spaceship repairs—"

Brooke interrupts her: "Beki, please don't worry about the mechanics or any of the logistics of the voyage. We've already taken care of everything. We have technology and equipment that your world has yet to discover and will probably never discover."

Beki sits back down as she looks around at the other astronauts with a puzzled expression on her face. Her companions seem equally confused and lean forward in their seats, almost in unison, as they eagerly wait to hear more from Brooke.

Brooke continues, "Your spaceship will look the same, but it's now controlled by our technology and our team. All you have to do is enjoy the wonderful trip back home. We'll use the same technology and team to bring you back to Eartha and then back to Earth again. You only need to follow our instructions, and you'll be just fine—actually, even better than your definition of 'fine.'"

Beki smiles and gives the astronauts a thumbs-up, and they all relax. Brooke takes her seat as she motions to Robin to speak. Robin walks to the front of the room while Brooke advances to a new slide, which shows an outline of several actions. Robin points to the slide and says, "Ladies, there are seven items listed here that cover all you must do to support our mission. Please pay close attention as I walk you through each item."

The astronauts lean forward in their chairs, all eyes on the screen, as they await Robin's words.

"Item one: Beki will continue to be commander of the spaceship, but I will be in control of the journey back to Earth.

"Item two: You will land the spaceship at the destination we've selected, in the state of California.

"Item three: Beki will exit the spaceship first, to a mass

greeting from military personnel, government intelligence, reporters, and many others. Your return home is a really big deal because you've been gone for four months and your space center lost the ability to track your orbit after three months. Beki, you will smile joyfully when you step out of the spaceship and will share how happy you are to be back home. You'll talk about the journey of your lives and say you can't wait to tell the world about it. They'll think you've truly gotten a glimpse of heaven. The others will follow you in this order: Vivian, Gwen, Cristina, and Lillian. None of you will speak until the appointed time. You will appear tired and weak, because that's what expected from spending this much time in the galaxy with no communication or typical resources from your national space center. But they will discover soon enough that you're in excellent health.

"Item four: After you've received medical examinations and clearance, you will be called into a debriefing with military leaders and government intelligence leaders. They will want to hear about your journey and will ask questions like, 'Where have you been for the past four months?' 'How did you veer off course? 'Why did we lose contact with you?' 'Did you come in contact with other beings?' and 'How would you describe your mental state?'"

Gwen raises her hand and asks, "How will we know how to answer these questions?"

Robin quickly responds, "We will give you all the answers you'll need."

Gwen shakes her head and asks, "But how are you going to speak for each of us? What if we're in different places? We're not robots you can program."

Robin smiles and exchanges a knowing look with the other Supreme Highnesses as she says, "You will never have to worry about how to answer questions, or about what to say to reporters or anyone else, for that matter. We will make sure you always say the right thing. That is, you'll respond in a manner that fully supports our mission."

Beki jumps in and asks, "Does that mean you will program us to say exactly what you want us to say?"

Robin looks to Edith, and Edith responds, "'Program' sounds a bit harsh. Let's just say we're helping you with your words so that you don't ever have to worry about your speech being off course from the mission."

Lillian frowns, with deeply furrowed brows, and comments, "Sure sounds like programming to me."

Robin ignores her and says, "Let's continue with item five: You will create excitement about the opportunity for a small group of citizens to join you on your return voyage to Eartha. We will coordinate a nationwide invitation for citizens to self-nominate for the mission. No one on Earth will be able to select these individuals, which is the course of action your government would take, if allowed, and which would result in the very rich being the first visitors here. That won't happen. Instead, an open lottery will allow people to submit their names, and thousands will self-nominate to join you. You will draw the names during a nationally televised program. Don't worry, because we've already selected five people who will be part of this first mission. You will announce their names as the first visitors to Eartha, and they will be overjoyed, even as many others experience disappointment."

Gwen raises her hand to ask, "Who are these five individuals, and how were they selected? I'm curious how you even know them."

Before anyone can answer, Vivian raises her hand and asks, "And what if we draw the wrong names? When is our return trip scheduled? What if the government doesn't let us come back here?"

Edith says, "First of all, you'll draw the names that we've selected, and your government will totally support this voyage and future voyages."

Lillian almost jumps out of her chair to ask her question: "Wait a minute—you said we had to make one return trip, and now you're talking about *other* trips? That's not right!"

Edith waves her hand, as if to dismiss Lillian's reaction. "Yes, there will be future voyages, but, as promised, you will make only one return trip. Other astronauts will be trained for the future voyages. You will never have to worry that we will break our promises to you."

Gwen has a distant look in her eyes as she tries to digest all of the new information from the Supreme Highnesses, especially the idea of a return voyage and having to take five new people to Planet Earth. Then she asks, "What if the government changes its mind about a return voyage, and what if the five guests aren't allowed to make the trip? What if they don't want to come to Eartha? Are we going to be responsible for handling things we have no control over or authority to make any decisions about? I'll do what's necessary to go back home, but I'm downright worried about how many things could go wrong—and then what? Will you hold us captive or kill us if your great mission fails?"

Lillian lowers her head and stares down at the conference room floor. The light around Edith disappears, and she nods at Robin to continue. Robin says, "Item six: Your return trip to Eartha will be scheduled one year after your return home. We'll have everything set up for that mission, including ensuring that the five selected guests are ready for the voyage."

Beki shakes her head in amazement. "It took us at least four years to prepare for our voyage into the galaxy, and now five people who have never traveled in outer space are coming back with us to Eartha after less than one year? That doesn't make sense. I don't think it's possible."

Robin responds, "I'm sure it doesn't make sense in your world, but it's totally possible in ours. We could actually have you come back in two months, but we want to give you time to reconnect with your loved ones. There's also some additional preparation for future missions that we will accomplish while we're on Earth."

Cristina quickly raises her hand and asks, "What does 'while we're on Earth' mean? Are you going to follow our every move, as you're doing here? Will we ever have any privacy again?"

Edith answers, "Of course you will have plenty of privacy, but please understand, we'll be with you the entire time you're back on Earth. However, you'll feel our presence only when it's needed for the mission. I'll emphasize again that if at any time you're tempted to deviate from any aspect of the mission, then you'll know that we're with you. The best way to ensure your privacy is to make sure you always stick with the plan."

Cristina lowers her eyes and slowly nods her head as she absorbs Edith's comments and says to herself, *I definitely won't ask any more questions.*

Robin begins speaking again and says, "Lastly, we go to item seven: You will never, ever have a conversation with anyone about your experience here. Not with family, friends, lovers—no one. If you're tempted to share your experience, we'll make sure that you never have that temptation again."

Silence fills the room until Vivian raises her hand and asks, "I want to make sure I hear you correctly. Do you mean that if I say the wrong thing about my time here, something dreadful will happen to me?"

Robin responds, "Let's not waste time discussing the consequences if you attempt to deviate from the plan. Yes, such an act of resistance would be punishable, but we're very confident that each of you will be in full compliance. We thank you in advance for your commitment to achieving our mission and the important role that each of you will play." Robin nods at Edith and then walks back to her seat.

Edith stands and says, "Ladies, now that you've been informed about your role in support of the mission, please let me know if you have further questions."

The astronauts quickly raise their hands, and Edith points at Beki to speak. Beki says, "Time is passing quickly, and I need to know what we have to do to prepare for our departure in two days. You said our vessel will be run with your technology. As the captain of our spacecraft, I'd like to know what that means for us and the roles we've had on past voyages. Do we need to learn anything new?"

Catherine stands and says, "Good question, Beki. You

won't have to do anything but enjoy the ride. The spaceship has already been programmed for your return trip home. We retrofitted the same space suits that you wore when you arrived here, and they will look exactly as expected, given your voyage and time in space. You will be able to share what you experienced as captain of the vessel before and after you arrived here. We know there's a lot for you to digest, and you keep hearing that we've got everything covered, but believe me, we really do. The voyage back home will be as comfortable as riding in those nice, colorful vehicles that you drive on Planet Earth."

Catherine takes her seat, and Edith says, "Thank you, Catherine. Any other questions?"

Lillian raises her hand and now speaks in a more contrite tone. "May I ask how you will equip us to answer all the questions that we know everyone will ask when we get back home?"

Lucy steps forward and answers, "Another good question. We know the questions before they're asked, and we will use what people on Earth call mental telepathy to transmit the answers to your thoughts; then you will respond accordingly. You may have heard of this technique, which is thought of as a form of science fiction in your world. However, in our world, it's very common."

Gwen raises her hand and asks, "I hate to ask this again, but does that mean you will control our minds? That really scares me, which is why I keep asking about it."

Lucy smiles and says, "Perhaps it's a stretch to say we're controlling your mind; we like to think that we're helping you with the words that are necessary to support the success of our mission. In any matters not related to the mission, you will still have control of your thoughts. Think of us as being like the people who write speeches for your politicians, except instead of giving you words on paper, we transmit the words through telepathic waves. It's much more effective than paper, and people will be in awe of your brilliance as you respond to questions with tremendous poise and intellect. You'll be viewed as scientific geniuses, and everyone will want to see and hear you because of your eloquence and charm. Trust me, you ladies will be bigger than any of the superstars currently on Earth. You will also become very rich. People from across your planet will be excited and very curious about your venture into an unknown world that so far has been only a part of their imagination. That means you will be paid substantial sums of money to share your stories, to speak to groups across the globe, and even to have popular movies made about your journey to our planet. Does that answer your question?"

Lillian nods her head vigorously and smiles broadly as she says, "Sounds great to me. I love the idea of being rich and a superstar! I'm totally in."

As Lucy takes her seat, Edith thanks her and asks the astronauts, "Any other questions?"

The astronauts shake their heads and almost in unison say, "No, we're good!"

Edith replies, "Well, okay, then I believe it's time for our final preparations for your return trip home. Let me thank you again for your willingness to support our mission. We are deeply grateful to you."

The other Supreme Highnesses stand in solidarity and show the astronauts unfamiliar, ritualistic hand gestures. Their palms face down, just above their waists, and they each lift both hands up and down four times. They then turn their palms over and extend them to the astronauts, waving their right hands in a circle two times. The astronauts stand still, mouths open, as they gape at these rapid motions.

After this demonstration, the Supreme Highnesses stand at attention, like soldiers, while Edith speaks: "Brooke and April will escort you back to your quarters and help you prepare for the voyage home."

The astronauts wait as Brooke and April step forward and then follow them to their glass quarters. Brooke feels the tension among the astronauts and says, "Ladies, you have nothing to fear. Everything is going to go perfectly, so relax."

Vivian looks over at Brooke and thinks, *Easy for you to say.*

Brooke and April merely smile as they take in Vivian's thoughts without comment.

8 Finally, the Trip Home

The astronauts' final two days on Eartha fly by, and departure day finds the women chatting busily about what might be different about traveling on a space shuttle that is totally beyond their control. Vivian and Lillian link arms and dance around in a circle as they listen to Gwen singing off-key lyrics with a catchy beat: "We're going home, yes, we are. Earth is waiting for us, yes, it is. The world will know us, yes, they will. Gonna have money, hope we will." They all break into laughter at Gwen's antics as they celebrate the fact that it's finally time for them to board their space shuttle. Their bright pink launch and entry flight suits look the same as when they landed on Eartha, but when they put them on, they don't feel the roughness they're used to from previous voyages. Lillian rubs the fabric gently and says, "Wow, this suit is so comfortable and so soft. It reminds me of the blue pajamas that we wore in our glass room. I feel the same warm hug from it, and, for some strange reason, it reassures me that everything will be all right. It's a feeling of comfort but also safety. It's hard to explain, but I definitely feel it."

The other astronauts also rub their own space suits, and Gwen crosses her arms in a self-embrace and beams.

Beki takes command on the flight deck, in front of the windows, as she did previously, with Lillian as the pilot. The other three astronauts take their positions middeck, lying on their backs—the best posture for humans to handle g-force. On previous Earth launches, once they've walked through the shuttle hatch to their seats, they've sometimes waited in place for a few hours for everything to check out, as the space center could cancel a flight up to the last minute if the weather was bad or something else went wrong. They wait one hour, thirty minutes, ten minutes, one minute, and then it's only seconds until takeoff. Momentarily, the auxiliary power units start. At six seconds, they hear the deafening roar of the main engines and feel the shuttle shake and shudder.

At zero, the rocket boosters light and off they go. They're going one hundred miles per hour before they've even cleared the tower. They get up to three Gs for about two and a half minutes and then feel as if their body weight has increased by at least three times. In an interview, Beki said she felt like an eight-hundred-pound giant was pressing against her chest with all of his weight and she wanted to yell, *Get off me!*

In eight and a half minutes, they've accelerated from zero to more than seventeen thousand miles per hour and leave the earth's atmosphere. The astronauts feel a sense of calm come over them when the loud noises and shaking stop once the engines cut off and the fuel tank is gone. They've described a quietness that's greeted them as they've entered space and known they had a successful launch. Beki shared in that same interview that one of them, usually Lillian, mutters, "Thank you, Jesus! We made it! Thank you, Lord!"

The Eartha team is meticulous as they finish preparing the astronauts for their return trip to Earth now. They carefully buckle them into their seats and gently place their helmets on their heads, as if the astronauts possess a fragileness they must protect. The astronauts check their oxygen tanks and other gear and take deep breaths as they prepare for the riveting effects of previous Earth launches. After they're confident that everything is perfectly in place and good to go, the Earth team salutes the astronauts with thumbs-ups and waves goodbye as they exit the shuttle. The astronauts return the gestures and give the team their best smiles. Lillian and Cristina lift their bodies and yell, "Thank you!" in unison, because the team really has been attentive to their every need. Then they lie back in their seats and prepare for the intense pressure of the g-force on their bodies as the auxiliary power starts. Their helmets contain an integrated audio system with high-quality speakers that enable them to communicate with each other. They hear Lillian praying out loud: "Lord, please get us home safely. Thank you for being with us, and protect us as we leave this planet."

They can't hear the countdown but know that it's only a matter of seconds before takeoff. Suddenly they feel the spaceship lifting, but this time there's no g-force of eight-hundred-pound giants pressing their bodies into their seats. There's no deafening roar of the main engines, and they don't feel the shuttle shake and shudder, the way they have on previous earth launches.

Then, suddenly, a most interesting thing happens. The astronauts hear a familiar voice through their helmets, but not a voice from the space center on Earth. It's Edith, saying, "Ladies, you're on your way home, and we want you to be comfortable throughout your journey. Your trip is a short one, so no need to take off your helmets and space suits."

Cristina struggles to sit up and then mutters aloud, "Something isn't right here. This whole thing doesn't feel right. Nothing is this perfect. I think we're still on Eartha and this is a game they're playing with us. We're never going home. We're going to die here."

Beki immediately responds with words of reassurance: "No, Cristina, we're in orbit and we're headed home. This launch is just different from what we're used to. There are powers and technology on Eartha that are unexplainable, but trust me, we have every indication that we're on our way home."

Cristina says, "Okay, if you say so, but I won't believe it until we land on Earth."

Another familiar voice speaks through their helmets and to Cristina in particular, as Brooke says, "Hello, ladies, I can understand your concern and anxiety about the launch from Eartha. You are indeed headed home, and you'll be there in much less time than you've experienced on any of your previous space flights. Please don't be afraid, Cristina. A request to trust us is not something you want to hear, but please try. Everything will go as planned, so get ready for your big arrival and the fanfare that comes with it. Remember, we're with you every step of the way to ensure that all goes well."

Cristina lies back down, and as she takes deep breaths, her arms come to rest beside her hips and her shoulders become more relaxed.

About twenty minutes after launch, Gwen says to Beki, "Hey, Captain, don't you think it's okay to remove our flight suits? I'd like to change into something more comfortable."

Beki looks outside the window and says, "You can change now. I know Edith said we have a short flight, but I believe we have at least four more hours before we enter Earth's atmosphere, so, by all means, everyone get comfortable."

The astronauts hear Brooke's voice again. She says, "You really don't have time to change from your flight suits, because you're going to enter Earth's atmosphere in less than an hour."

Beki responds, "Wait, that's not possible. Our flight to the Planet Zuko took us one month. We're traveling faster than the speed of sound, and I'm calculating four hours, at a minimum, before landing, Our spacecraft will disintegrate with any faster speed."

Brooke chuckles over the speakers and says, "Please let me remind you that the spacecraft looks the same as when you landed on Eartha but is now using Eartha technology. You will reenter Earth in exactly forty-five minutes."

Cristina calls out, "I don't understand. Will we enter the earth differently because of Eartha technology? We need friction to slow the shuttle down so we don't crash."

Brooke interrupts Cristina and speaks a bit more sternly. "Let me make this plain once again: We have everything under control. You will make a perfect landing. Instead of worrying about something you can't control, I suggest you spend your time thinking about how you will react when the hatch opens and see people around the globe watching your exit from the shuttle. We've made sure that the national space center, American dignitaries, and global news outlets and media know about your arrival. We've also notified global dignitaries, international space organizations, and world-renowned scientists about your voyage home. All of Planet Earth is awaiting you."

Lillian asks Brooke, "Why would we worry about what to say to people? I thought you were going to control our actions when we get home."

Edith's voice, gentle but stern, now comes through the astronauts' helmets. "We've explained that we will help you with the right messaging, but you can exercise free will in your actions, as long as you don't say anything that doesn't support our mission. So go ahead and do what comes naturally when you arrive after an extended time away. Be happy to be home and to see your loved ones. Let everyone see your joy. We just want you to talk with much enthusiasm about your time on Eartha. That's when we'll supply the words that you will speak. Now, stop asking questions, because you're almost home, just as we promised."

Lillian smiles and says, "Wow, we're entering the earth's atmosphere, and I can see the heat, but where's the force of gravity pressing against our chests? We usually feel a tremendous heaviness—my watch and my papers start weighing a ton—but that's not happening. Something's not right!"

They hear Brooke's voice again as she says, "Ladies, you're just about to land, and remember, Eartha's technology is much more advanced than what you're used to experiencing, so enjoy the reentry. Welcome home!"

Lillian deploys the landing gear, and the orbiter touches down. A parachute also deploys from the back to help stop the orbiter. The parachute and the speed brake on the tail increase the drag on the orbiter. The orbiter stops about three-quarters of the way down the runway. The sound of the shuttle landing on a solid surface is audible, and Cristina's eyes well up as she shouts, "We made it back!" All five astronauts begin to cheer, and each of them joins Cristina in shedding tears of joy.

9 THE ARRIVAL

After the astronauts have gone through their shutdown procedures and disabled the orbiter, they prepare to exit the shuttle. A cheering crowd of personnel from the National Space Center, a ten-person medical team, and at least twenty members of the media surround the vehicle, with cameras flashing and videos capturing the astronauts' successful landing.

The hatch opens, and Beki is the first to exit. Her legs are wobbly as she climbs out of the spacecraft, and she has trouble standing as her balance system adjusts from weightlessness to gravity. As she closes her eyes and grabs hold of the door frame to keep from falling, a member of the space center team rushes up to help steady her until she regains her composure.

Questions begin coming at her from all directions, but she still doesn't feel coherent enough to speak intelligently. A reporter forces his way close to Beki, pushes his microphone at her, and says, "You've been gone for more than four months, and for a while, no one knew your whereabouts. Tell us about your journey."

As afraid as Beki is that she won't be able to speak with

any clarity, she hears herself saying with confidence and absolute coherence, "We had an amazing journey. Please give my travel companions an opportunity to exit the spacecraft. We've been away for months, and they're as eager as I am to once again touch American soil."

The space center team moves the reporters away from the spacecraft and then assists Vivian out of the vehicle, followed by Gwen, Cristina, and Lillian. No sooner has Lillian exited than the reporters jostle their way back to Beki. One asks, "How did you end up on this Planet Eartha?"

Beki replies, "A mechanical failure caused our vehicle to veer off course, and we literally crash-landed on Planet Eartha. Thankfully, none of us sustained any major injuries, although there was significant damage to our spacecraft. We were suffering from dehydration and nausea and scared out of our wits, thinking that when we exited the spacecraft we would meet our end being attacked by alien creatures of all sizes and shapes. We had all kinds of space-alien images in our heads from watching lots of science fiction movies."

Before Beki can finish, another reporter pushes his way close to her and yells, "What did the creatures on the planet look like? How were you able to survive as humans on another planet? Did they give you oxygen to breathe?"

Beki smiles as she responds, "We were surprised when we were greeted by beings who looked like us. They had the same physical features, spoke the same language, and quickly alleviated our fears. They also breathed the same air as we do on Earth. We soon discovered a place of unimaginable beauty that is very similar to our planet, but without any pollution."

Another reporter asks, "What was the place like, and how did you breathe their air?"

Beki continues, "The air, the atmosphere, was just like ours on Earth. Words are inadequate to describe Planet Eartha's beauty, pristine waters, and bright blue skies, so clear that at nightfall the stars twinkle and dance around as if directed by a master choreographer. The wonderful beings there welcomed us and nursed us back to health. We would not have made it back home without their kindness. We look forward to returning and hope that we can launch a spirit of connection between our planet and Planet Eartha. It should be on everyone's bucket list. We can assure you that once you visit this amazing place, you just won't return home the same."

An aggressive journalist pushes his way in close to Beki and asks, "How will people get to this Planet Eartha? It's not like they can hop on a commercial flight."

Before Beki can answer, a space center staffer cuts off the reporters and signals for the medical team to bring a gurney to transport Beki to a waiting ambulance. The team helps Beki onto the gurney and rolls her through the open double doors in the back of the ambulance.

A reporter then shoves his microphone into Vivian's face and says, "Tell us more about this planet. Is it really as amazing as your captain says?"

Vivian hesitates and then surprises herself by beginning to speak. "As Beki said, words are inadequate to describe that amazing planet. As a woman of faith, I felt as if I were in heaven. It was so tranquil and just brought warmth to my heart. To tell you the truth, I didn't want to leave."

Cristina looks back in disbelief at Vivian's words. The medical team waves the reporters away as the rest of the astronauts are placed in the waiting ambulances.

Once Cristina and Vivian are in another vehicle, with two space center attendants checking their vitals, Cristina looks over at Vivian and intends to say, "Really? You didn't want to come back home? Have you lost your mind? You couldn't wait to leave that planet." Instead, the words she speaks also don't match her thoughts. "Vivian, I had the same feelings about leaving Eartha. I can't wait to go back there."

One of the two attendants says, "Wow, I hope there will be an opportunity for other people to go to Eartha. I'll be first in line. I've heard that there might be other planets where life exists, but I always thought they would annihilate earthlings. I can't wait to hear more about this place."

Cristina and Vivian exchange looks that hover between fear and happiness to be back home. They both think about things to say to each other but decide to say nothing because their words might not reflect their actual thoughts.

Lillian and Beki are riding in a different vehicle with two space center attendants. Lillian thinks, *I can't believe Beki said those things. The girl obviously didn't have control of her words.* She looks over at Beki and decides to ask her, "What led you to speak so glowingly about Planet Eartha? You couldn't wait to get back home." Instead, the words from her mouth are not aligned with her thoughts. She actually says, "Beki, I'm so glad you told people about Planet Eartha. Your excitement was over the top, and you were telling everyone about Eartha before you could even enjoy the first breaths of the earth's atmosphere. That was truly amazing."

One of their attendants says, "I was thinking the same thing when Miss Beki spoke. That had to be a very special place for her to talk so glowingly about it as she was exiting the shuttle after such a long journey. I sure hope to go there one day. Just think, we've been told for ages that there's probably no other life in the galaxy like humankind. I can't wait to hear more about this planet. You women are my heroes, and I suspect people across the globe feel the same way. It's awesome to be in the same vehicle with you—just awesome!"

Beki mutters, as she tries to keep her heavy eyes open, "Thank you so much, but I think I'll rest quietly for the rest of the trip to the space center. I'm awfully tired, and I know the others are as well."

Lillian nods and says, "Yep, I feel the same way. I think I could sleep for at least two months."

Upon hearing this, the two attendants quietly continue monitoring Beki and Lillian's vital signs as the two women close their eyes to signal that they want to talk no further.

10 The Eartha Story

The astronauts spent several days reconnecting with family and friends from whom they've been separated over the past five months. They relish the warm hugs and strong embraces from loved ones. Family meals where everyone asks about Planet Eartha quickly become a favorite pastime, and the astronauts savor every morsel of homemade seafood casseroles, hearty beef stews, roasted chicken and cornbread dressing, perfectly grilled T-bone steaks, and collards with ham hocks. They spent hours chatting with friends, catching up on the latest hot gossip about who's dating whom and who broke up with whom, what new restaurants have opened, whether the tall, curly-haired bartender with the angel tattoo is still working at their favorite bar, and who missed each other the most. Even during those conversations, though, the mission is always on the astronauts' minds, along with the tasks that the Supreme Highnesses are expecting them to execute to perfection.

After the dining and chatting subside, a whirlwind of media tours begins to satisfy the insatiable national appetite for every possible detail about the astronauts' trip to Planet Eartha. Beki in particular is invited to appear on television stations globally, but the astronauts are not allowed to address international media or travel outside the United States. They are told this is for national-security reasons, but the astronauts' safety also plays a big part in the space center's decision to restrict their travel.

On one major news network, Beki and her fellow astronauts are invited to tell the nation about the people of Planet Eartha. The news anchor begins the interview by barraging Beki with question after question: "Everyone is very curious about the beings on Planet Eartha. What do they look like? Were you frightened when you first landed? Do they speak our language? Are they intelligent beings, or are they primitive compared to humans?"

Beki chuckles and says, "Let me start with the fact that the people of Eartha look exactly like humans on Earth, and much like us in the United States. They speak English fluently and are extremely intelligent. Their technology is vastly superior to ours. Three months wasn't long enough for us to learn everything about Eartha, but we were very impressed with its unique architecture, advanced technology in data management and communications, and environmental protection. We weren't sure what to expect when we landed there, but they were most gracious from the very beginning in assuring us that we weren't in harm's way."

The anchor asks, "Do you feel that they're a threat to Planet Earth?"

Beki responds, "Absolutely not! In fact, they are very interested in getting better acquainted with the people of our planet. They've never been here before and are eager to have visitors from Earth. However, they're not interested in visitors who are high-powered political leaders. They want to see Americans of different backgrounds, cultures, and professions." Beki is aware that these words are coming quickly and are not her own, but she has no control of what she's saying, nor over the enthusiasm in her voice.

The anchor says, "You've been back home for three months, and I understand the National Space Center has already approved you to make a return trip to Eartha in about nine months. I can't overstate the enthusiasm and interest of millions who would love to join you. It's ingenious that the space center has launched a lottery to select the first batch of lucky travelers to Eartha. I'm sure that countless people will apply, but I understand that you can take only a very small number with you. How will you manage the selection process?"

Beki answers, "Great questions! First of all, we're grateful that the space center leadership and our government agreed so quickly to have citizens join us on the return trip to Eartha. To create a fair selection process, the National Space Center has introduced a nationwide lottery for which people can self-nominate. Unfortunately, we can take only five people on the first return trip. A computerized selection process will select the five names, which the astronauts will then announce. We anticipate other trips once those five lucky people have an unforgettable experience during their time on Eartha. By the way, we will continue to use the lottery system for future visits."

The anchor says, "I'd like to hear from our other famous astronauts now. Tell us, how was the time on Eartha for you? What was most impactful for you? Let's start with Cristina."

Cristina smiles at the anchor as she says, "I can truly say

that the visit to Eartha was one of the crowning experiences of my life. It was life-changing for me in that I learned something about myself that I was oblivious to before, and that was my judgmental nature. I met people who looked a lot like me but were very different in that they saw only the good in us. Too often on Earth, we look for what's wrong with people and categorize them based on our personal standards or on their physical characteristics, and I didn't find that to be true on Eartha.

Vivian doesn't wait to be invited to speak and comments, "The women there genuinely cared about us, even though we were from a different planet. I was worried about my life when we landed on Eartha. I wasn't thinking about the fact that they could have been just as worried about these five unknown beings who sprang in from the galaxy. What harm or danger might we have brought to their planet? I learned so much about kindness and acceptance, in a way that I hadn't seen on Earth for some time. That said, in spite of our flaws on this planet, there will never be any place as wonderful as Planet Earth, and we're so glad to be back home."

The anchor says, "Kudos to you, Vivian, a true American, and thank you, Cristina. Now, let's hear from Gwen."

Gwen looks at the anchor without smiling and says, "It's hard for me to describe my experience on Planet Eartha. It's one of those things where you have to have been there to fully understand it. Cristina spoke about kindness and acceptance. What was most impactful for me was the Earthans' lack of pretense and arrogance. They could have kept us on their planet and not allowed us to come back home, but they didn't do that. They were curious about our planet and in awe of our space technology, yet they have their own superior technology. They were never once condescending to us but were very helpful in repairing our spaceship so that we could safely make the trip back home. Our ship was heavily damaged from being off course in the galaxy, and they knew exactly what to do to help us get back to Earth. We didn't even have to ask them. For me, that took selflessness to a new level, and, of course, we made it home safely, with no glitches."

The anchor turns from Gwen and says, "Well said. Now, let's hear from Lillian. Tell us what was most impactful for you during your time on Planet Eartha."

Lillian nods to the anchor and says, "Wow, there are so many things that I could highlight, but there's one in particular. I loved the diversity of the people, yet it wasn't something they called attention to. We noticed it because intolerance of differences is such a big issue in America and throughout the world. Millions of people have been killed on Earth because of their race, religion, gender, sexual orientation, or other physical and social differences. Not once did we have to answer questions about our race or gender during the time we were on Eartha. The Earthans did ask us many questions about life on Earth and the daily routines of our people, but they never asked what it was like to be a woman or a woman of color. We could just feel their genuine caring for us as humans, humans who were lost in space and desperately wanted to get back home. They heard from us that Earth, and America in particular, has some flaws, but they knew without a doubt that we loved our country and our world and that there's no other place we'd want to live in the universe. I sincerely believe they respected that and that it's why they helped us come home. Each of us feels indebted to the women on Eartha for their selfless act in enabling us to be here today. They wanted nothing from us in return."

For a brief moment, undetectable to the anchor or the television audience, Lillian looks up, as if in an attempt to see where the words she has just spoken came from. But she just as quickly regains her focus and smiles charmingly at her global audience.

The anchor beams at Lillian and then says to his viewers, "This Planet Eartha sounds amazing. I don't know about you, but I can't wait to make a trip there. These five great Americans have experienced something that no one else in the world has experienced: a new planet and new beings. We salute you, and, for the umpteenth time, we welcome you back home. We look forward to hearing about your return trip and also from the five people who will be joining you. Until tomorrow night at the same time, America, stay safe and share the love!"

Once the cameras are off, he turns to the astronauts and says, "Thank you so much for a very interesting session. America thanks you, and I believe the world thanks you. You are probably the most popular humans on the planet right now. It was like climbing Mount Kilimanjaro without a guide to get you on my show. Everyone wants a part of you and to be with you. I just heard that Paris Fashion Week has offered you a selection of the designer clothes of your choice. Is that true?"

Lillian responds, "Yes, they did, but we're inundated

with offers, and of course we're in no way trying to profit from our voyage. We're just happy to share our experience with our fellow Americans and the whole world."

The anchor looks at the women with true admiration and says, "You ladies rock. Please feel free to come back on my show anytime."

They all shake hands and exchange hugs with the anchor and then exit the set. Lillian looks down at her $2,000 red-bottom shoes and smiles as she walks away.

Each of the astronauts receives words of encouragement in her thoughts from the Supreme Highnesses. They hear, "Great job! We're so proud of you all. We told you that you'd be famous, and now you know that we keep our word. Rest well, because tomorrow is another full day, as the lottery has closed and will be the most popular event in American history. We can only imagine your excitement, as you'll soon get to announce the five visitors to Eartha. Of course, we know that they've already been chosen, but no one else on Earth will ever know that. Don't worry about a thing, because we have everything perfectly planned for you and you'll continue to be shining stars. Congratulations!"

11 The Selection of the Five Winners

After two months of open nominations and millions of entrants for the journey back to Eartha, the day has finally arrived for the astronauts to publicly announce the five winners of the National Space Center lottery in Livingston, Texas. Beki, Vivian, Gwen, Cristina, and Lillian are all there for the huge event. In front of a global television audience, each of the five women will announce one of the winners, chosen through a highly secure and computerized process.

Beki and Vivian arrive ahead of the others and have a chance to chat in a large blue waiting room before the big drawing. Vivian whispers to Beki, "I can't believe all of the things that have been coming out of my mouth. I feel like a complete phony, and there's nothing I can do about it. How are you feeling?"

Beki glares at Vivian and answers with words that her narrowed eyes intentionally betray, "Everything is going well with me. I'm really enjoying the opportunity to tell people about Planet Eartha. I know we had some challenging experiences there, but, in a weird sort of way, I look forward to going back." Beki then puts her index finger to her lips to match the gaze in her eyes that tells Vivian to watch her words.

Vivian gets the message and says, "I guess you're right. We really were treated very specially, and I shouldn't complain. I'm just anxious about taking another voyage away from my family. I hope this will be the last one for me and that I can then return home and be a super wife and mother, instead of a super-famous astronaut. Being famous is not all it's hyped up to be."

Lilian, Cristina, and Gwen soon walk into the blue waiting room as well, but before they can begin talking, Beki cautions them to watch their words by quickly pressing her thumb and forefinger together and making a zipping gesture across her mouth. She touches her firmly pressed lips with her index finger and then says, with false excitement, "Well, ladies, this is the big day we've been waiting for, and I hope you're as excited as Vivian and I are."

Vivian's facial expression doesn't match the zeal in her voice as she chimes in, "I know these five lucky people will be out of their minds with happiness about being selected for the trip."As Vivian speaks, a tall, slim woman wearing a dark blue National Space Center polo shirt, with a welcoming twinkle in her eyes walks up to them and says, "Ladies, you're about to make five unknowns the happiest people on Earth. Let me introduce myself. I'm Sally Pender, the lead program manager responsible for preparing the five civilians who will be joining you on the voyage back to Planet Eartha. I've heard so much about you, and it's my pleasure to finally meet you. It's kind of strange, but I feel as if we've met before. Probably just my imagination, though. I'm not going to take up any more of your precious time. Have a wonderful day, and we'll definitely see each again soon." Her now piercing eyes create an uneasiness that lingers after she turns and walks away. There is no doubt in the minds of the five women that Planet Eartha is very much present and controlling the selection process.

A tall, middle-aged gentleman then walks briskly into the room with a smile that fills the space with warmth and eases the tension the previous visitor left. In a booming, welcoming voice, he says, "Hello to the world's superstars! Are we ready for the biggest event ever to hit the planet, and are you ladies as excited as I am? I couldn't even sleep last night; I tossed and turned so much that my wife finally kicked me out of bed. I've had five cups of coffee today, not to keep me awake but actually to calm my nerves. There must be a thousand reporters outside, from every news channel on the planet. Everyone wants to know who the lucky five will be, so let's not keep the world waiting. Please join me in the auditorium. There will also be about one hundred reporters waiting for your entrance." He stops for a moment and looks apprehensively at each of the women, who are now wide-eyed. He then lowers his voice to a more calming tone as he says, "Hey, everything is going to be fine, so don't be nervous. I assure you that you have nothing to worry about. Everything is so well planned that it's going to go off like clockwork. I'll be with you the entire time." He then winks, and his hand gesture reminds Beki of one that she remembers seeing during one of the meetings on Eartha.

They enter the auditorium, which is filled to capacity and abuzz with chatter, laughter, and high anticipation.

People stand and cheer as the astronauts enter the room. The emcee, a stately, white-haired man wearing a blue National Space Center shirt and a huge smile, walks up to the podium on the stage and tells the audience, "Let's give a hearty welcome to the most famous women in the nation. No, let me change that—the most famous people in the nation and the world."

The astronauts wave to the crowd as the cheering, whistles, and applause reach a fever pitch. The emcee motions for the astronauts to join him on the stage and to take their seats in five chairs arranged in a half circle. As the women seat themselves, the emcee begins speaking. "Ladies and gentlemen, thank you for joining us today as we announce the winners of the most sought-after trip in world history. Five lucky people will join these amazing women on a return flight to Planet Eartha. I'll be totally truthful and let you in on a secret: If there had been any way that I could have cheated to become one of the five, rest assured that someone would be calling my name today."

Peals of laughter flood the auditorium, and the astronauts quickly exchange glances as they force spurious smiles, knowing that the five visitors to Eartha were determined long before this fictious selection event.

The emcee continues, "We're not going to delay what millions of people are glued to their televisions, computers, laptops, smartphones, and every other mobile device to learn: who will be the lucky five. So, let's get down to business. Okay, guys, bring out the magic machine, and let's call out the lucky winners. Each of our highly esteemed astronauts will reveal the winners to the world. Hey, sound people, can we get a drum roll?"

As if on cue, twenty uniformed percussionists from one of the local colleges march into the room and fill the auditorium with a drum roll that causes everyone to jump to their feet. The emcee beckons for Beki to come forward. He then touches the magic machine, actually a touchscreen computer, as she steps forward, and on the screen appears a name that's visible only to the emcee and Beki. "Ladies and gentlemen, astronaut Beki Peters will announce the first winner."

Beki looks at the name on the screen and shouts the name of the first winner. "The Honorable Morcus Bottomy, from Hudson, North Carolina."

The emcee says, "North Carolina is home to a very happy man. Thank you, Ms. Peters."

Next, the emcee calls out, "Astronaut Gwen Hall, please come up and announce the second winner."

Gwen walks up to the podium, looks at the name on the screen, and calls out, "Mr. Wyatt Stone, of Canterville, New Jersey."

The emcee is almost leaping with excitement, so much so that he has to keep wiping his face with his handkerchief and his armpits now have large circles of sweat under them. "Congratulations, Mr. Stone," he says. "Sir, you have hit the jackpot!"

The emcee continues, "Astronaut Lillian Thomas, come on up here and announce the third winner for us."

Lillian joins Beki and Gwen at the podium. She looks at the name on the screen and yells out, "Ms. Sweetie Harris, from Los Angeles, California."

The emcee yells out, "All right, Ms. Sweetie, this is sweet news for you!"

Next, he announces, "Astronaut Cristina Ramirez, come on up here and announce the fourth winner."

Cristina approaches Beki, Gwen, and Lillian. She sees the name on the screen and shouts at the top of her voice, "Mr. Jorrome Smithy, of Brooklyn, New York!"

The emcee claps his hands and shouts, "There had to be a New Yorker in the mix. Well, good for Mr. Smithy." He then says, "Astronaut Vivian Willingham, you have the honor of announcing the final winner. Come on over here."

Vivian walks to the podium and looks at the name on the screen. She then shouts to the audience, "The final winner is"—she pauses for effect—"the Almighty Apostle Henry Bendy, from Arlington, Texas."

The emcee shouts, "What, an apostle? Well, bless my soul. This man must have said some powerful prayers!"

Scattered laughter comes from the audience, mixed with groans from some nonwinners. The emcee continues, "Ladies and gentlemen, I'm sad for those of you who had your hopes up and didn't get selected, but huge congratulations to the five winners. Please, one more round of applause for our five amazing astronauts. Aren't they the greatest?"

The audience stands and once again extends thunderous applause for the astronauts as the women exit the stage. At the exit from the auditorium, the tall woman who greeted them earlier in the waiting room makes a failed attempt to smile as she says, "Well done, ladies. I'm sure the winners can't wait to meet you so they can learn more about the Planet Eartha. I've seen your interviews, and it sounds like a great place to visit. Anyway, I'm sure this has been a whirlwind day for you. Please take care of yourselves; I imagine you have a lot of preparation ahead of you." She makes eye contact with each astronaut, showing the same twinkle in her eyes, and then walks away briskly.

Beki begins to say something but quickly changes her mind. Lillian says, "I'm tired, and I'm going home to get some sleep. See you later." With that, the astronauts give each other hugs and walk off to their waiting automobiles.

12 MEETING THE FIVE WINNERS

The National Space Center mails letters of official notification to the five winners who will accompany the astronauts on the return voyage to Planet Eartha. After the winners were announced during the globally televised lottery selection event, they immediately gained extensive notoriety, becoming hometown heroes and the envy of people all over the world. Now, the time has arrived when they will meet the astronauts and begin to prepare for their trip, gathering at the National Space Center for their first meeting.

The astronauts are winding down their whirlwind media tour, as organizing for the voyage to Eartha will soon occupy most of their time. None of them are looking forward to the trip, but they clearly understand that it is a decision beyond their control. It's also clear that there will be consequences for failure to comply with the commands of the Supreme Highnesses, although God only knows what those consequences might be. The Supreme Highnesses have vast, mysterious powers that are unmatched on Planet Earth. They are capable of implanting thoughts in the astronauts' heads and causing them to speak words that burst forth with the intellect and fluency of the world's brightest minds. They caused the astronauts' spaceship to veer off course in the galaxy and then land on their planet. Unquestionably, they have eyes and ears everywhere in the universe, so there's no escaping their wrath if the astronauts cause any deviation or pose a threat to their earthly mission. Fear of the Supreme Highnesses' wrath is what drives the astronauts to stay the course set before them, and what causes them to travel without hesitation to the National Space Center to meet the lottery winners.

The astronauts arrive at the space center at different times for this first meeting. Cristina and Lillian arrive first. Lillian has taken full advantage of offers from top fashion designers to supply her with a wardrobe for her media tour. Her navy suede, red-bottom heels are the first to emerge from the private limousine service that picked her up at the airport. She is conservatively but stylishly dressed in a navy designer pantsuit, a white silk blouse, and a single-strand diamond-and-pearl necklace with matching earrings. She epitomizes the glitz and glamour that the Supreme Highnesses promised the astronauts would enjoy.

Cristina slowly emerges from the limousine with less fanfare but looking equally chic in a dark brown pantsuit and a cream silk blouse with a lace collar. She may not have Lillian's pricey shoes, but she's carrying a designer purse that retails for at least $4,000.

Beki, Gwen, and Vivian arrive in the second limousine and are also elegantly attired. Beki exits the car wearing a custom-tailored black blazer with cream slacks and black-and-cream slingback heels. She's also wearing designer sunglasses that recently gained attention in the fashion world when they were first worn by a famous actress during Paris Fashion Week. Gwen gets out next, in a dark gray pantsuit with a tailored white blouse and a large square silk scarf with white peonies imprinted on a navy background with a bright yellow border. She is carrying a black quilted lambskin Chanel handbag.

Vivian gracefully exits the limousine so that she's offering a prime view of her long, shapely legs, the result of her daily five-to-seven-mile runs, just in case a photographer happens to be nearby. She's wearing a black tweed designer jacket with a matching skirt that falls just above her knees and black open-toe stilettos. She stops for a moment to check her diamond-studded Rolex wristwatch to make sure she's on time for the meeting but also to call attention to this luxurious piece of jewelry.

While the astronauts are not happy about their return trip or the control that the Supreme Highnesses have over their lives, they're certainly enjoying the perks of being so famous that everyone wants to be seen with them. Designers are competing with each other to get the astronauts to wear their clothing lines, perfumes, and other products. They're also being paid six-figure fees for their media appearances, and the National Space Center is allowing them to keep the big paychecks. There's one question each of them asks herself daily: *Is it worth all of this glamour and glitz to lose our freedom and our very thoughts to become pawns for the Supreme Highnesses?* The answer is always the same: *We have no choice, so we might as well enjoy it.*

The lottery winners arrive at the space center feeling eager to meet the astronauts and to let everyone know how special they are for having been selected. They bring egos that are as big as the Planets Earth and Eartha combined. They walk into a large conference room, where the five astronauts and several National Space Center employees are waiting their arrival. Judge Morcus Bottomy and Mr. Wyatt Stone are each over six feet tall and began bonding during their ride together from the airport. They enter the room with shoulders back, heads held high, to accentuate their height advantage over the other two men, while surveying the room to see if all eyes are on them. Judge Bottomy walks right up to Vivian, extends his hand, and seemingly ignores the other four astronauts.

Ms. Sweetie Harris enters the room in head-to-toe designer attire, and as one of the Space Center staff greets her, she says, "Thank you, young lady. Please be a doll and get me a bottle of water at room temperature. Traveling always makes me thirsty. You all will have to make sure there's plenty of water at room temperature on the spaceship."

The staffer looks at Ms. Harris in disbelief and replies, "I'm sorry, but we don't have any bottled water, as we're trying to save the planet. There's a water fountain right outside the conference room."

Ms. Harris scans the staffer with equal disbelief, rolls her eyes, and whispers, "Whatever," before sauntering over to where the astronauts are standing. Judge Bottomy is now engaged in conversation with Gwen, and Mr. Stone is chatting away with Cristina. Beki sees Ms. Harris and walks over with an extended hand to greet her: "Welcome. You must be Ms. Harris."

Ms. Harris tries to appear nonchalant and not show excitement as she says, "Oh, please call me Sweetie, and it's my pleasure to meet the captain of the ship. Your people must be so proud of you. You are a credit to your race."

Beki's neck stiffens, and she narrows her eyes and her lips tighten as she says, "I hope you mean that I'm a credit to the *human* race. Glad you could make it here, and congratulations on being one of the lottery winners. Please excuse me."

As Beki quickly turns and walks away, Ms. Harris shrugs her shoulders and mutters to herself, "Those people can't even take a compliment—too darn sensitive, if you ask me. They probably made her the captain as an affirmative-action requirement. They think they're so special, but their men love women like me. At least, I thought they did. No, I'm not going there today." Ms. Harris then looks for another astronaut and smiles as she walks toward where Vivian is chatting with a couple of space center staffers.

Mr. Jorrome Smithy walks into the conference room and scans the space to see who might be the most important person for him to meet. He eyes Beki and then sees a stately National Space Center staffer wearing a navy blazer with a black badge emblazoned with four gold stars and a gold-threaded border. Mr. Smithy assumes he must be the most important person in the room and walks over to him. "Hello," he says. "I'm Jorrome Smithy, one of the lottery winners. I can't thank the center enough for selecting me to visit Planet Eartha."

The staffer shakes Mr. Smithy's hand and says, "Nice to meet you, sir. I'm Lemont Kingsley. The selection process was totally random, so you're lucky to have been selected.

Millions of people were hoping to be one of the five winners."

Mr. Smithy asks, "So, tell me what your role at the space center is, Mr. Kingsley; I see you're wearing a very impressive badge."

Mr. Kingsley smiles and answers with pride, "Yes, I'm head of security, and I earned my stars by making sure everyone is safe when they visit the center."

Mr. Smithy's demeanor suddenly changes from leaning forward with interest to engage Mr. Kingsley as a staffer with power and authority who might bolster his stature among the five lottery winners to abruptly stepping back and wrinkling his nose in disappointment that Mr. Kingsley does not meet his expectations. Mr. Smithy pauses briefly before saying, "Oh, head of security? That's a nice job. But who heads up the space center?"

Mr. Kingsley senses Mr. Smithy's disappointment and points to his right as he steps back from Mr. Smithy and says, with narrowed eyes, "Oh, you're looking for Ms. Donna Watters. She's the lady in the navy polo shirt and khaki slacks."

Mr. Smithy nods and says, "Thank you," as he turns and walks toward Ms. Watters and joins the people standing around her. He literally pushes his way directly in front of Ms. Watters and introduces himself with an attention-getting, booming voice and a broad smile. "Hello, you must be Ms. Watters. I'm Jorrome Smithy, one of the five lottery winners. It's such a pleasure to meet you."

Ms. Watters makes eye contact with Mr. Smithy, and it appears as if she's almost looking through him and sensing his intentions, as she says, ever so hurriedly, "Welcome, Mr.

Smithy." She then turns around to continue speaking with the group around her and says, "My apologies; I believe one of you had begun asking a question."

Mr. Smithy lowers his head, and his face turns crimson with embarrassment, as he has nowhere to hide after being summarily dismissed by Ms. Watters.

Next, everyone's eyes turn toward the entrance to the conference room, where some sort of commotion appears to be happening. A man, soon to be known as the Almighty Apostle Henry Bendy, is standing in the doorway with a male companion and raising his voice at a staffer over something that she's said to him. He's scowling and protesting that the man with him, whom he announces as his armor bearer, is being denied entry. The armor bearer is holding the Apostle's hat, coat, and briefcase. Another space center staffer quickly rushes over to the entrance and greets the Apostle. "Welcome, sir. I'm so sorry, but only the lottery winners are allowed entrance for security reasons. I hope you understand."

The Apostle's brows raise and his lips tighten, and he points his index finger in the face of the staffer as his baritone voice commands, "My armor bearer goes everywhere with me and has never been a security risk or denied entrance anywhere. I've been to the Vatican, and he's accompanied me even there, where they have incredible security for the Pope."

Ms. Watters hears the commotion and quickly walks over to the Apostle. With a gentle smile and in the softest tone but with eyes of steel, she says, "Sir, we understand your disappointment; however, you are free to change your mind about joining the trip to Planet Eartha if you won't be able to attend this meeting without your armor bearer."

The Apostle remains tight-lipped and then gestures to his armor bearer to take a seat in one of the chairs in the hallway outside the conference room. He then enters the room with the two staffers.

Beki walks over to the Apostle and reaches out her hand to greet him as she says, "Hello, sir, you must be Mr. Bendy. Welcome! We're so glad you could make it."

The Apostle, still furrowing his brow, gives Beki a loose handshake and says icily, "Thank you, but I prefer 'Almighty Apostle Henry Bendy,' if you don't mind."

Beki feels his coldness and responds, "Why, yes, Almighty Apostle Henry Bendy." She turns to the other astronauts, who are now standing nearby, raises both hands, and shouts, "Ladies and gentlemen, may I have your attention? The Almighty Apostle Henry Bendy has arrived."

The Apostle's face relaxes, as he expects the kind of fanfare and applause that usually happen when he's introduced to an audience. Instead, much to his disappointment, everyone glances briefly over at him and then turns and continues their conversations.

Ms. Watters smirks and makes direct eye contact with the Apostle as she nonverbally messages him, *The Almighty Apostle Henry Bendy may be special in other venues, but he is nobody special in this room.* She turns and walks back to join one of the other staffers, who immediately hands her a folder. The Apostle watches as she leaves with a stare so cold that it makes ice seem warm. He regains his composure and saunters over to one of the animated conversations, where Ms. Sweetie Harris has full command.

Ms. Watters walks to the head of the conference table and calls out to the group, "Ladies and gentlemen, please take your assigned seats."

Judge Bottomy immediately frowns when he sees that he's sitting near the back of the room, whereas the Apostle's face lights up as he finds his seat positioned near the front of the room and close to Vivian. Ms. Sweetie Harris raises her voice in a way that garners attention when she finds that her seat is in a prominent place at the table. "Thank you so much. I like sitting where I can see everyone." She looks around at the other winners to see their reaction and is especially pleased when she sees the frown on Judge Bottomy's face.

Mr. Smithy walks to his assigned seat near the center of the long table without comment and makes no eye contact as he pulls out his chair. Mr. Stone walks to his chair, and as soon as he learns that he's the closest to Beki, he looks down at his newfound friend Judge Bottomy and shrugs his shoulders and gestures with open hands, as if to say, *Man, I didn't ask for this great seat.*

Once the astronauts and the space center staffers have all sat down, Ms. Watters pulls her shoulders back and stands tall as she calls the meeting to order. She speaks with a more genteel tone as she says, "Today is indeed a special day, as our amazing astronauts meet with the five citizens selected from millions of entrants to make the journey to Planet Eartha. Talk about winning the jackpot—you folks have actually struck gold." This comment leads to a few chuckles around the table. She continues, "You've had the opportunity to meet each other informally, but I'd like each of you to briefly introduce yourself so we can learn just a bit more about you. We'll start with our lottery winners, who from now on will be referred to as the Travelers, and we'll end with the astronauts. Who would like to start?"

Judge Bottomy quickly raises his hand to be the first to speak. After a lengthy introduction, he is followed by Mr. Stone, Ms. Harris, Apostle Bendy, and Mr. Smithy. The astronauts have little time left to introduce themselves as the Apostle and Ms. Harris have no idea what the word "brief" means. Mr. Smithy tries to hide his displeasure at Ms. Harris and the Apostle's extremely long-winded introductions, but the scowl on his face and his cutting comments when it's finally his turn to speak say it all. "Well, ladies and gentlemen, judging by the length of the last two introductions, the space shuttle to Eartha will not lack hot air. I'll show more courtesy and keep my introduction short and sweet, so the astronauts have ample time to introduce themselves." However, instead of doing just that, he says the following, which doesn't sit well with the other winners. "I am truly honored to be in the midst of such amazing astronauts. I am humbled by your accomplishments, and nothing I have to say about myself is worthy of mentioning here. I look forward to the journey to Eartha and just want to use my time to salute the five greatest astronauts on Planet Earth."

The space center staff break out in applause, and the other Travelers have to join in or risk being seen as selfish. Mr. Smithy smiles broadly and clasps his hands in a prayer-like gesture next to his heart as he not so subtly checks out each of the Travelers around the table to see if they're showing any sign of jealousy about his well-received words. He even turns red-faced as he feigns embarrassment from the attention he's getting.

Ms. Watters stands at the front of the table and, trying to hide her annoyance with Mr. Smithy and the rest of the Travelers, says, "Thank you for your introductions and comments. We don't have very much time left in today's meeting, and we must cover some key information in preparation for your journey to Eartha. We had planned to have the astronauts introduce themselves, but they don't really need introductions, since they're the most well-known people on Planet Earth right now." Heads nod in agreement around the table as she picks up the remote control in front of her, turns to the screen, and begins a slide presentation featuring details on what the Travelers will experience as they prepare for the most important venture of their lives. She ignores a voice in her head that whispers, *What is that thing in your hand? It's so primitive!*

13 Preparing the Travelers

It's been five months since the five Travelers were introduced to the astronauts and their preparation for the voyage has been a major challenge for all involved. The competition has been fierce among the Travelers to determine such questions as who is the greatest athlete, whom the staff converse with the most, and who is the most intelligent. One of the Travelers' first competitions required them to run four miles in half an hour. While such a target may have been easy to achieve for younger astronauts in great physical condition, the space center staff imagined this to be a major challenge for the middle-aged Travelers. Each of them trained vigorously to build up both their endurance and their speed, by running one mile, then two, struggling with three, and finally reaching four miles at the end of three weeks. When the four-mile competition at the space center's outdoor athletic track was officially timed, Mr. Stone came in fifth place, followed by Ms. Harris in fourth place, Judge Bottomy in third place, Apostle Bendy in second place, and Mr. Smithy proudly in first place.

Mr. Stone stamped his foot and huffed and puffed in anger to the timer, "You need to test that Smithy, because he may have taken some performance-enhancing drug." He then said of Apostle Bendy, "It's hard to compete with those people, because they run fast anyway."

Apostle Bendy came close to losing his religion as he stepped up close to Mr. Stone and snapped back at him, "Don't you dare go there with me. You are a pitiful, sore loser. Just accept that you came in last."

Mr. Smithy chimed in, "Yeah, get over it!"

A staff member blew his whistle loudly to bring things under control. He frowned and whispered to his fellow staffer, "These people are driving me crazy! Do they ever get along with each other?"

In another physical competition, the Travelers had to swim a mile in forty-five minutes. Ms. Harris raised her hand when the competition was announced and boasted, "Maybe I should sit this one out. I was a Junior Olympian swimmer until my early teens and was a star on both my high school and college swim teams. I'd hate to make these boys feel bad when they lose to a female."

Mr. Stone burst into laughter as he said, "You did all those things before you surgically altered your entire appearance. I know I can beat you swimming, so please don't drop out. I've never had the privilege of swimming with a real-life plastic woman."

Ms. Harris placed her hands on her hips and responded, "Okay, Mr. Thinks He's So Handsome. I will take much pleasure in beating your flat butt."

Mr. Stone immediately responds, "Let's not talk about butts. Yours is so fake, it might deflate in the pool."

The guys laugh at Mr. Stone's comments, and Ms. Harris flips her middle finger at them and says, "Okay, boys, we'll see who has the last laugh."

The space center staffer throws up his hands and shouts, "No more fighting, please! Can't we have one day when you all get along?" He then slams his clipboard on the table and takes a deep breath as he says, "Okay, the swim meet is scheduled within one week, so you don't have a lot of time to practice. I suggest you spend more time in the pool and less time badgering each other. We're done for the day, so get some rest." As he's putting away training equipment, he mutters to himself, "God help us if these loonies are going into space. I feel so sorry for those nice astronauts."

A week later, the swim meet takes place at the space center's outdoor, Olympic-size swimming pool. It is fifty meters long and twenty-five meters wide, with ten lanes, and is often used by Olympic swimmers who train year-round at the facility. The male Travelers are warming up on one side of the pool. All eyes are suddenly on Ms. Harris as she appears, wearing a leopard-print swimsuit. She avoids making eye contact with the male Travelers and does her warm-ups on the side of the pool opposite them. Several of the space center staff have come out to watch the race, as rumors have circulated throughout the center about Ms. Harris's challenge to the fellows, and some have even bet on the outcome.

As a crowd gathers around the pool, the five Travelers walk over to their designated lanes. Ms. Harris begins lifting her shoulders and swinging her arms to further loosen up. The other Travelers stare at her, and Mr. Stone begins to mimic her. The others begin laughing but quickly stop when one of the staff members blows a whistle to get the Travelers' attention. The young man speaks through a megaphone and tells the Travelers, "Lady and gentlemen, we are ready to begin the competition. I'll give you a couple of minutes to get on your meet blocks. Ready, set, go!"

The travelers dive into the pool, and Mr. Stone leads the pack by about ten meters. Judge Bottomy is a close second, Apostle Bendy is third, and Mr. Smithy and Ms. Harris are last. As they make the first turn, Mr. Smithy moves to third and Ms. Harris is still last. They begin the last lap, and suddenly Ms. Harris gains steam and moves from last to fourth to third and then to second. Judge Bottomy moves up to first. As they reach the finish line, Judge Bottomy touches first, and Ms. Harris is a very close second. Mr. Stone comes in third, Apostle Bendy is fourth, and Mr. Smithy is dead last.

Judge Bottomy jumps out of the pool and starts the pre–swim meet routine that Ms. Harris was doing before the competition began. Ms. Harris gets out of the pool, places her hands on her hips, and stares at Judge Bottomy with raised brows and a curled lip. She then says, "Well, you barely won, and anyway, you're a lot taller than I am, and your long arm just outreached mine. So stop gloating!"

As the other Travelers jump out of the pool, Mr. Smithy has a big grin on his face and says, "Well, I slowed down to let you guys win, and I'm glad that Judge Bottomy pulled through for us guys."

Ms. Harris looks at Mr. Smithy and says, "Shame on you! You're a loser. Just deal with it!" She then walks away with exaggerated movements of her hips and shoulders.

The staff member watches the other Travelers leave the

pool area, then walks over to a group of space center staffers who have gathered to watch the competition and says, "You see what I've had to deal with? These folks grate on my last nerve. Their trip to Planet Eartha can't come too soon."

The other staffers laugh, and one of them says, "I think you're in good company, my man. We all look forward to their liftoff."

In spite of their constant bickering, and to the space center staff's surprise, the Travelers manage to master all aspects of their physical training with the help of the Supreme Highnesses, who have used their powers to intensify the Travelers' physical prowess. The Space Center staffers are amazed by how quickly the Travelers master the physical requirements for their voyage. One staffer, speaking on the condition of anonymity, describes their progress as nothing short of miraculous, saying he's never seen such rapid progress. "These people are like machines when it comes to mastering each physical goal. It's like something or someone is controlling their bodies. Never, ever did we think they'd be ready to meet the tight deadline for the voyage. After all, they're mostly middle-aged, and even astronauts in training in their thirties and early forties have not met such stringent physical requirements. All I can say is that the right people won the lottery and it will be interesting to see how they manage the voyage, which is only a week away. If I didn't know better, I'd say that they're really not human but bionic beings. But they've been tested from head to toe, and they're definitely human—though perhaps 'superhuman' is a better word."

The Travelers gather with the astronauts in the large

conference room for their weekly update. For some reason known only to him, Judge Bottomy now sees himself as the leader of the Travelers and seats himself near the head of the large conference table next to Beki. The astronauts have watched the drama among the Travelers for comic relief, as each has tried to jockey to be closest to Beki. There has been one exception, and that's Ms. Sweetie Harris, who never seems to get over what she considered a snub from Beki when they first met. She has instead tried to build a relationship with Ms. Watters. Unfortunately for Ms. Harris, her blatant attempts to curry favor with Ms. Watters have had the opposite effect. Ms. Watters recently described Ms. Harris to one of her staffers by saying, "That woman is the epitome of wickedness. Just the sight of her makes my blood boil. There's a special place for women like her, and who knows—one day she just might go there."

As everyone takes their seat, Ms. Watters stands at the front of the table and looks around the room, as if mentally taking attendance. After the usual opening pleasantries, she asks the Travelers a question: "Well, lady and gentlemen, are you ready for the trip of your lives?" After a resounding "yes" from the Travelers. Ms. Watters continues, "The time is passing so quickly, and you've digested loads of information, mastered physical challenges, and surprised your instructors with your strong performances. We are now entering the last days of preparation, and then we're off to Planet Eartha." Ms. Watters realizes what she just said and immediately corrects herself. "I'm so excited for you that I just joined your voyage. No, I meant to say that *you're* off to Planet Eartha." Ms. Watters's comment isn't lost on the astronauts, who exchange curious glances, and their exchange isn't lost on Ms. Watters, either.

Ms. Watters continues with new details for the Travelers. "Once you land on Eartha, each of you will be greeted by your host. I'm sure that you will have the experience of your life, probably one you never ever imagined or dreamed would be possible for you. It's very likely that you'll return from Eartha very different people than you were when you left Planet Earth, because of your amazing experiences." Ms. Watters pauses for effect and then makes eye contact with each of the Travelers.

Ms. Sweetie Harris raises her hand and, at Ms. Watters's prompt, asks, "Ms. Watters, have you ever gone on one of these space voyages?"

Ms. Watters smiles as she says, "No, I haven't, but who knows—maybe one day I'll be able to answer yes, I have traveled to the galaxy from Earth. I must admit that I'm quite envious of you Travelers and the adventure that awaits you. Now, let's get back to business, because we have much to do in the final phase of our preparation for launch. I'll ask Beki, our esteemed captain, to review the launch procedures with you again. I know you've heard them at least a hundred times, but I promise you, you want to be perfect in this area."

Beki stands and walks to the front of the room. She pauses for a moment as she looks around the table at each of the Travelers. She takes a deep breath when she thinks about traveling into space with a group of personalities that are already grating on her nerves, when they haven't left Earth. Her thoughts race about Judge Bottomy, trying to be in charge; Mr. Stone, wanting everyone to know that he has a superior intellect; Ms. Harris and her air of superiority to Beki; the Almighty Apostle Henry Bendy, pretending to be close to sainthood; and dear Mr. Smithy, who's always trying to outdo the others. *They're all wicked to the core, yet I have to get them safely to Eartha,* she thinks. *I should just walk out of the room and say, "To hell with this!"* But she can't do that, so she takes another deep breath.

Ms. Watters senses that something isn't quite right during Beki's lengthy pause and quickly says, "Let's take a quick break, folks. We've had a week of very long days, and we're all tired." As people head out of the conference room, Ms. Watters's eyes never leave Beki.

Vivian also senses something is amiss when she sees Beki grabbing the edge of the table. She approaches her friend and asks, "Beki, can I get you a glass of water? You look exhausted. If you like, I can cover this section with the Travelers. I know this stuff backward and forward."

Beki lifts her head and says, "I'm okay. This has been a very full week, and I just need a good night's sleep."

Ms. Watters appears, her eyes still zeroed in on Beki, and says, "Don't worry, Vivian. Beki will be fine, but please do be so kind as to get her a glass of water."

Beki looks straight ahead and says with a smile, "Yes, I'll be fine."

Ms. Watters nods and gives Beki a thumbs-up.

By the time everyone returns to the conference room, Beki has regained her composure and, shoulders back and a smile on her face, says to the Travelers, "Now that I've had a chance to catch my breath after a very full week, let's get down to business. You've all had a chance to see the inside of the space shuttle we're taking to Eartha. You should know that this is one of the largest shuttles we've ever launched from Earth; it can accommodate ten passengers. I will now show you how you'll be seated on the shuttle." She grabs the remote and opens a slide that shows the ten seats inside the shuttle. Beki continues, "The front two seats are for the captain and the pilot. The next area will have an astronaut and two Travelers. The next—"

She's suddenly interrupted by Mr. Smithy, who asks anxiously, glancing around the room, "Do you mind identifying the Travelers who will be seated in each section? I'm sure we'll all find that very helpful."

Beki looks over at Ms. Watters who gives her another thumbs-up signal, and Beki responds without making eye contact with Mr. Smithy. "Yes, of course I can do that." She uses a laser pointer on the clicker and says, "Mr. Bottomy and Apostle Bendy will be seated in the second row of seats, with one astronaut; Ms. Harris and Mr. Stone will be seated in the next row, with one astronaut; and you, Mr. Smithy, will be in the last row, with one astronaut."

Mr. Smithy's face is now crimson, and his jaw tightens as he shouts, "I have a problem with being seated in the last row. Did you just arbitrarily make that decision because I asked you to identify where each Traveler would be seated? Am I now being punished for asking a question?"

Ms. Watters motions to Beki that she will respond and says, "Mr. Smithy, there is no punishment behind your seat selection. The selections were actually made based on the fitness and weight of the Travelers, in addition to their areas of expertise. The astronaut seated with you is the one who helps manage very sensitive communication equipment.

You were chosen for your seat because of your strong background using sophisticated communication technology, in the event that the astronaut needs some assistance."

Mr. Smithy tries to recover and says, with a hint of chagrin, "Well, it's not that I'm concerned about where I'm seated. I just wanted to make sure that I wasn't being punished because I asked Captain Beki a question. I seem to be the only one who asks a lot of clarifying questions, but that's just my nature."

Judge Bottomy whispers to Mr. Stone, but loudly enough for everyone to hear him, "Sometimes you should keep your big mouth shut."

Mr. Smithy turns toward Judge Bottomy, eyes bulging as he snaps, "You have some nerve! You pig face, always trying to take control."

Ms. Watters stands and shouts, "Stop it! You won't have a seat at all if you keep this up. You're behaving like five-year-olds. Actually, I should apologize to five-year-olds for insulting them with that comparison. It's not too late to cancel this mission, and I won't hesitate to do so if there are any more outbursts. Do I make myself clear?"

When she receives no response, Ms. Watters again asks, "Do I make myself clear? I want an answer from each of you!"

Mr. Stone says, "Yes, you're very clear."

Ms. Harris scowls, while looking directly at Mr. Smithy, and says, "Yes, and I apologize for any misbehavior by my fellow Travelers."

Apostle Bendy says, "Yes!"

Judge Bottomy looks down at his folded hands and says, "Yes."

Mr. Smithy's eyes become teary as he mumbles, "Yes, my apologies. I try to say things or ask questions that I know my fellow Travelers are thinking but are too afraid or too timid to ask."

Ms. Watters shakes her head in bewilderment and raises both hands in the air in an *I give up* motion.

At her own risk, Beki asks, "Are there any other questions about the seat assignments?" When the Travelers are silent, she says, "I take your silence to mean you have no further questions. One more thing before I turn the meeting over to Ms. Watters: Cameras are not allowed on Planet Eartha, so please do not bring any photography equipment. It won't work there anyway. Thank you. Ms. Watters, I will turn the meeting back over to you."

Beki takes her seat as Ms. Watters walks to the front of the room. She makes eye contact with each of the Travelers as she says, "Gentlemen and lady, being selected to join the most famous astronauts in the world on the journey to Eartha is the gift of a lifetime and should be accepted with humility and tremendous gratitude. You should have noticed the fatigue of our astronauts, who have had to work ten times harder than you over the past few months. You saw it in Captain Beki's face earlier today. They are doing everything possible to make this a perfect mission for you. I expect each of you to do the same. There will be no more outbursts and no more squabbling about anything, and I do mean *anything.* We are so close to launch, and if there was ever a time for unity, it's now. Please, make it clear to your fellow American citizens that you are more than the right lottery winners and are true winners in life. Make America proud of you! You are now dismissed, and we will reassemble tomorrow morning as we begin the final week of preparation before launch. Enjoy the rest of your day."

The Travelers, escorted out by Ms. Watters, leave their seats and head toward the door, not speaking a word to each other. Once they've all left the room, Lillian says to the other astronauts, "You mean we have to travel into space with these loonies?"

Beki, now fully composed, throws up her hands in a gesture that says, *Yes, we do!* and they leave the room in silence.

14 Planet Eartha, Here We Come!

The big day has finally arrived. The Travelers are so excited that they're even being civil with one another. The space center team has helped everyone into their latest-edition space suits. The suits are one-piece, lightweight, form-fitting, and much more comfortable than those of even five years ago. The helmets and visors are also built into the suits, unlike the detachable helmets of the past. The gloves allow the astronauts to work with touchscreens, much to the delight of Beki and Lillian. Once the shuttle is in orbit, the astronauts don't have to change into bright orange flight suits, like earlier astronauts did on past voyages. They can now wear the newer space suits for the duration of their journey.

The space center team begins testing the communication system within the helmets to make sure they're working perfectly for each of the astronauts and the Travelers. Beki and Lillian are doing their final equipment checks, and Beki in particular is more lively today, making more small talk and even exchanging smiles with the Travelers. She decides to offer words of praise to the Travelers, as they still have about two hours before launch. "As we prepare for liftoff, I want each of you to know how well you've done with your preparation. I admire the commitment you've shown to physical conditioning and to all of the studying required as you've absorbed a ton of scientific information. We've had our emotional ups and downs, but today we're on our way to an amazing destination, and I'm proud to be your captain. And now, I will ask the other astronauts if they have anything they'd like to say to you."

Lillian speaks first. "It's a pleasure to be the pilot of the shuttle that will take the first Travelers to Planet Eartha. You are the first nonastronauts to venture into the galaxy to a previously unknown world. How exciting for each of you. I encourage you to see this trip as an opportunity for learning, discovery, and, most of all, enjoyment. Thank you!"

Vivian goes next: "I'm so pleased to join you on this journey. You have amazing things in store for you, and I know you will love Planet Eartha just as much as we loved it during our visit. Best of luck to each of you."

Gwen says, "Wow, it's hard to believe how far we've come since that first meeting in the conference room. The moment we selected your names as lottery winners, we were happy for each of you, and we're even happier for you now that you will have this incredible experience. Our goal is to get you there and back safely, and we promise to do just that."

Cristina follows and says, "I echo what has already been said, which is what happens when you're preceded by people like my smart colleagues. I encourage each of you to enjoy yourselves and, during your visit to Eartha, to think about what you'll bring back to your fellow Americans. As has been said multiple times, this is the gift of a lifetime, so make the most of it. Let's shake a leg!"

The Travelers raise their hands and wave in appreciation, since their space suits prevent them from applauding.

The space center team continues testing the Travelers' and astronauts' helmets to make sure that they can communicate with each other. After that's successful, they exit the shuttle and close the hatch. The Travelers and astronauts lie on their backs in order to handle the g-force. About half an hour later, anxiety fills the shuttle among all who are aboard. Lillian says her usual prayer: "Lord, keep us safe on this journey to and from Planet Eartha. We thank you for this opportunity. Amen!" Thirty minutes pass by, then ten minutes, then one minute, and then it's mere seconds to takeoff.

Although the Travelers have experienced simulated takeoffs, there's nothing like the real thing. Mr. Stone, who fears death, begins to perspire and says a short prayer: "Jesus, keep me safe. Amen!"

Ms. Harris closes her eyes and does something she hasn't done in forty years: She begins to pray, too. "Lord, I hope you still know me. Please keep us safe. Amen!"

Apostle Bendy says, "Lord, you know me as your devoted servant. I ask you, in the name of Jesus, to give us a safe voyage to and from Planet Eartha. I love you and praise your holy name. Amen!"

Judge Bottomy is making every attempt to stay calm, but even he turns to prayer: "God of heaven and Earth, keep us safe on this journey. You know me, and you know that I've done good things all my life. Thank you for watching over me. Amen!"

Mr. Smithy's nervousness also causes him to turn to the Lord. "Dear God, thank you for allowing me to be here on this voyage. I pray for my safety and everyone's safety. If anything goes wrong, please let me live to be able to tell about it. I promise to always praise you for allowing me to come out of this journey with the fame and glory that I'm worthy of. Thank you, and amen!"

At six seconds, they hear the deafening roar of the main engines and feel the shuttle shake and shudder. At zero, the rocket boosters light, and off they go, reaching one hundred miles per hour before they clear the tower. Each of them feels their body weight increase at least three times as the eight-hundred-pound giant known as g-force presses against their chests. Ms. Harris almost passes out from fear. Judge Bottomy suddenly has to urinate, and as much as he tries to hold it, it just starts flowing. He's so glad that he's wearing a MAG, a maximum absorbency garment, which is really an adult-size diaper that allows astronauts to urinate and defecate during liftoff or landing. Thank goodness for him that he only has to pee.

In eight and a half minutes, the shuttle accelerates from zero to more than seventeen thousand miles per hour and leaves the earth's atmosphere. Then that wonderful quietness greets them as they enter space and feel the relief of a successful launch. They suddenly hear Lillian's prayer through their helmets: "Thank you Jesus! We made it! Thank you, Lord!" Apostle Bendy joins Lillian with his own prayer of thanks: "Thank you, Lord. I'm happy if the pilot is happy. Amen!"

Beki says to the Travelers, "My friends, you are now in orbit and on your way to Planet Eartha. We should arrive in about six hours. Feel free to make yourselves comfortable, and try to relax and take a nap if you feel like it. We have everything under control. Before you know it, we'll be landing on Eartha. Do you have any questions?"

Ms. Harris raises her hand and asks, "What happens when we land on Eartha? You said we will each have hosts, but will either of you remain with us?"

Beki says, "Good question. We will of course remain on Eartha with you, because we're bringing you back home. However, we want you to have plenty of time to get to know Eartha for the two weeks that you're visiting, so we will see you only when you're ready to return home. Don't worry, though, we'll keep track of you at all times."

Ms. Harris says, "Thank you! I feel better knowing that."

Mr. Stone raises his hand and asks, "We didn't bring any clothes with us, and I want to make sure they know our sizes and styles. After all, they've never been to Earth."

The astronauts exchange smiles, and Cristina answers, "Don't worry about your clothes. The people of Eartha dress a lot like us, so you won't be surprised to learn that they know all about you and your sizes. They're so excited about the first visitors from Earth who are regular citizens."The Apostle asks, "Did you see any places of worship on Eartha? I'd love to attend one of their church services."

Lillian answers, "We didn't check out their churches, but I imagine they have some form of worship. They were very ethical and kind people, and there's goodness at their core."

Judge Bottomy asks, "Were there any judges among the people you met?"

Beki responds, "I believe there are judges there, and I'm sure you'll get a chance to meet them."

Not to be outdone, Mr. Smithy, who always seems to wait to have the final thought or question, asks, "What will each of you do while we're spending time with our hosts?"

Gwen answers, "We'll get to enjoy time with some of the people we met previously, and we'll also do much more sightseeing than we did during our last visit. There are some sights there that you'll never see on Earth."

Beki chimes in, "As we've said before, Eartha will be an unforgettable experience for each of you, and I'm sure you'll bring back lifelong memories of this journey when you return to Earth. Now, I suggest you take some time to rest up before we land."

15 Welcome to Eartha

About five and a half hours into the flight, Beki begins to prepare both the astronauts and the Travelers for their arrival on Planet Eartha. All the passengers assume the landing position, and as they enter Eartha's atmosphere, the astronauts wait to hear the loud noises they heard when they landed on Eartha over a year ago.

The Travelers' hearts begin racing and their breathing becomes heavy as they start to feel the heaviness of tumbling into Eartha's atmosphere. Beki speaks calming words to them: "The sensation you're feeling, of falling rapidly from about thirty-one miles, is very different from what you felt during launch. Remember your training, and this will pass quickly. Closing your eyes and taking deep breaths will be helpful. We're almost at ground level. You'll probably hear various rhythmic thumping sounds when we land, but they're all part of Eartha's landing routine, so don't be frightened by the noises."

Lillian yells out, "T-minus thirty seconds!" The shuttle touches down on Eartha, and the barely audible sounds that the astronauts heard on their previous journey begin: *thump, thump-thump, thump-thump-thump.* The sounds grow louder, like iron fists banging against empty metal pots: *clang, clang-clang, CLANG-CLANG-CLANG.* Unlike the even louder noise before, the hypnotic sound grows softer—*clang-clang, clang-clang-clang*—until it is barely audible again. Then the astronauts hear a familiar voice, undetectable to the Travelers, as Edith speaks: "Welcome back, ladies! We've looked forward to your return. We'll open the hatch shortly to officially welcome our new visitors. Beki, you will exit first, followed by the Travelers; then the rest of the astronauts will exit."

Beki says to the Travelers, "Welcome to Eartha! We will exit the shuttle in about ten minutes."

Mr. Smithy can hardly contain his excitement as he yells out, "We made it! We made it! I can't believe we're here. You astronauts totally rock!" He then begins waving his hands in appreciation, since he still can't applaud with a space suit on, and the other Travelers join him.

Ten minutes race by like one, and they're all watching the closed hatch intently, waiting for it to open. Suddenly, the hatch begins to open and four members of Eartha's space team peer into the shuttle. One yells, "Welcome to Eartha! We will help you out. Please move toward the opening."

Beki climbs out first, following Edith's orders, and breathes in the clean, fresh air of Eartha. She's followed by Ms. Harris, Apostle Bendy, Judge Bottomy, Mr. Stone, and, lastly, Mr. Smithy.

As the astronauts busily complete the landing routine, the Travelers take deep breaths of the pollution-free air and are wide-eyed with curiosity as they take in the beauty of Eartha and its majestic mountain ranges. A recent rain has left triple rainbows with arches of red, orange, yellow, green, blue, and violet. Ms. Harris looks around and says, "Darn, I wish I had brought a camera. This place is even more beautiful than the astronauts have been describing."

Apostle Bendy lifts his hands to the bright blue sky as he says, "You didn't tell me that we would be visiting heaven."

Ms. Harris can't stop looking up into the sky, either, and comments, "This sky is so blue that it reminds me of the gorgeous sapphire in one of my necklaces." She turns to her fellow Travelers and says, "Have you ever seen anything so beautiful? I love the sprinkling of white clouds; they look like cotton balls. And I can't wait to get a closer view of those majestic mountains. Apostle Bendy, I'm with you—I feel like I'm in heaven."

Apostle Bendy quickly turns to Ms. Harris with narrowed eyes and pursed lips, as he retorts, "You have no idea what heaven looks like, because you're not a woman of faith."

Mr. Stone glares at Apostle Bendy and shushes him as he says, "Give us a break, man. If you can think it's like heaven, then so can she. Don't bring your holier-than-thou attitude to this planet."

Beki overhears their conversation and says, "I can't believe you guys. For heaven's sake, we'll have none of that here."

The Eartha space team assists Lillian, the last astronaut out of the shuttle, and greets each person with a handshake and a smile. A woman wearing a badge imprinted with TEAM LEADER says, "Welcome to Planet Eartha. We have been looking forward to your arrival. Please follow me to the vehicles that will take you to the Eartha Space Center lounge. Hop into the vehicle of your choice, and you'll be there in about five minutes.

The Travelers all walk over to the vehicles, climb into what look like souped-up golf carts, and wait for team members to drive them to the lounge. The team members move away from the carts once all of the passengers are onboard and wave goodbye. Judge Bottomy sees them back away and says, "Who's going to drive us?" As if on cue, the driverless vehicles respond to the words "drive us" and begin moving, making absolutely no sound as they glide toward the space center lounge.

Along the way, the Travelers see the distant skyline of towering buildings that seem to touch the deep-blue sky. They are welcomed by a gentle breeze that carries the fragrance of lavender blossoms. They see five huge banners at least fifteen feet high that read WELCOME, EARTH VISITORS!

The vehicles pull up to the front entrance of the space center, and the riders are greeted by a new space center team, who assist them in getting out of the vehicles. The team members yell in unison, "Welcome to Eartha!"

The team leader, a woman with reddish-brown, shoulder-length hair, says, "Please follow me; the lounge is a short walk away."

The space center is massive and roughly ten times the size of the National Space Center on Earth. As the Travelers walk up to the entrance, they see twenty-foot, decorative, wrought-iron doors with geometric symbols. To their surprise, the doors move upward, unlike the automatic doors on Earth that slide sideways. Judge Bottomy enters cautiously, looking up the entire time he walks through the entrance, as if the doors might come crashing down on him.

The Travelers have heard the astronauts say that the people of Eartha look like people on Earth, but they didn't expect such identical features. Judge Bottomy whispers to Mr. Stone, "One of the space center team looks like a cousin of mine, but she's better looking than my cousin, who has a crooked nose and eyebrows that have grown together. I'm not prejudiced against women, but don't you think it's rather strange that everyone who has greeted us is a woman?"

Mr. Stone mutters to Judge Bottomy, his lips barely moving, "You're right. I haven't seen a single man since we landed. I sure hope there're some men here."

Mr. Smithy overhears the conversation and says, "Don't worry, guys, you can count on men being here, because there's no way that women could have the engineering expertise and high-level design skills to create these massive buildings and driverless vehicles. No way, so stop worrying."

Lillian also overhears the conversation and snaps, "Good grief, don't you ever quit? Don't you dare bring that chauvinistic talk here. You guys get on my last nerve!"

Mr. Smithy gives Lillian a look of disdain and starts to speak but then lowers his head and says nothing.

The ten Supreme Highnesses are lined up in pairs, wearing their matching, midlength, unbelted black dresses as they greet the astronauts and Travelers entering the space center lobby. They warmly welcome the astronauts with unexpected hugs and then reach out to shake the hands of each of the Travelers.

Ms. Harris smiles at the Supreme Highnesses and can hardly keep a straight face as she checks out their attire and thinks, *What in the world are these women wearing, and why don't they have on makeup. They could have at least taken the time to get their hair styled. I can't believe I don't see one piece of jewelry. What a weird bunch. Have they no shame greeting guests from another planet in those drab, shapeless dresses? I hope they're not expecting me to change into those ugly sacks.*

Edith speaks to the visitors on behalf of the Supreme Highnesses: "We are Planet Eartha's Supreme Highnesses, and we welcome our newest visitors from Planet Earth, who have joined the astronauts on their return voyage. Please follow me to the lounge so you can make yourselves comfortable and we can introduce ourselves more formally. You'll be here for about an hour, and then your hosts, whom you'll get to know shortly, will take you to your hotel so that you can unwind and rest up for dinner."

The Travelers are openmouthed and wide-eyed at the grandness and splendor of the space center, with its twenty-foot pillars, glass walls, and elegantly carved wooden benches. The massive structure has an open atrium with visibility to all five floors of the center, and a most unusual flowering tree that stands from floor to ceiling in the center of the lobby courtyard. Its thick branches explode with purple, pink, and white rose-like blossoms.

The Supreme Highnesses watch the visitors as they check out the space center, and Edith says with pride, "This facility was built in just six months. Our architects and builders used only the most energy-efficient materials, and the sun is the sole source of energy for this building. Of course, it's but one of many magnificent structures on Eartha."

Judge Bottomy says, "You must have architectural geniuses here in order to build such an amazing structure in six months. Maybe we can meet your chief architect to gain information that we can take back to Earth."

Edith reads between the lines of Judge Bottomy's inquiry, detecting his hope that he will meet the "man" behind this work. She gives him a tight smile as she responds, "Oh, we'd love for you to meet the lead architect for this structure and others that are much more impressive than the one you're in. *She* would enjoy sharing with you how *her* work is not only the best on Eartha but the best in the entire galaxy."

Judge Bottomy lowers his head but still manages to make eye contact with Mr. Stone and shrugs his shoulders as a way of communicating, *I'm not sure about this place.*

The visitors and the Supreme Highnesses reach the lounge, and it, too, is equally grand, featuring views of the huge flowering tree and stylishly furnished with chairs and sofas that are upholstered with a dark brown fabric that looks like the finest grade of leather. Computer stations throughout the room are easily accessible to staff and visitors. As the Travelers walk into the elegant foyer, an alarm sounds continuously, indicating new entrants who must go through a screening process. April steps over and touches the keypad with her finger, and the alarm speaks the words "All clear. Please proceed."

The group goes into a conference room with a large mahogany table in the center. High-backed seats of the same fabric as the couches and chairs in the lounge display their unique computerized capability as they turn around and greet each person by name according to their assigned seat.

Apostle Bendy wears the broadest smile he's had since he joined the Travelers at the National Space Center when his chair boldly announces, "Welcome, Almighty Apostle Henry Bendy. It is my pleasure to seat such a distinguished man of honor."

After the chair greetings, Edith walks to the front of the room and again welcomes the Earth visitors. "We can't begin to contain our enthusiasm about your being with us, or how pleased we are that you had a safe journey. You must be quite tired, and I know you want to remove your space suits at the earliest opportunity. We're not going to hold you here long but want to take the time to introduce your hosts for this visit. We'll have plenty of time to get to know each other over the next two weeks. We're already acquainted with the astronauts but would like our Travelers to briefly introduce themselves, and then we'll introduce your hosts for this visit." Beki stands and, to her surprise, utters words she would never say on her own. "Before the Travelers speak, I just want to say on behalf of the astronauts that we're so happy to be back on the Planet Eartha and to bring these five guests with us. It's been great getting to know them and to see their excitement about coming to this beautiful place."

Lillian gives Beki an incredulous stare, with her mouth open and her eyebrows raised, as she thinks, *Really? Are you kidding me? You hate these five despicable creatures!*

Beki averts her eyes from Lillian's gaze as she says, "I know you want to hear from our other guests, so I'll take my seat."

Apostle Bendy, on a high from his great chair introduction, says, "I'll go first. My name is the Almighty Apostle

Henry Bendy. I'm the senior pastor of a megachurch with more than thirty thousand members in satellite churches across America. I was called to pastoral service thirty years ago, at the tender age of nineteen, and I've preached the good news of Jesus Christ ever since. It is my pleasure to be here. Thank you!"

Cristina looks over at Apostle Bendy and thinks, *He forgot to add that he's an arrogant, holier-than-thou preacher who acts like he's on his way to sainthood. I bet the good news he's preaching is about himself.*

Ms. Harris says, "I'll go next. My name is Sweetie Harris. I'm an international entrepreneur and fashion designer specializing in a clothing line for women of all ages, but primarily between thirteen and twenty-five. Customers around the world quickly snatch up my apparel to join an elite group of fashionable and hip young women. I'm a strong advocate for building girls' self-esteem in a world where the media pummels them with images that wreak havoc and make them unhappy with their young bodies. I promote hope, joy, and self-love!"

Beki smiles, but not out of respect for Ms. Harris, as she thinks, *Hello, Eartha, meet Ms. Bionic America, Planet Earth's ambassador for plastic surgeries. She's right about self-love, because she's full of it.*

Mr. Smithy stands to introduce himself and says, "Hello, ladies, and thank you for welcoming us to Eartha. I'm Jorrome Smithy, a prominent real estate investor. I have the honor of placing people in some of the finest properties in the United States. I won't brag, but I've received numerous awards for my efforts to provide affordable housing for the poor and people with disabilities. I also volunteer with the homeless, especially veterans of our military. It's my pleasure to be a visitor on Planet Eartha."

Vivian coughs to conceal her laughter as she thinks, *He won't brag? Give me a break! The man's ego is bigger than Earth, Eartha, and all the planets in the galaxy combined. Where did these five creatures come from?*

As Mr. Smithy finishes, Judge Bottomy stands and says, "Thank you for your warm welcome. I am the Honorable Judge Morcus Bottomy and have served on the judicial bench for three decades. I am strongly committed to dispensing justice in the juvenile court system. I love young people, regardless of race, creed, or color, and have done my best to be fair and even to try new ways to avoid incarceration of first offenders who've committed minor crimes. I serve with honor and integrity. I look forward to learning as much as possible while I'm on Planet Eartha, to take back with me to Earth."

Lillian exchanges glances with Cristina as she thinks, *There is nothing honorable about this old goat, from what I can tell so far. I wonder why in the world the Supreme Highnesses selected him for this journey.*

Lastly, Mr. Stone stands while saying, "Good afternoon, ladies—at least, I think it's afternoon. I'm excited to be in your beautiful world. I am a well-respected movie producer and have won many awards for my work. I am also a philanthropist who gives a large portion of my wealth to help the poor and disadvantaged. I've been married to an amazing woman for twenty-five years and have four wonderful daughters. I'm missing them a lot right now. I'm so pleased to have been selected to visit your planet. Thank you!"

Gwen keeps a straight face as she thinks, *Did he just say "well-respected"? There's something about this guy that I really don't trust. He's hiding something, and I wonder if that's why he was selected with those other yahoos.*

Edith stands and says, "Thank you all for your fine introductions. We're very fortunate to have visitors of your caliber, and we'll do our best to ensure that you have experiences deserving of your standing. Now, I'll introduce you to your hosts so that you can get to your hotel and get some rest before dinner. We don't use last names here, as you do in your world, so you'll learn only the first name of your host. Judge Bottomy, your host is Carmen."

Carmen stands and walks over to stand behind Judge Bottomy's chair. As the other hosts are named, they, too, each stand behind the chair of their assigned Traveler. "Ms. Harris, your host is Gail." "Mr. Smithy, your host is Robin." "The Almighty Apostle Bendy, your host is April." "Mr. Stone, your host is Felicia."

Edith announces, "Now that the hosts are in place, we have transportation waiting at the front entrance to take you to your hotel. You will find clothing and a light snack in your rooms."

Ms. Harris asks Edith, "Pardon me, but did someone give you our sizes ahead of time? As a fashion designer, I'm just curious how you know our sizes and our taste in clothes."

Before Edith can respond, Cristina rolls her eyes at Ms. Harris and says, "Look, you don't have to worry about a thing. Rest assured, everything was perfect for us during our last visit—food, clothes, everything—and I'm sure it will be the same for you."

Edith smiles at Cristina and says, "Thank you, Cristina. We will certainly take good care of our Travelers."

The five hosts escort the Travelers and astronauts to the front entrance of the space center and into a dark blue vehicle that appears to be a hybrid of a limousine and a small airplane. They quickly learn that it's a smart, driverless vehicle that speaks to the passengers once the doors are closed. "Welcome, passengers from Planet Earth. You will arrive at your hotel in exactly fifteen minutes. Please sit back and relax." The vehicle begins moving slowly and then lifts above the ground as it takes flight. Once they're out of the center campus, they connect to a thoroughfare with other flying vehicles. The Travelers are again wide-eyed as they take in the architectural genius of city skyscrapers that reach above the clouds, some appearing to be more than 150 floors. The futuristic buildings come in all designs, from towering pyramids of steel to walls of textured glass that give the illusion of movement.

In the midst of so many amazing structures, Mr. Stone is still fixated on the fact that he hasn't seen one male since the Travelers landed on Eartha. He frowns and mumbles to Judge Bottomy, "Man, we're in deep trouble if we're the only men on this planet."

Judge Bottomy winks as he says, "Don't get paranoid on me; this could mean heaven on Eartha for us. Although the women look a bit plain so far, if you ask me. That said, a piece of tail doesn't have to be beautiful." They both laugh as the vehicle pulls up to a grand hotel that blends glass and mosaic stone to create the illusion of diamonds set in geometrical patterns similar to those on the wrought-iron doors of the space center entrance.

The vehicle lowers for a smooth landing in front of the hotel. A couple of bellmen in dark blue suits rush to open the doors to the vehicle and help out the passengers. Mr. Stone's eyes brighten and his smile is utterly gleeful upon seeing the two men. He turns to Judge Bottomy and says in a joyous tone, "Finally! I knew there had to be some men around here."

He greets one of the bellmen: "Hello, sir. It's great to see that there are males on Planet Eartha."

He almost urinates in his space suit at the bellman's response. In a clipped, staccato voice, the man says, "Welcome to the Eartha Palace. Please let me know if I can assist you in any way. I am here to serve." The bellman then turns to the Almighty Apostle Henry Bendy and says in an identical voice, "Welcome to the Eartha Palace. Please let me know if I can assist you in any way. I am here to serve." Both of the bellmen continue this greeting to each of the travelers and astronauts. Judge Bottomy's face turns red, his jaw drops, and his eyes widen as he watches the bellmen and whispers to Mr. Stone, "Oh my God, I don't believe this. These guys are fricking robots!"

At this point, the hosts separate the astronauts from the Travelers. It's a good move, because Beki especially is looking for a reprieve from the Travelers, all of whom are now showing signs of fatigue: droopy eyes, slumped shoulders, and more frowns from the men. In spite of her desire to get away from them, she offers words of encouragement. "Please get some rest! We'll join you at dinner tonight, and you'll get to taste the best food ever. Too bad we can't capture a photo of us in our space suits."

Ms. Harris groans, "Are you kidding me? I would never

agree to a photo the way I'm looking now, in an outfit that I've been wearing for almost twelve hours?"

Mr. Stone's immediate, rude response speaks to both his fatigue and his annoyance with Ms. Harris as he says, "Oh, please. Your plastic face would look exactly the same later on, so that shouldn't have stopped you from taking a photo if we'd had a camera!"

Ms. Harris's head swivels as quickly as the girl's head in the movie *The Exorcist* as she snaps, "You have some nerve talking about a plastic face. You certainly weren't born with that chiseled chin and almost perfect nose."

Beki jumps in and sharply rebukes the two Travelers through clenched teeth: "Are you really going to misbehave in front of our hosts? Remember, it's not too late to have you locked in a room so you miss out on all the activities. Now, control yourselves! You're embarrassing us all." She shakes her head.

April, who has now taken on the leadership role in the absence of Edith and Brooke, observes the Travelers' behavior and motions to Felicia to intervene. Felicia walks up to the Travelers and says, "You've had quite a journey today, and your hotel rooms are ready and waiting for you.

The Almighty Apostle asks, "Don't we have to check in and get our room keys?"

Felicia chuckles at the question and then answers, "No, sir, we don't use room keys here. I have your room number, and when you walk up to the door, it will open based on facial recognition. While we were out here, the bellmen already scanned your faces, so you're ready to go."

The Almighty Apostle raises his hands to the sky and shouts, "Hallelujah! Let's go!"

As the group enters the hotel lobby, they gape at the beautifully carved wood-grain tables and benches. Like the space center, the lobby has an enormous atrium with a magnificent flowering tree in the center that extends the full height of the building and is covered with snow-white flowers that look like chrysanthemums. The ceiling is all glass, and the sun beams through the tree, giving it a divine aura.

Mr. Smithy asks Robin, his host, "Do all of your large buildings have trees in their lobbies? Do you folks worship trees? Seems like they are a big deal here, so that's why I'm asking."

Robin responds, "No, we don't 'worship' trees, per se, but yes, all of our buildings have them. It's one of the ways we recognize and honor the precious gifts of nature, whose beauty we do everything possible to preserve. Our lush forests, all of our pure waterways, our clean oceans, and our clear, deep-blue skies all reflect our care for the environment. Is that what you do on Planet Earth?"

Mr. Smithy stares back at Robin and opens his mouth to speak but quickly closes it and says nothing.

April senses the tension and provides additional instructions. "We will return to take you to dinner at six o'clock this evening. You have clothing in your room properly labeled for this meal and other activities."

The hosts step aside and begin walking toward the lobby entrance as the Travelers and astronauts proceed to their respective rooms. The hosts gather in front of the lobby before heading to the Supreme Highnesses' headquarters. Robin breaks into laughter as she says, "Wow, do we have our work cut out for us. Can you believe how these characters introduced themselves? You would think they were some of the most honorable people on Planet Earth, instead of the wicked creatures we know them to be."

Felicia chuckles and adds, "I loved it when the guys realized that the bellmen were robots. They're still looking for the men who are behind all of our amazing architecture and advanced technology. All I can say is, those boys will very soon have the chance to see firsthand what real woman power is about."

All the hosts join in the laughter as they board their waiting vehicle.

Ms. Harris walks up to the door of her room on the second floor, and it opens shortly after it recognizes her face. Her hands cover her mouth as she takes in the plush beauty of the two-room suite. She walks over to a glass wall that overlooks a lush garden, filled with low-lying and towering plants in varying shades of yellow, orange, and red; multiple breeds of cacti; and trees with thick green leaves of different sizes. She decides to check out the closet and finds a classic pantsuit that is exactly her size and in her favorite shade of burgundy. She doesn't yield to the temptation to try on the outfit, though; instead, she walks into the bathroom. Again, her eyes fixate on deeply stained oak surfaces that would typically be tile or marble in luxurious baths on Earth. The super-plush monogrammed towels are so thick and cuddly that she decides to immediately run bath water in the large, curved stone tub. As she removes her space suit and sinks into the warm, lavender-scented water, she says to herself, "This is truly heaven on Eartha!"

Mr. Smithy, who has a strong interest in architectural designs and interior decor, has broken away from his fellow Travelers and is walking around the hotel lobby, taking in its beauty. He walks over to one of the wooden benches and rubs the fine texture, thinking about how he might be able to replicate this material in his luxury buildings. He finally walks to his room on the twentieth floor, and as he looks out on structure after structure of varying architectural designs, he says aloud, "There must be men on this planet. I don't think women are capable of such innovation. I'll have to be craftier in asking where the men hang out. I don't think those dumb robot bellmen can tell me."

16 A Dinner for the Ages

The Travelers and the astronauts meet in the front lobby at fifty minutes after five o'clock. The hosts, led by April, enter the lobby at exactly six o'clock. They are wearing simple, ankle-length dresses that are full and beltless, but this time they come in a diverse array of colors. They don't embody the media's definition of beauty on Earth—heavy makeup, false eyelashes, plumped lips, and eye-catching hairstyles—but their poise, grace, and elegance perfectly define how true beauty should be perceived on any planet.

April greets the Travelers and astronauts and says, "I hope you all had a chance to get some rest. We have a nice dinner planned for you, and our transport is waiting."

The same hybrid limousine is parked at the hotel entrance, and once the passengers are in, it speaks to them again in a deep male voice. "Welcome back, passengers. You will arrive at your destination in ten minutes. Please sit back and relax."

The Travelers again gaze at the skyline. Its mostly glass buildings reflect the reddish rays of the sunset, and the city lights begin to make their appearance to brighten the skies. Although many vehicles are darting around in the skyways, not a sound can be heard inside the transport besides the passengers' breathing and their bodies shifting in their seats as they take in the beauty all around them.

They arrive at a one-story building that lacks the grandeur of the space center and the Eartha Palace. They exit the vehicle, and, to their surprise, they walk into a small but elegant lobby with an array of tables and benches of wood with grains similar to those at the Eartha Palace.

The hosts lead them through a narrow hallway, past several offices, and they enter a large conference room at the end. It has a floor-to-ceiling rear wall made of glass that reveals the city lights and the choreography of twinkling stars that dance around the turquoise moon, with its silver ring. The Travelers are mesmerized by the view of both the city lights and the stars as they take in this atmospheric beauty. The Almighty Apostle Bendy walks up to the glass wall and raises his arms in reverence as he says, "This is God's universe, and I feel His divine presence in this space."

Edith walks over to the Apostle and lays a hand on his shoulder as she says, "You're right, sir—this *is* God's universe, and we always treat it with the utmost reverence."

All of the Supreme Highnesses are dressed in the same simple, ankle-length, colorful dresses that the hosts wear. The five hosts join the other five Supreme Highnesses as they extend greetings to the visitors. The sound of a faintly ringing bell catches everyone's attention. Edith announces, "Ladies and gentlemen, dinner is ready. We will now move to the dining room next door." At that moment, a side wall slides upward and reveals a dining room with table settings for twenty people. The savory aromas wafting from the lavish buffet in the rear of the room overwhelm the visitors, and their salivary glands go into overdrive. The banquet offerings are an array of delicacies that include assorted seafood, poultry, and red meat. The desserts include mouthwatering fruit-filled crêpes, assorted cakes and pies, fruit tarts, and chocolate and vanilla pudding.

The visitors pile their plates with food and are ushered to their assigned seats. It is no coincidence that Ms. Harris and Mr. Stone are seated on opposite sides of the table. While they eat, the visitors barely even make small talk, only commenting periodically on the meal. Edith observes the Travelers' hearty appetites and says, "Please, help yourselves to seconds. Delicious food is one of the joys of our planet."

Judge Bottomy nods and says, "You are so right. The food is absolutely delectable." He and Mr. Stone clean their plates and head to the buffet area for second helpings.

Ms. Harris can't refrain from saying, "Thank you for the kind offer, but the snacks in my hotel room were so filling that it's hard for me to even think of another serving. I don't want to appear greedy."

Beki looks at Ms. Harris and shoots daggers through her narrowed eyes, daring Ms. Harris to speak another word.

Of course, Mr. Stone can't help himself and shoots back at Ms. Harris, "It's a good thing some of us don't go for seconds, especially if the size we're wearing is already too small."

Edith clears her throat and exchanges glances with the other Supreme Highnesses. They all look down at their plates, trying to ignore both comments, but April, Gwen, and Brooke have to place their napkins close to their mouths to hide their giggles. Beki gets Mr. Stone's attention and throws him the same threatening look that she gave to Ms. Harris.

After the meal, Edith invites the visitors back to the large conference room. This time, the astronauts are seated together next to the Travelers, with Edith and Brooke at opposite ends of the table. Edith stands and begins the discourse. "It's such a pleasure having you all here tonight. We hope you enjoyed your dinner." After she introduces each of the Supreme Highnesses by name, she continues, "We were chosen by majority vote to govern our planet for ten years. It was an honor to be chosen in a very fair and objective process, and we serve with pride, integrity, grace, and humility. We love our people and give them the best leadership and support we can offer. We connect with them on a regular basis."

Mr. Smithy raises his hand and says, "Something has been bothering me and, I know, others since we landed on Eartha. Do you have any men on this planet? I haven't seen one yet who wasn't a robot."

April answers, "We have a small male population on our planet, but we make no apologies for the fact that Eartha is a planet governed by women, with a population that is ninety-eight percent female. In addition to our male robots, we have men who visit Eartha for scientific research, for employment, and to study at our excellent universities."

Mr. Stone raises his hand and asks, "About those robots: Do you by any chance turn humans like us into robots?"

All of the Supreme Highnesses begin to laugh, and Edith explains, "Please, gentlemen, you have nothing to fear. We have the technology to make robots of all kinds, and we never, ever use humans or any other living species."

"Whew," Mr. Stone exclaims. "I was getting a bit worried."

Brooke responds to Edith's nod and stands to speak. "We know that each of you brings a unique background and experiences from Planet Earth, and we're pleased that we'll have the opportunity to get to know one another better. You are our special guests, and we want to make the most of each day you're with us. Beginning tomorrow morning, each of you will meet your host in the hotel lobby at a designated time to begin your personal welcome to Eartha. We really want you to take something special back to Earth with you. You'll need your energy for all the things we have planned for you, so please, get a good night's sleep and enjoy the delicious hotel breakfast buffet. Our dear friends and astronauts, you will have a well-deserved day of leisure tomorrow and then will enjoy the special tours and activities that we've planned for you the following days. All of you will have busy schedules and probably won't reconnect until perhaps a day or two before you travel back to Earth. Again, thank you for joining us for dinner, and have a good night."

The Supreme Highnesses rise, along with the Travelers and astronauts. Felicia escorts all of the visitors to their waiting vehicle for transport back to the hotel. The Travelers are all talking at once as they anticipate what tomorrow will bring for each of them. Judge Bottomy can't contain his curiosity as he asks Felicia, with the brightest smile he can muster, "Can you give us a clue as to what we can expect tomorrow, if that's not asking too much?"

Felicia returns his smile and responds, "Oh, I don't want to spoil it for you. Just know that it will be an unforgettable experience for each of you."

Judge Bottomy turns to the other Travelers and shrugs his shoulders as he says, "Well, I tried."

17 The Reckoning—Wyatt Stone

Mr. Stone's designated time to meet his host is at eight o'clock in the morning. He dresses after a nice, long shower and thinks about what the Supreme Highnesses may have planned for him today. He thinks, *I know I've asked some challenging questions, but they didn't seem to mind. I believe today will give me something very special to take back home. I can see myself being interviewed on all of the major networks and global news shows. I can make a lot of money off this trip. My fame will also help my recruiting efforts, as young women and girls will want to be with one of the most popular guys on Earth. Look at how the whole world fell in love with those female astronauts. With my good looks, I know all the talk shows will want me, over the others, to represent the Travelers.* He holds up the outfit that was selected for him and thinks, *I like the casual look they chose for me. I wonder who told them that I like polo shirts and jeans. They even got the color right, since I prefer lighter shades that highlight my nice tan.* As he stands in front of the mirror, admiring himself, Mr.

Stone says out loud, "You are one good-looking dude. Now, let's go and capture the hearts of those plain ole broads."

When he enters the lobby at seven fifty-five, his host, Felicia, is there waiting for him. She waves at Mr. Stone and says, "Good morning, sir. You look very refreshed. I hope you had a good night's sleep." He smiles at Felicia as he says, "Come, now, let's drop that 'sir' thing. I like first names, just as you do on Eartha, so please, call me Wyatt. And yes, I had a great night's sleep. I can't wait to see what you ladies have planned for me today."

Felicia smiles back with a twinkle in her eyes as she says, "Okay, Wyatt, it's a big day indeed, so let's be on our way."

They arrive at the Supreme Highnesses' headquarters, and Felicia leads Mr. Stone down the narrow hallway into a different large conference room. In the front of the room is a projection screen that measures at least 150 inches. Mr. Stone sees the Supreme Highnesses seated around a U-shaped table as he enters. He smiles and lifts his hand to wave at the women around the table, and Brooke says, "Good morning, Mr. Stone. We are so happy to see you. I hope you had a good night's rest. This is a special day for you, and we are grateful for your presence. We have a seat of honor for you right up front." As Felicia comes forward, takes Mr. Stone's arm, and escorts him to a seat at the head of the U-shaped table, Brooke continues, "We also have a special surprise for you, because we know you've come a long way and miss your family."

Felicia walks over to a panel and presses a button, and the room darkens as a rear view of four young girls riding bikes appears on the screen. They're in a very affluent-looking neighborhood with well-manicured lawns and modern and Victorian mansions with both city and ocean views. Mr. Stone's eyes widen, and he leans forward in his chair as he realizes his daughters are on the screen. He turns around to the women and points to the screen as he says, "Hey, those are my daughters! You know where I live and my family? I didn't know you had all of that information. You're seeing my two sets of twins, Kelly and Karen, age nine, and Maria and Marla, age eleven. My sweet girls—I miss them so much."

The women don't respond or show any form of emotion; they keep their eyes focused on the screen showing the four pretty girls with their long blond hair blowing in the wind as they ride their bikes. After getting no reaction from the women, Mr. Stone slowly turns around to look at his children again.

Suddenly, a black van with darkly tinted rear windows appears, heading toward the girls. The van pulls up so close to them that two of the girls begin to have trouble steering their bikes and both tumble to the ground. Kelly yells to her sisters riding ahead, "Maria, Marla, help us! That car almost hit us! Help!" The two older sisters are riding a couple of yards ahead of the younger ones and immediately turn their bikes around at the sound of their sisters' cries for help.

Mr. Stone is beside himself with concern. He jumps up from his chair and yells, "Oh my God, what is happening there? I know that black van. They need to run as fast as they can. Where are the neighbors? Can you make them hear me from here? I need to warn them. They're in danger!"

The women continue to look stoically at the screen and remain unresponsive to Mr. Stone's cries for help.

At that moment, the driver stops the black van close to the fallen girls, and two men, one white and one Hispanic, jump out of the van and run toward them. They grab the arms of the two girls on the ground, who are now kicking and screaming, "Don't touch us! Leave us alone! Help! Somebody, help!"

The other two girls jump off their bikes and run toward their sisters. The two men quickly kick the bikes away from the girls on the ground and grab the screaming girls, who are now trying to bite and kick to get away.

The men turn and run to the van's open rear door and literally throw the screaming girls into the back. The other two sisters run toward the van, screaming at the top of their lungs, "Stop! Somebody, help! Please help us!"

The two men now run toward the other sisters and grab them as they struggle to free themselves. They throw the two screaming girls in the back of the van with their sisters and quickly slam the door. The girls' muffled screams remain audible as the van drives away.

By now, Mr. Stone is pacing frantically, rubbing his head, and clenching his fists as he screams, "Where are my neighbors? Why isn't anyone trying to help them. Call 911! Those men will do horrible things to my daughters. I have to stop them!" He then breaks down sobbing and falls to his knees, with his head in his hands.

Felicia pauses the video as it captures a still shot of the van driving away. She turns to Mr. Stone and watches him weep for a couple of minutes. She then says forcefully to the weeping Traveler, "Wyatt Stone, stand up! Right now!"

Mr. Stone looks up at Felicia with the curious eyes of a cowering puppy and slowly rises to his feet. Felicia then advances to another slide, which shows the faces of hundreds of young girls. The next slide shows a breakdown of some ominous statistics, and she reads them aloud to Mr. Stone. "Wyatt Stone, you have masterminded the trafficking of more than two thousand young women and girls, some as young as six years old. Your human-trafficking empire sold them as sex slaves, slave laborers, and much worse. Two thousand young human beings had their lives taken away from them by you and your evil empire. You never wept for them like you just did for your daughters—not one tear.

"Now, Wyatt Stone, the Supreme Highnesses are pleased to announce that today is your day of reckoning. You have personally molested and sexually assaulted well over two hundred young girls. How could you, especially when you hold your own daughters so dear? How dare you have such disregard for human life?"

Mr. Stone makes an attempt to speak, but Felicia points her finger at him and says, "You have no voice today. You will speak only when we give you the opportunity to speak."

Mr. Stone lowers his head and looks down at the floor, and Felicia continues, "Over the past ten years, you have made more than four hundred million dollars from trafficking young girls of all ages, races, and backgrounds. They have been transported from the United States to all parts of Earth. You even partnered with an international trafficking empire to import more than five hundred young girls into the United States, primarily as sex slaves. You, Wyatt Stone, did this, and you never shed a tear of remorse. You bought a beautiful mansion, luxury cars, and expensive jewelry, took exotic vacations, and showered your twins with material gifts that are every child's dream. You've lived a great life by torturing young girls, and now you will witness what happens to those girls through the suffering of your own daughters—the daughters whom you love so very much!"

Mr. Stone pleads, "I'm so sorry. I won't do this again. Please don't hurt my daughters. Take my life, but don't let my girls go through this pain."

Felicia ignores Mr. Stone's pleas and continues, "It's too late for that." She then starts another video on the screen. It shows the four girls now huddled together in the back of the van as the two men pull them out and usher them into what looks like a well-maintained office building. One of the girls screams, "You can't do this to us! Our dad will be very angry. He has guns and he will shoot you guys!"

The men laugh and say, "Who cares about your dad?"

Another girl adds to her sister's comments as she yells, "Our dad is a very rich man, and he'll get you for this. His name is Wyatt Stone, and no one messes with him."

The men look at each other and smile mischievously as one says, "Wyatt Stone captures little girls like you all the time. He sells pretty little blond girls for a big payday. Anyway, he can't do anything right now, because he's on another planet. That sounds funny, because Wyatt Stone has always been on another planet. I wish I could see his arrogant face right now." The other man laughs heartily at the comment.

Mr. Stone is now as white as a ghost, and he stares pitifully, weeping at the screen in his feeble state, and slumps to the floor.

Felicia still shows no mercy and continues the video as the women watch in total silence. The video shows the shaken girls being taken into a room where a white woman wearing a crisp white blouse and jeans welcomes them. "Well, well, who do we have here? Aren't you ladies a pretty sight for sore eyes." She high-fives one of the men and says, "Wow, you hit the jackpot. Four pretty little blondes, and I can tell they're virgins, which is going to bring smiles to our favorite client." She runs her hands across the chests of the girls, and one slaps her hand away. The woman looks at the girl and immediately smacks her across the face and then grabs her chin and yells, "You little snobs are nothing here! You will not speak, and you will never, ever touch me or any of the men here. Do you understand?" The girls say nothing, and she slaps a second one. "Now, do you understand? Answer me!"

The girls are all crying again, and they respond in one voice, while lowering their heads, "Yes."

Mr. Stone can't take anymore, and he crawls on his knees to Felicia and begs, "Please, don't let this happen to my girls. They're so innocent. They're so young. You have no idea what will become of them. Their lives will be ruined. Please!"

Felicia looks down at Mr. Stone and scowls, then says coldly, "Get up! You have caused more than two thousand girls to experience much worse than what your daughters are experiencing, so don't you dare speak about how young they are or how their lives will be ruined. No, no, no—you will watch so that you feel the pain so many other parents have felt about the loss of their young daughters. You will watch, and you will remain silent. Why? Because human trafficking is too horrible for words. We will leave you here, and you will continue to watch everything that happens to your daughters. We'll come back in two days to check on you."

Mr. Stone yells, "Two days! You can't do this to me. What if I have to go to the bathroom? Will I have any food?"

Felicia answers, "You'll have neither, because the girls you trafficked often went without food, proper sanitation, or sleep, and never had their basic needs met. You'll have to experience it for only two days, but those two days will be a living hell for you."

Mr. Stone responds in almost a whimper, "This is cruel. I thought Eartha was supposed to be a planet of love and kindness. You broads are crazy!"

"No, Mr. Stone, we're not broads, and we're certainly not crazy," Edith says, as she rises from her seat. "It's because of our love, kindness, and caring for human life that we invited you here."

Mr. Stone snaps, "You didn't invite me here; I won the lottery to get here."

Felicia responds, "You're here because we wanted you here. You and everyone with you."

Mr. Stone attempts to speak again, but Felicia shushes him as she places her finger to her closed lips. Two male robots, who look incredibly human, walk into the room as the ten women prepare to exit. The robots stand on both sides of Mr. Stone, facing the screen, while he continues whimpering on the floor. Felicia says to Mr. Stone, "Wyatt Stone, we will see you in a couple of days." The women then walk out of the conference room, leaving Mr. Stone speechless and slumped on the floor, staring at the screen through his tears.

18 The Reckoning—the Almighty Apostle Henry Bendy

The Almighty Apostle Henry Bendy is freshly showered and kneels next to his bed to pray. "Lord, thank you for allowing me to make this voyage to another planet that you made with your own hands. You could have allowed a million others to be selected, but you chose me. For that, I am truly grateful. I pray that today will be one of the most incredible days of my life. Help me to be exposed to the raw truth of this planet. I am your representative, and I've always tried to do everything you asked me to. I know there is a reason you chose me to be here, and I pray that I get to understand that purpose. I pray for this planet and the nine people traveling with me. Let me be able to tell the story of Eartha to millions of current and new followers when I return home. I pray that my ministry will be even greater than ever before and that my popularity grows across the globe. Not that I'm seeking fame, Lord, but I just want to bring more people to you. Again, thank you for this day."

The Apostle rises, walks over to the closet, and selects a beige, long-sleeved, silk barong tagalog shirt with an embroidered front design. This formal dress shirt, worn by wealthy Filipinos, has always been one of the Apostle's favorite fashion choices. A perfectly sized pair of black dress shoes is there, along with a pair of nicely tailored black slacks. He glances at himself in the mirror after dressing and says to himself, "Praise the Lord for these good looks. I'll have those plain Janes eating out of my hand." He glances at the clock next to his bed and says to no one in particular, "I'd better grab some breakfast, because April will be waiting for me in the lobby at ten o'clock. I definitely don't want to be late." He then takes one more satisfied look at his reflection in the mirror and heads down to the hotel restaurant.

The Apostle walks into the hotel lobby at nine fifty and sees April walking through the front entrance at exactly the same time. She waves at him and says, "Good morning, sir. You look very refreshed. I hope you had a good night's sleep."

The Apostle doesn't make eye contact with April when he responds, with a slight edge in his tone, "I slept well. I'm not one for small talk, and my main focus right now is meeting with the Supreme Highnesses and learning more about Planet Eartha."

April nods and says, "Of course, and I assure you that the Supreme Highnesses are waiting for you as well. It's a big day, so let's be on our way."

They arrive at the Supreme Highnesses' headquarters,

and as they enter the building, April leads the Apostle down the narrow hallway into another large conference room. There is a projection screen in the front of the room that is the same size, 150 inches, as the one that Mr. Stone is now viewing in the other conference room. April opens the door, and the Apostle sees the Supreme Highnesses seated around a U-shaped dark mahogany table as he walks in.

Brooke greets him at the door, as he appears to be taking in both the size of the conference room and the women around the table. "Good morning, Almighty Apostle Bendy. We are so happy to see you. I hope you had a good night's rest. This is a special day for you, and we are grateful for your presence. We have a seat of honor for you right up front." April takes Apostle Bendy's arm and escorts him to a seat at the head of the U-shaped table. He scans the room while he's walking, with a cross between a scowl and an attempted smile on his face.

Once he takes his seat, April walks over to the wall panel and presses a button that slowly darkens the room. A video begins, and a magnificent megachurch appears on the screen. The camera pans the church campus to capture its expansiveness. It's situated on twenty-five acres and has its own bank, restaurant, fitness center, heated indoor pool, and lake surrounded by tall, lush cypress trees. Apostle Bendy turns around with a puzzled look at the women around the table and exclaims, "That's my church! How did you get this video of our campus?"

April walks close to where Apostle Bendy is sitting and says to him, "This is a live stream of activities taking place today at your church. I think you'll be very interested in what's happening."

Apostle Bendy sits back in his chair in an erect position with his shoulders back, his lips tight, and his steely eyes zeroed in on the screen.

The live streaming continues in the main sanctuary, where several hundred people are gathered to hear a young man speaking. They greet him with chants: "We love Pastor Monty! We love Pastor Monty!"

Pastor Monty, wearing a striped, long-sleeved shirt and jeans, waves at the crowd and shouts, "We have endured almost three decades of the Almighty Apostle Henry Bendy's greed and corruption. He has lived the good life. No, it's better than the good life. He's lived a great life on the backs of this congregation. He has a gigantic mansion with fine cars and a private jet, while far too many members of our congregation are barely making ends meet. We even have members who are homeless, but does he care?"

The people shout, "No, he doesn't care!"

Apostle Bendy stands up and shouts, "I do care! What is he talking about? He's trying to take over my church. God has allowed me to prosper, and he's just jealous. I need to stop him. You have to let me speak to my people!"

April pauses the streaming, walks over to Apostle Bendy, and says, softly but firmly, "Sir, you need to sit down. You will watch every minute of what's happening at your church without further outbursts. Do you understand? Every minute. Now, please, sit down."

Apostle Bendy clenches his fists but does as she asks.

April walks back to the panel and restarts the live streaming. The young man's voice is filled with emotion as his tears begin to fall. "The Almighty Apostle Henry Bendy cares only about himself. What man of God refers to himself as the Almighty Apostle? Who made him almighty? It's his selfish acts of arrogance and pride. That man has stooped so low that he's taken advantage of our members who have fallen on hard times. He has his own form of slave labor as they work at his house and don't get paid one dime. He exploits our people every way that he can. The man doesn't even have a conscience. He comes here every Sunday, wearing his expensive robes and fine jewelry, and sits on that gold throne and claims to be one of God's anointed. He doesn't worship God. He thinks *he's* God. We can't allow him to prostitute the word of God for his own greed. We've tolerated his unthinkable behavior far too long. You, as children of God, deserve better, God *wants* you to have better.

"The Apostle's special council is made up of men who are his puppets, and he rewards them handsomely. They won't make the right decision, so I'm asking you today to remove the Almighty Apostle Henry Bendy as the leader of this church, God's holy temple. I believe he left the planet for a reason, and we need to make sure that if and when he comes back, he is no longer the leader of this church."

Apostle Bendy jumps up from his chair and shouts, "I've seen enough! I've seen enough! That young hooligan is trying to take over my church while I'm away. I've always been suspicious of him. He's going to be so disappointed, because I know my people love me and won't let this happen. I'm one of the most popular religious leaders in America, maybe on Earth!"

April stands in front of the U-shaped table and speaks to the Supreme Highnesses. "Ladies, Apostle Bendy believes his congregation loves him so much that they would never toss him out. I think he should hear from some of his members whom Pastor Monty called to the front of the sanctuary to share their opinions about Apostle Bendy. Would you like to hear from them?"

"Yes!" the other Supreme Highnesses yell.

The Apostle screeches, "Go ahead and listen to them. My wife is sitting there, and they love us both. They wouldn't say anything negative about me or my wife. We've done so much for our church and our congregation."

April levels the Apostle with her gaze as she says, "Apostle Bendy, the Supreme Highnesses have spoken, and more than one thousand people volunteered to share their opinions, but only a hundred were selected. You will not leave this room until you've heard all one hundred of them. You will listen with no interruptions and no comments."

"Wait a minute!" the Apostle shouts. "You can't keep me here against my will. That's kidnapping. I thought you women were supposed to promote goodwill and make this visit memorable for us. You're treating me like a criminal. Are you treating the white Travelers this way? I certainly doubt it. I'm seeing wickedness here that turns my stomach. You women should be ashamed of yourselves."

April shakes her head at the Apostle's verbal rant and speaks to him in a voice filled with raw anger: "I won't dignify your comment about your treatment because of your race, for we despise racism in any form. How dare you, one of the worse hypocrites we've ever seen, chastise us about wickedness and tell us we should be ashamed? You scum of Planet Earth. You used the Bible to exploit innocent people. Who are you to pressure people, in the name of your Jesus, to work at your home without pay? You have the gall to lie to people during your large gatherings about healing the afflicted, when you hire actors to pretend they're paralyzed in wheelchairs. You go through this theatrical demonstration of laying your hands on their heads and then telling them to stand up and walk. You are a despicable man, and you will suffer the consequences of your wrongdoing. The Almighty Apostle Henry Bendy, today is your day of reckoning. Now, sit down! You will listen to all one hundred comments from people speaking truth about what they think of you. You'll learn that you're not loved anywhere near as much as you believe, sir. Two members of our robotic security team will keep you company as you listen intently. We will come back to see you in a couple of days, once all one hundred people have spoken."

The conference door opens, and two security robots enter the room. They walk over to Apostle Bendy's chair and stand on each side of him. Apostle Bendy sits erect again, with his eyes now focused on the screen. He looks to neither the right nor the left as Pastor Monty asks the first person to go to one of the microphones stationed throughout the sanctuary and share their personal experience in dealing with Apostle Bendy.

A gentleman, probably in his early sixties, slowly walks up to one of the microphones. He looks around at the large audience, clears his throat, lowers his head, and then stands silently, as if he's afraid to speak. Pastor Monty encourages him: "Come on, Brother Bell, you have nothing to fear. We all want to hear what you have to say, so don't be afraid to speak up."

The predominantly Black audience, in their usual church cadence, say, "Come on, Brother Bell, speak the truth!"

Brother Bell lifts his head, and the words begin to flow with pent-up anger and passion. "I was dealing with the loss of my job of fifteen years as a chef. I've always tithed a tenth of my earnings, even when I could barely make ends meet. I was desperate to find work to feed my family. I asked for a meeting with the Almighty Apostle Henry Bendy, hoping that I could find some work around the church, since we have several facilities. If necessary, I was willing to mow lawns or wash dishes in the church restaurant.

"When I met with the Almighty Apostle Henry Bendy, I told him about my dilemma. He asked me if I was a good chef. I told him that I was an excellent chef and had won local competitions because of my skills. He told me that he had the perfect job for me and to come to his home the next morning. I was thrilled and thanked God for His wonderful servant.

"I showed up at the Apostle's home, his huge mansion, the next morning and rang the front doorbell. A maid answered the door and directed me to the back door. I walked to the back door, and another worker directed me to the kitchen, where I would be given instructions. A person in a chef's uniform met me and told me that he was the head chef and that I would be working with him. I was so excited. He and I prepared daily menus that week, and let me tell you, I'm talking about the best seafood, pastas, salads, pastries—we did it all. I typically worked twelve hours a day. At the end of the week, I was looking forward to getting a paycheck, since my house note was due. No paycheck on Friday, no paycheck on Saturday, and then no paycheck on Sunday.

"When I reported to work on Monday, I asked the head

chef about my pay. He looked at me and said, 'What paycheck?' I said, 'The paycheck for my work as a chef.' He laughed and said, 'Oh my goodness, didn't you know you're not being paid? This is one of the ways you're contributing to the church when you can't afford to pay your tithes.'

"I was mortified and felt such frustration and anger. I tried to meet with the Almighty Apostle Henry Bendy, but I couldn't get an appointment. I ended up losing my home, and my wife left me after four months of unemployment. I don't wish the man any harm, but the Almighty Apostle Henry Bendy is pure evil. He basically used me and others at his mansion as slave labor. I hope and pray that the people here today will make sure that he doesn't get the opportunity to lead this church or any other church. He is not a man of God, and he will one day pay dearly for his wickedness.

Apostle Bendy maintains his stoic expression and says nothing. April says to him, "This is just the beginning. You have ninety-nine more testimonies, and we'll see when we return if you still believe that your congregation loves you so much."

The Supreme Highnesses exit the conference room, leaving Apostle Bendy alone to watch the screen with his two security robots and hear with absolute clarity what his congregation really thinks about him.

19 The Reckoning—Sweetie Harris

Ms. Sweetie Harris typically lingers in bed most mornings because she's not an early riser. Today, however, she awoke early with high anticipation about what's in store for her when she spends time with the Supreme Highnesses. She loves the fact that such strong women are in control of Planet Eartha, but as far as she's concerned, they could do so much more to improve their appearance. She cringes every time she sees them in those drab dresses and no makeup. With the right help from her, they could improve their looks 1,000 percent.

She peeks in the closet and checks out the clothing they've selected for her, and says to herself, "My goodness, it's hard to believe that such plain Janes could choose outfits that I would have chosen myself. I guess they just don't show their good taste in their own wardrobe."

She removes a dark blue dress with small white flowers from its silk clothes hanger and immediately feels the softness of the fabric and presses it against her cheek. She smiles at the sheer pleasure of its texture. She pulls the dress over her head and stands in front of the mirror to admire how it flatters every inch of her shapely body. It certainly was well worth the tens of thousands of dollars she's invested in tummy tucks, breast implants, butt injections, and having a couple of ribs removed to create her signature small waist and oversize buttocks.

Ms. Harris glances at the clock near her bed and realizes that her host, Gail, will be meeting her in the hotel lobby in less than an hour. She applies her makeup, fumbling a bit with her false eyelashes while thinking, *I bet those men didn't have to go through anywhere near what I've had to do this morning to achieve these awesome results. Those scum-bags, especially that Wyatt Stone character. He disgusts me with his inflated ego. I can't stand that guy!* She takes one last look in the mirror and heads to the lobby to meet Gail.

Ms. Harris walks into the elegant lobby at twelve noon on the dot and finds Gail waiting for her. Gail waves at Ms. Harris and says, "Good afternoon, Ms. Harris. You look very refreshed. I hope you had a good night's sleep."

Ms. Harris is more focused on Gail's attire than on her greeting, thinking, *Here she is again, wearing another unim-pressive outfit. I was hoping things might be different today. My goodness!*

She manages to say, "Well, hello, Gail. It's so good to see you. I slept like a baby, and I'm so excited about your plans for the day. You look nice today. I've tried going without makeup, but it doesn't work for me."

Gail ignores Ms. Harris's comments and says, "Let's get going. You have a big day ahead of you. Our transportation is waiting out front."

As they're entering the vehicle, Ms. Harris asks, "Do you mind telling me where we're going today?"

Gail answers, "Oh, we wanted it to be a surprise, but I guess I can tell you. We're going to one of the largest health expositions on Planet Eartha. We know you have an interest in the health of young girls, and this will give you a chance to see the wonderful work we're doing."

Ms. Harris takes in the response and says to herself, *Really! A health fair is what they thought I'd enjoy? I was sure they were going to give me a chance to show off my Planet Earth beauty.* Instead, she says, "Sounds wonderful. I look forward to it."

Intuiting Ms. Harris's thoughts, Gail says, "Rest assured, you will certainly be the center of attention at this event."

Ms. Harris gives Gail a broad smile of satisfaction as she thinks, *Now,* that's *what I'm talking about.*

They arrive at a massive structure where thousands of people have gathered. The building has walls of curved glass and steel, which appears to be a popular architectural design on Eartha. As they exit the vehicle, Ms. Harris makes sure that any spectators catch a glimpse of her well-toned, long legs before her curvaceous body emerges. As Gail watches Ms. Harris's dramatic exit, she rolls her eyes but says nothing.

Gail escorts Ms. Harris to a large conference room inside the building, and when she opens the door, Ms. Harris sees the Supreme Highnesses seated around a beautiful, U-shaped mahogany table.

Brooke says, "Good afternoon, Ms. Harris. We are so happy to see you. I hope you had a good night's rest. This is a special day for you, and we are grateful for your presence. We have a seat of honor for you right up front."

Ms. Harris glances around the room, presses her palms against her hips—something she does routinely when she has an audience—and says, "Thank you all for having me here."

Gail shows Ms. Harris to her seat in the front of the room and then walks over to a panel and waves her hand as a large screen descends from the tall ceiling.

A video begins, showing Ms. Harris's website and an advertisement that depicts an overweight, unsmiling, olive-skinned teenage girl with dark brown hair, sad eyes, thick thighs and waist, and acne on her chubby face. She is wearing a one-piece bathing suit with a skirted bottom. The caption underneath her photo reads, "Do you want to look like her?"

Next, a thin, shapely teenage girl in a bright orange bikini with flowing blond hair, bright blue eyes, and perfect skin and teeth appears on the screen, along with the caption "Or do you want to like her?"

Ms. Harris then makes an appearance, touting the value of her products. "I know who you want to look like, all one million of you. You want to look like this young lady."

The blond teenage girl reappears on the screen, with a smile that shows her perfect white teeth, and says, "Hello, girls, I'm Ashley."

Ms. Harris continues, "Let me tell you how you can have this body. All you need to do is try my special weight and digestive aids, and you'll begin seeing results in less than ten weeks. If you want quicker access to stunning good looks, here's a list of my highly recommended medical professionals who are among the best in the country in breast, chin, or cheek enhancement; eyelid, neck, and brow lifts; tummy tucks; liposuction; and more. There's absolutely no reason for you to look like this." The overweight teenager reappears on the screen.

Ms. Harris continues, this time sitting on a high stool that accentuates her shapely legs, with Ashley standing next to her, "You think Ashley was born with this awesome body? She only wishes. She achieved it through a combination of my weight aids and cosmetic surgery. I know that exercise and eating right are so important, but for most of us, they don't lead to this gorgeous figure." She gestures to Ashley's body. "Ashley is a cheerleader. Her phone is constantly ringing with calls from boys asking her out, and she's also a part-time model. She doesn't live off lettuce and eats a healthy diet, but no harm to her if she decides to eat a juicy burger and fries. My weight aid devours those calories, so it's the same as eating lettuce, but without the hunger."

Gail stops the video at that point and speaks directly to Ms. Harris. "Ms. Harris, did you know that one hundred thousand teenage girls have experienced dangerous side effects from your products? Some of those side effects were so severe that they caused the death of two hundred girls. And did you know that one hundred girls committed suicide because they couldn't get a body like Ashley's?"

Gail pauses and shakes her head before continuing, "Ms. Sweetie Harris, you need a dose of your own medicine, and today is the day. Ladies, we've heard straight from the mouth of Ms. Harris, with no redeeming grace. Shall we put our plan into action?"

The Supreme Highnesses all say, "Yes!"

Edith adds, "Yes, and to the fullest extent. There's no mercy for this one, but let's be kind. She's been sitting there for a while, so please show some respect and at least give our guest a glass of water. We've had the pleasure of sipping our own cold water and haven't offered Ms. Harris any."

Ms. Harris turns around to Edith and says, "Thank you. I'm very thirsty. At least one of you has some manners."

Laura gets up, pours Ms. Harris a glass of water, and hands it to her. Ms. Harris takes a long drink and empties the glass. As she takes a deep breath, she places both hands against her forehead and says, "I don't feel quite right," then lapses into unconsciousness.

When Ms. Harris wakes up, she opens her eyes and, as she looks around, sees that she's no longer in the conference room. She realizes that she's in a well-lit, mostly glass-walled room instead. Her body feels different, but she's not sure exactly why. Her eyes are closed as she runs her hands across her chest and is shocked to discover that one breast is much larger than the other. It's as if one breast is a triple-D cup and the other is an A cup. Her hands move down to her waist, and that's still the same, but she makes another discovery as she touches her hips. One is a normal size, and the other is protruding abnormally. In fact, as she slowly raises herself up to a kneeling position and touches her buttocks, she finds that one buttock is much larger than the other. She stands facing the back wall and looks down at her legs, and one leg is also grossly oversize. When she turns around to face the glass front wall, she realizes that hundreds of people are gawking and pointing at her.

Ms. Harris tries to scream, but no sound comes out. She begins sobbing as she takes in the transformation of her once coveted body. Lucy, one of the Supreme Highnesses, is standing outside the glass wall and pointing at Ms. Harris as she speaks to a crowd of hundreds of teenage schoolgirls. "This woman is an example of someone who ingested harmful products and underwent dangerous cosmetic surgeries to make her body conform to the white media's definition of female beauty on Planet Earth. Her now misshapen body is what happens when you allow others to define who you are. She allowed herself to become an aberration, instead of accepting the beautiful body that her God gave her. Look at this pitiful human being and see the sadness in her eyes as her tears flow like water from a broken dam."

Lucy asks the crowd to walk over to a stage, where four young ladies wearing colorful pastel blouses and dark slacks are waiting. She gestures at them and says, "These women all have different skin colors, different body types and sizes, and different hair textures and styles. But look at them. Watch how they move, the look of happiness in their eyes, the way they stand with pride and dignity. They love their bodies just as they are. They are healthy young women with a purpose far greater than living out someone else's jaded and warped definition of beauty—unlike the poor creature on the other side of the hallway, who's experiencing disfigurement from attempts to alter her form. I applaud them."

Ms. Harris hears Lucy's comments and tries to scream again, but only her tears of distress continue to flow. Lucy walks the crowd back to Ms. Harris's glass chamber, where Ms. Harris is now pounding on the wall and crying out, "You wicked, evil women! Look what you did to my body! I've only tried to help girls look their best. I'm not a bad person. I love people, but I can't help it if some are better than others. What's wrong with helping people look their best and not get stuck with bodies they don't like? I've made so many people happy. You're looking only at the negative side of my work, not the good side. Please, I want my body back the way it was when I arrived here. It's not right what you've done to me."

She hears a familiar voice coming through the ceiling of her chamber, as Edith says, "Ms. Harris, you still don't get it. You caused so many young girls and women to hate their bodies because of your definition of beauty. You peddled your useless products and promoted unnecessary and dangerous surgeries for your own gain. Yet you feel no remorse for what you've done. Look at those people out there, staring at you as an abnormal being. That's exactly how you caused teenage girls and young women to look at themselves—at their healthy, beautiful selves. You are a murderer and a destroyer, not just of lives, but of dreams and bright futures. Think about what would happen if you returned to Planet Earth in your current condition. You would be on display in those events you earthlings call circuses. People will gawk at you and taunt you, just like teenage girls on your websites taunt other girls who don't fit the images you promote. Shame on you, Ms. Sweetie Harris. Shame on you! This is your day of reckoning."

Ms. Harris cries out to Edith, "I will do better—I promise. I've learned my lesson, and I now know that the things I've done were wrong. Please, just give me back my normal body. Please!"

Edith laughs. "Your 'normal body'—is that what you really want? You haven't had a normal body in twenty-five years. What you're really asking for is your synthetic, manufactured body. Maybe you'll get it back, and maybe you won't. You'll have some time to think about it over the next couple of days as you remain in this glass chamber and experience what it's like to be seen as an aberration. We'll talk then and determine what the future holds for you. Oh, and one more thing: We have two lovely guests to keep you company while you're in here."

Suddenly, in the rear of the chamber, two female robots appear, with perfectly shaped bodies like the one Ms. Harris had before her disfigurement. They are wearing stylish black designer knit dresses that fit snugly around their hips and fall below their knees, as well as six-inch stiletto heels.

Ms. Harris looks at the robots and puts her hands to her mouth and says, "What the hell! How dare you put these things in here with me? Haven't you tortured me enough with what you've done to my body? You evil witches!" She again pounds frantically on the glass wall with both fists and screams, "You can't do this to me! I will tell everyone on Earth about this. Let me out of here! Please, please." She breaks down sobbing under the watchful eyes of the two robots, who stand quietly, looking out at the crowd through the glass wall. A new and larger group gathers around Ms. Harris's chamber to listen to Lucy again explain the difference between Ms. Harris and the young women on the stage nearby.

20 The Reckoning—Judge Morcus Bottomy

Judge Bottomy jumps out of the shower shortly before he is scheduled to meet Carmen in the hotel lobby for what will most surely be a day for him to shine by showing off his superior intelligence to the Supreme Highnesses. He's had a hearty breakfast in his room, and now, while drying himself, he thinks about what the day's plans might entail. *I'm certainly the smartest of the Travelers, so they'll probably want to know what it's like being a distinguished judge on Planet Earth. After talking to that arrogant nigger preacher who calls himself the Almighty Apostle, and to that fake Miss Plastic America, they probably think we earthlings are the dumbest beings in the universe. Stone and Smithy aren't that much better. The Supreme Highnesses will be impressed with my intellect and my experience as a no-nonsense judge. I don't regret one bit the number of kids I've locked up. Society is in a much better position with them off the streets. Anyway, it's not good to keep a Supreme Highness waiting, so I'd better hurry. I definitely don't want*

Carmen to think I don't value her time. Who knows what that odd-looking bunch of women might do to a man like me?

He walks out of his room and takes the elevator to the lobby, where Carmen is waiting for him. She waves at the judge and says, "Good afternoon, sir. You look very refreshed. I hope you had a good night's sleep."

Judge Bottomy greets Carmen in a cheerful tone. "Good afternoon, Carmen. I did sleep well. It's so good to see you. I'm excited to meet with the Supreme Highnesses so we can get to know each other better."

Carmen responds, just as cheerfully, "I assure you that the Supreme Highnesses are excited about spending time with you today. It's a big day, so let's be on our way."

They arrive at the Supreme Highnesses' headquarters and head to another large conference room. A 150-inch projection screen, the same size as the one that Mr. Stone and Apostle Bendy are now viewing in the other conference rooms, hangs on the wall. Judge Bottomy sees the Supreme Highnesses seated around a U-shaped dark mahogany table as he walks into the room.

Brooke greets him at the door, and he suddenly has a good feeling about what the day holds for him. "Good morning, Judge Bottomy. We are so happy to see you. I hope you had a good night's rest. This is a special day for you, and we are grateful for your presence. We have a seat of honor for you right up front. Carmen, please escort Judge Bottomy to his chair."

Carmen takes Judge Bottomy's arm and leads him to a seat at the head of the U-shaped table. He smiles continuously and nods to the women, trying his best to get

Edith's attention, recognizing that she's the supreme leader, but Edith does a good job of avoiding contact by engaging in a conversation with one of the other Supreme Highnesses.

Once Judge Bottomy takes his seat, Carmen walks over to the wall panel and presses a button that slowly darkens the room. A video begins, and Judge Bottomy's courtroom appears on the screen. A robed African American judge is talking to a white bailiff.

Judge Bottomy looks at the screen and frowns as he says, "Hey, that's my courtroom. What's that guy doing there? How did you get a video in my courtroom? I don't allow videos."

Carmen says, "This is a live stream in your *former* courtroom."

Judge Bottomy jumps from his chair and snaps at Carmen, "What do you mean, my *former* courtroom? I am—"

Carmen interrupts him, "Judge Bottomy, please take your seat. This is the time for you to watch and listen. You are not holding court here. Right now, I am the judge and these nine ladies seated at the table are the jury. Now, please sit!"

Judge Bottomy's lips tighten, and his cold-eyed stare at Carmen has no effect on her stance, so he slowly sits down.

As the streaming continues, the group can hear the conversation between the judge and the bailiff. The judge says to the bailiff, "This courtroom has been assigned to Judge Bottomy for at least two decades. I was surprised to get the call to move in here after so many years. Do you know what happened?"

The bailiff answers, "Well, you didn't hear this from me, but that Bottomy was as mean as a snake, and he was especially cruel to young Black boys. He is a stone-cold racist. We'd have boys come in here with no priors, for minor shoplifting, and sometimes, because of poverty and no representation, they'd be forced to accept a plea deal when it was doubtful that they'd even committed a crime. Bottomy would give them harsh sentences regardless. I've seen a fifteen-year-old Black kid come before him who was a straight-A student and was arrested for allegedly spraying graffiti at his school. The kid denied that he committed this act and had some strong witnesses who supported his innocence and gave him terrific character references. I personally believed the kid, but Bottomy gave him two years in juvenile detention. I personally followed up on the boy, and he wasn't the same kid who walked into this courtroom two years earlier. He had become hardened, and I believe he now has a criminal path ahead of him, instead of college. I pray that I'm wrong. Bottomy could easily have released him or sent him to a diversion program. He just seemed to have this evil streak in him whenever a Black boy came to court.

"On the other hand, he was super lenient with the white boys. I've seen some monsters come in here, like a kid who attacked his mom and dad with a hammer. Bottomy assigned him to counseling, instead of sending his sorry butt to juvenile detention until he was eighteen. That kid eventually murdered one of his friends over a lost bet. The world is a better place now that Bottomy is not on the bench."

The judge shook his head and said, "I heard he was tough, but I had no idea he was such a racist."

Judge Bottomy stands up and rams his right fist into the

back of his chair, which looks lightweight but is actually made of steel. As he nurses what may be a broken hand, he yells out, "That guy is a liar! I'm not a racist! Someone has to keep those young Black thugs in check, and I took on the job of getting that done. The streets are safer because of how I dispensed justice, stopping these degenerates before they became adult criminals."

Carmen glares at Judge Bottomy as she says, "You're a despicable man, and you've been a force for injustice far too long. Today, Judge Bottomy, you will see firsthand what injustice looks like as you experience the hell your son will experience, the hell you've caused for thousands of young men of color. Sit back down, because there's more in store for you." She adds sarcastically, with a slight smile, "By the way, how's your hand? I hope it isn't broken."

Nursing his right hand, Judge Bottomy takes his seat as the streaming continues. The judge is seen walking back to his chamber, and shortly thereafter, the courtroom begins to fill with lawyers, courtroom staff, and spectators.

After a series of hearings, the next case to come before the judge involves a young white male, around sixteen years old. He walks awkwardly, shuffling into the courtroom because of his leg irons, with his head bowed. He's handcuffed and wearing an orange jumpsuit, and as he takes his seat next to his lawyer, he's visibly shaken, his face streaked with tears. Judge Bottomy screams, "No! That's my son! Why is my son in this courtroom? He's a straight-A student and has never been in any kind of trouble. He comes from a good family. This is wrong! I need to stop this hearing."

Gail signals with a hand gesture for Judge Bottomy to stop talking.

As the door to the judge's chambers opens, the bailiff announces, "Please rise. The Court of the Third Judicial Circuit, Juvenile Division, is now in session. The Honorable Chawn Jankins is presiding."

Judge Jankins enters the courtroom and sits on the bench. He looks out at the defendant, now squirming in his seat, and then reviews the petition for this disposition hearing, where he will make a decision about the minor's future treatment, care, or punishment.

Judge Jankins speaks to the defendant's lawyer and says, "The defendant, Jeremy Bottomy, has been charged with shoplifting in a local game store. He pleaded not guilty. The store cameras show him putting something in his backpack, but it's not clear what he took. The police searched the backpack and found a game DVD that belonged to the store. Several character witnesses have spoken on his behalf, and I thank them for taking the time to support this young man. Mr. Bottomy also has no prior criminal record. I understand, however, that he has been rude to court officials. One official said that while he was walking the defendant into the courtroom, the defendant warned him that he'd better be careful because his dad is a big-time judge. Mr. Bottomy, please stand up."

Jeremy's lawyer nudges him, and he slowly rises from his chair. Judge Jankins says, "Young man, I understand that your father is a judge, and that would certainly work in your favor if he were handling this case. However, he's not the judge in this courtroom. In fact, I understand that he's even on another planet. So today, I'm the judge. After weighing every aspect of this case, I've reached a decision and hereby sentence Mr. Bottomy to two years in juvenile detention. A change in your attitude, young man, could lead to less time served, and I hope that's the case. This court is adjourned." Judge Jankins gives Jeremy Bottomy one more stern look and then leaves the bench.

Jeremy Bottomy collapses on the floor and cries uncontrollably as the bailiff announces, "All rise!"

Judge Bottomy leaps from his chair with fire in his eyes and yells, "You dirty Black nigger! What's the matter with you? How dare you do this to my son? This is cruel and inhumane treatment! These are trumped-up charges! He's a good kid and should have been sent home for a minor offense. This is not a court of justice but the center of injustice. " He turns and looks at the Supreme Highnesses and screams at them, "You witches! You caused this to happen. I'm going to let everyone on Earth know how cruel you are and that no one should ever visit here again. You're heartless and evil bitches."

The women look at him stone-faced and say nothing. Then Carmen walks over to Judge Bottomy and gets very close to his face as she says, with a hardened stare, "You have some nerve to call us heartless and female animals. For decades, you've been cruel and heartless to young men of color, especially young Black men. You've given harsh sentences for the most minor offenses; some were not even guilty of a crime, but you didn't care. They wept before you, and you looked down on them from your mighty bench as if they were rubbish. Judge Morcus Bottomy, you will spend the next two days watching what happens to young men—including your beloved son—when they're unjustly incarcerated and sent to detention centers, how they're strip searched, how they're harassed, how their self-esteem is destroyed. You will watch, and you will not leave this room until we return. Now, sit down!"

Judge Bottomy is so angry that he spits in Carmen's face. To his surprise, the spit stops in midair and becomes much larger than what left his mouth. It turns into ugly, yellowish-green mucus with the most horrific smell and turns back full force into his own face, entering his nostrils and mouth. Carmen gives him a scornful smile while saying, "Don't forget where you are, Judge Bottomy. You're not dealing with helpless young men; you're up against the most powerful women in the universe. Don't ever show any form of aggression to us again. Do I make myself clear?"

Judge Bottomy gags and chokes as he mumbles, "Yes."

Carmen smiles again and says, "Good. Now, sit back down!"

Two robotic men walk into the room and stand on each side of Judge Bottomy's chair as he continues to gag from the horrible substance in his nostrils and mouth. He pulls out his shirttail and tries to wipe the gunk off his face, and blows his nose into his shirt, but the mucus stays in place.

Judge Bottomy takes his seat as the streaming continues and shows his son still crying uncontrollably as a guard yanks his arm and yells, "Stand up, you little scum, and stop crying, or I'll really give you something to cry about."

The boy struggles to walk in his leg irons and, in his weakened state, stumbles and falls. The guard puts his foot on Jeremy's back and laughs as he yells, "Didn't I tell you to stand up? Don't think your big-time judge daddy can help you now. He's a coward, anyway, always throwing his weight around. You're nothing but a fresh piece of meat back here. Now, get your ass up!"

Jeremy tries to stand, but the guard still has his foot on his back and continues laughing as he watches the boy struggle. Once again, Judge Bottomy weeps uncontrollably with his face in his hands and fresh tears mixed with the awful substance on his face. The Supreme Highnesses watch, still emotionless, and then turn and walk out of the conference room.

21 The Reckoning—Jorrome Smithy

Mr. Smithy is fully dressed in the tan khakis and pink-and-white, button-down oxford shirt that are a staple of his wardrobe. He rubs his hands against his thighs and then wrings his hands, a habit he has when he's nervous or anxious. Like the other Travelers, he is curious about the plans for his day with the Supreme Highnesses. He spent the entire night tossing and turning as he ruminated about his large real estate holdings and whether his team was making the right decisions during his absence. He looks in the mirror and frowns at his receding hairline while combing his hair and thinks, *I can't believe they knew my taste in clothes. Who knows what these women have in store for me today? I would rather have had a nice round of golf with some Eartha fellows, but they're nowhere to be found, unless I want to golf with robots. Wait until I tell the guys back home about this place. No way in hell am I gonna encourage them to come here. I'm surprised that Planet Eartha has advanced to this level without some form of male dominance. I bet male figures come in from other galaxies to provide intellectual talent. Maybe they're men disguised as women, just to test us. I hate the idea of having to spend time with them today, but, since I have no choice, I'll make the best of it.*

He glances over at the clock and decides he'd better rush down to the lobby to meet his host, Robin.

He steps out of the elevator into the elegant lobby, and Robin is already waiting for him to arrive. She rushes over to greet him and says, "Good afternoon, Mr. Smithy. You look very refreshed. I hope you had a good night's sleep."

Mr. Smithy lies, "Yes, I slept like a newborn baby. It's good to see you, and I'm so excited about what lies ahead for me today. It is truly an honor to be in the presence of the Supreme Highnesses."

Robin nods and directs Mr. Smithy to the front entrance as she says, "Okay, let's get going. You have a big day in store for you."

They enter the waiting vehicle and travel to the Supreme Highnesses' headquarters. When they reach the facility, Robin leads Mr. Smithy down the narrow hallway to yet another large conference room. Robin opens the door, and Mr. Smithy sees the Supreme Highnesses seated around a beautiful, U-shaped mahogany table as he walks into the room. Brooke greets him at the door as Mr. Smithy scans the room and can't help himself from wondering, *How do these women create these magnificent structures? There must be men somewhere.*

Edith extends her standard greeting to Mr. Smithy: "Good afternoon, Mr. Smithy. We are so happy to see you. I hope you had a good night's rest. This is a special day for you, and we are grateful for your presence. We have a seat of honor for you right up front. Robin, please escort

Mr. Smithy to his seat." Robin does as she's asked, and Mr. Smithy's chest puffs up as he walks with his chin up and a big grin on his face.

Robin goes over to a panel and waves her hand. A large screen descends from the high ceiling, and a magnificent mansion appears. Robin addresses the room: "Mr. Smithy has one of the most exclusive mansions in his state. As this virtual tour illustrates, he has spared no expense in acquiring original oil paintings, beautifully hand-woven Persian and hand-knotted Lazarus area rugs, multimillion-dollar chandeliers, and exotic plants from all over Planet Earth. His mansion has two custom kitchens with top-of-the-line Signature Kitchen Suite appliances, and ten luxurious bathrooms, where his vast collection of bonsai trees grows directly out of stone vanity countertops. The mansion also has three stunning swimming pools with waterfalls that put any luxury resort to shame."

Mr. Smithy sits up straight in his chair and crosses his legs at the display of his wealth. He can't help himself when he says, "Hey, where did you get this video? This mansion is my pride and joy. You should know that I personally assisted in decorating the entire place, down to the tiniest detail. Did you by chance see the statue by the main entrance? I thought since I work hard for my money, why put up a statue of some dead guy? Why not me instead?"

Robin advances the video so the Supreme Highnesses can see the statue and says, "Oh, you mean this piece? Rumor has it you paid the sculptor two million dollars for it."

Mr. Smithy shrugs and says, "Why not? I'm proud of who I am and what I've accomplished."

Next, Robin advances the video to show a series of deplorable, run-down apartment complexes, desperately in need of repair. The virtual tour enters one apartment where three small Hispanic children are watching television in the living room. The place is tidy but practically falling apart. The ceiling has missing tiles and exposed wiring. It's also bulging from water damage, and the walls are covered with actively growing gray and black splotches of thick, velvety mold. It's common knowledge that mold is highly toxic and causes long-lasting, serious health issues, especially for children, seniors, and pregnant women.

The mother of the children says to the camera, "I pay five hundred dollars a month for this dilapidated apartment because it's close to decent schools and there's a bus stop close by, which is important for me as a single mom with no car. I work two jobs just to get by and keep a roof over our heads. We've lived here for two years, and I've complained over and over about the mold, the broken toilet, the power outages, and so much more. The landlord doesn't care. You can go through each of the apartments here, and you'll see that they're all in the same horrible condition. I'm trying to save money to move, but I've had to pay for medicine for my children, who have asthma as a result of the mold." She tries to hold back her tears, but they begin to flow as she says, "If the landlord would just care one bit . . . He would never have his own family live under these conditions—never."

Mr. Smithy stands and turns to speak to the Supreme Highnesses, using hand gestures for effect. "You need to understand that those people don't know how to take care of property. I can go in and make repairs, and they'll be damaged in no time. That girl's lucky to have a place close to schools and a bus stop, so I don't know why she's complaining. She's worried about those kids, but she should have thought about them when she got knocked up three times. Give me a break that she's worried about the dangers of mold. Anyway, I've had health inspections done and they always give my buildings a passing grade."

"Isn't it true," Robin asserts, "that your brother-in-law heads up the city's inspection department and that's why you get passing grades? You live in an opulent mansion and have absolutely no concern for the poor people living in squalor in your apartment buildings."

Mr. Smithy shouts at Robin, "You don't know me, lady!"

"I know you better than you think," Robin retorts. "I know that you are a despicable human being who cares for no one but yourself. That statue of you is living proof of your narcissism and self-absorption. It's time that you learn why it's important to treat your tenants as human beings, not disposable objects."

Mr. Smithy rubs his receding hairline and asks Robin, "While you're ripping me a new one, can you at least give me a glass of water? I'm thirsty as hell."

Laura immediately stands up and pours a glass of water from the pitcher in front of her on the U-shaped table and brings it to him, saying, "Mr. Smithy, I apologize that we didn't offer you a drink. Please forgive our rudeness."

He nods and takes the glass of water, drinks it all in two gulps, and hands the glass back to Laura. Laura smiles shrewdly at Robin as she walks back to her seat.

Mr. Smithy feels different when he awakens a short

while later. He's lying on the floor, and as he raises himself up, he realizes that he's no longer in the conference room. A foul smell enters his nostrils, and he feels something crawling over his hand on the floor. He looks down and sees that it's a large rat. He screams and jumps to his feet. As he scans the scene, he discovers that he's in a filthy, dilapidated studio apartment. He sees a door and rushes over to escape, but the door disappears into a solid wall when he tries to open it. He shouts, "Where am I? What have you done to me? Let me out of here! You can't do this to me!"

He suddenly hears a familiar voice as Robin yells back, "Mr. Jorrome Smithy, welcome to hell. Today is your day of reckoning. You now have the opportunity to experience the horrors that your tenants deal with on a daily basis. We'll come back to see you in a couple of days. Make yourself at home."

As Robin's voice fades, two robots appear near the disappearing door, wearing head-to-toe hazmat suits with self-contained breathing apparatuses. They silently stand watch and say nothing to Mr. Smithy. Mr. Smithy screams, "What the hell! Robots have on hazmat suits in this squalor, and I'm a human wearing no protection? This is beyond cruel; it's inhumane!"

Mr. Smithy suddenly has to use the bathroom, and he heads to one that he sees across the room. He almost vomits when he enters. A disgusting smell slaps him in the face as he sees a toilet badly in need of flushing. He holds his nose and pushes down the toilet handle, and suddenly the toilet overflows and all of its putrefying contents puddle around him. He rushes out of the bathroom and decides to pee in the sink, which is clogged with its own decaying content.

At this point, he can't hold it any longer and vomits in the sink. He pounds his fists on the small table in the kitchenette, and the unstable structure crashes to the floor. He balls his fists and screams at the top of his lungs at the sagging ceiling, "You can't do this to me! Get me out of here!"

When he receives no response, he grabs the only chair nearby and sits down, beating his fist on the upper edge of the broken table. A curious rat watches him with interest and then quickly runs away as Mr. Smithy kicks at it with his foot. He screams again to the sagging ceiling, "You can't keep me here! I'll tell everyone on Earth that you women are really alien demons and that they'd better not ever come here. Do you hear me? No one will come back here! I'll get back at you if it's the last thing I do!" He then puts his head in his hands and weeps.

22 The Supreme Highnesses Reconvene

The Supreme Highnesses gather at their headquarters in one of the large conference rooms. Edith is at the head of the table and calls the meeting to order. "Well, Supreme Highnesses, what an interesting day. Our hosts have done a great job of giving our Travelers the opportunity to experience firsthand the horror, deceit, agony, and pain they've inflicted on others. They're lucky that it's for only a short time, if they cooperate. Hosts, please give us an update on your charges—quite an interesting cast of characters, indeed. It's hard to believe that there are worse earthlings you could have chosen. Felicia, please start us off with Mr. Wyatt Stone."

Felicia stands, walks over to the large projector screen, and touches the wall panel. The conference room where Mr. Stone is located appears on the screen. He's sitting with his head bowed as he watches live streaming of the men haggling over payment for his daughters. His daughters are huddled together in a corner of the room where the men are arguing. They are crying and holding on to each other for support. The seller is very agitated, and his voice is high pitched as he shouts to a potential client, "No way will I accept your cheap offer for these girls. You want to buy them as a package deal, then you gotta pay big money. Look at it this way, man: They haven't even reached puberty. They're virgins, and, most of all, they're white and blond. You've got to come up with more money, or no deal."

The potential buyer is equally agitated and shouts back, "You prick, give me a break! I tell you what—undress them so I can get a better look at the goods."

Mr. Stone's entire body shakes as he screams, "No, don't do this to my little girls. Please, don't humiliate them like this."

The seller says, "Okay, but I'll let only one girl take off her blouse, and that's it." He walks over to the frightened girls, yanks the arm of one of them, and pulls her over to the buyer, who wears a devious smile. The seller tells the girl, "Take off your top and your bra."

The girl pulls away from him and says, "No!"

The seller becomes more agitated and slaps the girl across the face. She recoils in tears, and then he grabs her top and rips it over her head. She's not yet wearing a bra, and her face turns beet red with shame and terror.

The buyer reaches out his hand to touch her budding breasts, and the seller slaps it away as he says, "No way! You don't touch or even sniff until we have a deal."

By this time, Mr. Stone is on the floor on his knees, with his hands in a praying position, as he looks up toward the ceiling and says, "Lord, I've been a horrible man, and I ask your forgiveness. Please, spare my daughters, and I promise you I'll be a changed man. Please, Lord, don't let those guys do further harm to my little girls."

Felicia stops the video while Mr. Stone is still on his knees, weeping uncontrollably. She smiles victoriously to the Supreme Highnesses as she says, "I believe we have a breakthrough!"

They all applaud, and Edith says, "Well done, my sister, well done! April, you're next."

April stands and walks over to touch the wall panel. The conference room where the Almighty Apostle Henry Bendy is located appears on the screen. Apostle Bendy is sitting with his arms folded, heaviness and despair etched on his face, as Pastor Monty calls up the ninetieth member to share her story about Apostle Bendy. An elderly woman with a cane can't make it to the stage, so Pastor Monty meets her in the aisle with a hug and helps her walk to a chair in front of the church. He holds the microphone close to her mouth so she can speak to the congregation.

"Good evening, my church family. I'm not a speaker, but I guess I have something that needs to be heard," she says.

Someone in the audience yells out, "Come on, Mother Brown, we want to hear from you."

She continues, "Thank you! I have known the Almighty Apostle Henry Bendy for thirty years, before he became known by that name. I knew him when he was just Pastor Bendy, living in a tiny apartment and barely making ends meet on a small church salary. That was when we were worshipping over at the storefront on 3800 East Green Street and had about fifty members. He was a good man back then, with his head on straight, and had plenty of ideas about how we could grow the church. I had a decent job at the time and had saved up about three thousand dollars by living a simple life with just the basics. That was a lot of money for a Black woman back then."

She coughs and takes a deep breath before continuing, "The Almighty Apostle Henry Bendy knew I had the money, because one day in prayer meeting I thanked God for blessing me with the gift of managing my money and shared how much I'd saved. He came to me about a week later and said that God had given him a vision, and in that vision, God told him to come to me because I was going to help grow His church. He said the vision was as clear as he was standing in front of me. I asked the Almighty Apostle Bendy what God said I was going to do, and he said that I was going to lend the church three thousand dollars to purchase a larger building. I can tell you that I wondered why God was asking me to lend him all of my savings without showing me that vision Himself."

After a brief burst of laughter in the audience, she continues, "Anyway, I've always tried to do what God expected of me, so I gave the Almighty Apostle Henry Bendy all of my savings. He promised to pay me back as the church's finances improved. I believed him, but to this day, despite all the money the church has, he has never repaid me one dime. I went to his office one time to ask about it, and he said he'd talk to the trustees, but he never got back with me.

"About ten years ago, I fell on hard times because of a back injury at work and ended up losing my house. I went to the Almighty Apostle Henry Bendy's office and explained how desperate I was for help, but he said it wouldn't be fair to the congregation for him to help me when other people were also facing hard times. I had to move in with my daughter and have been in her house ever since. But let me tell you, God will deal with that evil man, and hell will be even hotter when he goes there. That's all I have to say."

A couple of members jump up from the audience to help her to her seat. Amid loud applause and a standing ovation for Mother Brown, someone yells, "That alone is enough to get rid of the Almighty Henry Bendy. He's a pulpit pimp, and I won't even dignify that impostor by calling him an apostle. What he did to Mother Brown is hard to stomach. Pastor Monty, we need to make things right with Mother Brown."

The congregation gets on their feet and shouts, "Amen! Amen!"

Apostle Bendy drops to his knees and weeps so loudly that one of the two robots begins speaking: "Crying not helpful! Crying not helpful!" The robots move closer to where Apostle Bendy is still kneeling and look straight ahead.

Apostle Bendy lifts his hands to his chin in prayer and cries out, "Lord, please forgive me. I don't know what happened to me. How could I have been so cruel? People have poured their hearts out about my evilness. I love my church, your church, and just got caught up in the fame, the money, the material things, and lost my way. I replaced you with my own selfishness. I don't want to stay this way. I want to change. Please help me to change, to be the man of God that you want me to be. Please help me." He falls into a prone position and weeps again.

April stops the live stream and turns to the Supreme Highnesses and says, "I think we have a breakthrough here as well. It's hard to believe that a man of God can be the purveyor of such evil. The sad thing is that I saw so many men and women of God on Earth who are just like Apostle Bendy. They live in fancy mansions, wear designer clothing and expensive jewelry, and drive luxury cars, and God isn't their primary focus. Their focus is building megachurches, huge edifices that are larger than some of the sports arenas on Earth and that hold up to thirty thousand people. These so-called men and women of God take pleasure in being the center of the church, instead of their God being the center. They have some religious leaders who support politicians who lie, cheat, steal, commit adultery, and do all the things their Bible says is sinful. Yet they urge the people in their congregations to vote for them, just to add to the church leaders' personal power. Getting across to Apostle Bendy that he needs to change his behavior is a big step in the right direction, although there are many more steps to go."

The Supreme Highnesses applaud, and Edith acknowledges April. "My sister, you have done a great job, and a tough one at that. Thank you for your work. Next, let's hear from Gail."

Gail stands and walks over to touch the wall panel. Ms. Sweetie Harris appears on the screen in her glass chamber, where her disfigured body is being viewed by a large crowd of Eartha schoolgirls. A guide points to Ms. Harris and says, "Young ladies, the body of this woman from Planet Earth is an example of what happens when women don't love their bodies and use dangerous chemicals and surgeries to make their bodies conform to male standards. We don't do this awful thing on Eartha, because we love our bodies and no man defines us. On Planet Earth, there are women like Ms. Harris, and very powerful men, who make young girls feel ashamed of their bodies and hate themselves."

One of the girls raises her hand and asks, "How do they reach the girls on Planet Earth to cause them so much harm?"

The guide replies, "Great question. They use paper magazines, television, internet, and other primitive media to bombard girls like you with images of what they've decided are the perfect physical features for women. These images often depict women who've had all kinds of plastic surgery: their breasts implanted with a silicone substance, injections to create puffy lips, and, most disgusting, fake buttocks."

Another girl raises her hand and says, "I'm so glad we don't have this problem on Eartha. Are the people on Earth punished for such bad behavior?"

The guide answers, "You're right about such an issue not happening on our planet. The sad thing is that the businesses that market these products and services amass great wealth. Even more disgraceful is that the women with these fake bodies are on the covers of Earth magazines and have millions of followers on their internet sites. They are also seen with nationally and globally popular male entertainers or professional athletes, who are the reason they go through this physical mutilation. You should also know that Earth men don't experience the same pressure to take these extreme measures to change their bodies as Earth women do."

A young girl who looks to be about twelve years old

raises her hand and shouts, "I never want to go to Planet Earth! It sounds like a very scary place for girls like us." She points at Ms. Harris and again shouts, "This lady should be ashamed of herself!"

The guide smiles at the schoolgirl, pauses a moment, and says, "You're right, but I'm not sure she bears such shame. Ms. Harris is one of those people who promote these body images, and she has become very wealthy destroying the self-esteem of young girls. Unfortunately, many of those girls experience significant mental and physical health issues. Some of the girls have even taken their own lives."

Cries of "Oh no!" echo throughout the crowd. The guide walks across from Ms. Harris to the stage, where four young Eartha women, between ages sixteen and eighteen, wave and smile brightly at the schoolgirls. They are racially diverse and have healthy bodies of different sizes and shapes. They are wearing white blouses and loose-fitting, knee-length black skirts. "This is what we are about on Eartha. We don't use shame or ridicule to create fake body images for profit. On Eartha, we teach our girls to love their bodies, and if they have health issues, we encourage a healthy diet and a healthy lifestyle."

Ms. Harris hears the guide and begins screaming to the ceiling, as if hoping that Gail will hear her, "I never meant to harm anyone. I'm not a bad person. You have to believe me. I'll go back to Earth and I'll encourage young girls to love their bodies. I'll use my broad platform to promote truly healthy lifestyles, and I'll showcase girls and women of all sizes, shapes, and colors. I'll never, ever resort to body shaming again. I'll discourage girls from injecting harmful chemicals and going under the knife to alter their appearance. I'll tell my story about the harmful things I've done to my own body. Please, just restore my former figure, and I promise to make a big difference when I return to Earth. Please!"

Gail claps her hands and says to the Supreme Highnesses, "Ladies, I believe we may have another convert who will go back to Earth as a changed woman, especially if she gets her man-made body back. But we'll let her experience her disfigurement a while longer, so that she truly understands how young girls with perfect bodies are made to see themselves as disfigured. Yes, Ms. Sweetie Harris is going to become a *real* 'sweetie.'"

The Supreme Highnesses all applaud, and Edith says, "Gail, you've done an amazing job. Your idea of changing Ms. Harris's body was ingenious. Thank you! Now, let's hear from Carmen."

Carmen stands and walks over to touch the wall panel. Judge Morcus Bottomy appears on the screen, his face still covered with mucus, and still watching his son's introduction to incarceration on the large projector. His hands are folded beneath his chin, and his eyes are red and swollen from crying. He sees Jeremy Bottomy, in an orange jumpsuit, trying to adjust to being a resident in a juvenile detention center filled with 90 percent Black and Brown boys. As Jeremy walks into the cafeteria, his face is pale, his eyes wide with terror as they dart around the room. He's never been around so many boys of color before. At his elite private boys' school, there was only one Black kid and two Asians. Everyone else was white.

He walks slowly and cautiously, as if trying not to draw attention to himself. He picks up a plate and goes through the cafeteria serving line. As he reaches the end, he looks around for a place to sit. He sees a Black kid sitting by himself and decides that's the best place for him. He walks over to the table and pulls out a chair.

The kid looks up at him and says, "Hey, you must be new here. You must have done something terrible to wind up in this hellhole. We don't see many white boys here."

Instead of telling his story, Jeremy responds, "Why are you here?"

The boy says, "Man, I was homeless for three years, and one day I grabbed two pieces of fruit from a cart and then took off running. A cop was nearby and caught up with me and arrested me. I went before this horrible judge who my public defender said would give me a break because I was an A student and had never been in trouble before. Wow, was he wrong. That mean bastard sentenced me to two years in juvenile detention. I think he hated Black kids because so many of us got long sentences. They call him Wicked Bottomy. I hate him like I've never hated anyone in my life for what he did to me. That was so wrong."

Jeremy's face turns beet red, and he begins to vomit, causing a major stir in the cafeteria.

Judge Bottomy stands and caresses his stomach with both arms, as if that might help his son. "He speaks just above a whisper and says, "Please, God, don't let them know that Jeremy's my son. Please protect him."

As the boys watch Jeremy retching and shout their disgust, one of the kids who was in court with Jeremy recognizes him. He shouts out to the room, "Hey, that kid is that awful Judge Bottomy's son. He's the bastard judge that put most of us in here!"

The kid at the table with Jeremy stands and shouts, "You must have killed a lot of people, because your daddy would never have sent you here."

The kid who recognized Jeremy said, "His daddy wasn't the judge. He was sentenced by a brotha, a new Black judge."

Someone in the room yells out, "Hey, I think he should clean up his vomit."

Someone else says, "Yeah, you're right."

A group of boys rush over, grab Jeremy, knock him down into his vomit, and begin to drag his face through the repugnant slime. Judge Bottomy screams, "Where are the guards? Don't let them hurt my boy!"

Suddenly, the young boy at Jeremy's table shouts, "Stop it! Please don't do this. He's not responsible for what his horrible father did to us. I hate his dad, but I can't do this to his son. Come on, guys." He walks over and pours water into a napkin and starts wiping the vomit off Jeremy's face as Jeremy cries uncontrollably, with his head in his hands.

One boy yells, "Daddy's big crybaby. I'm not done with him. No, he's going to pay for what his daddy did to me."

Kneeling on the floor, cupping his face in his hands, Judge Bottomy cries out, "I'm so sorry for what I've done to these boys. I was taught to despise Black people. My daddy was a Klansman, and he said you should lock them up early, while they're young, and they'll be in prison for most of their lives after that. What have I done? How many lives have I destroyed? That kid saved my son, even after what I did to him. I'm a monster. I want to do better. I *have* to do better."

He glances over at the two robots, who are staring expressionlessly at him, and then looks up toward the ceiling as he says, "Ladies, I don't know if you can hear me, but I bet you can. Give me a chance to go back to Earth, and I'll do everything possible to help young men like the boy sitting with Jeremy and other Black boys that I've wronged. I'll let the world know that I gave harsh sentences to Black boys solely because of my racism. I'll do everything I can, even if I'm removed from the bench, to be an advocate for justice and fairness for young men of color. I'll advocate for diversion programs for first offenders of minor crimes. I'll take my crusade national. I promise you, I'll become one of the strongest advocates for social justice in the United States!"

Carmen raises her hands to the sky as she says to the Supreme Highnesses, "I was so worried, because of the racism at his core, that Judge Bottomy would be our biggest challenge yet. We will have to stay closely connected with him until his promises are indeed a reality, but today we see real progress."

The women applaud, and Edith acknowledges Carmen's work. "Carmen, you had a tough challenge, and you worked miracles. We're all so proud of you. Thank you! Lastly, let's hear from Robin."

Robin walks over to the wall panel and touches it. The apartment where Mr. Smithy is staying appears on the screen. He is still sitting in the unstable chair, with his head bowed and his hands curled in tight fists. He lifts his head and looks around the filthy, dilapidated space. He sees another rat dart across his foot, as if he's daring Mr. Smithy to come after him. A piece of the ceiling falls to the floor, adding to the labyrinth of clutter. Mr. Smithy slowly stands and opens the cabinet doors underneath the sink. One of the doors comes off its hinges into his hand. He looks at the decay below the sink and spots a plunger. He pushes the plunger into the drain and tries to force the putrid sludge into the pipes below. He suddenly shouts, "I hate this crappy place!" as the U-shaped pipe breaks at a rusted point and the sludge pours on the floor and covers his shoes. The odor is so overwhelming that he suddenly doubles over and retches.

As Mr. Smithy sits back down in the rickety chair, he hears a knock on the door. The two robots disappear as he opens it and sees a young, dark-skinned woman with a toddler standing there. She peers over Mr. Smithy's shoulder and says, "Wow, I thought my unit was bad. This place is awful. May I come in?"

Mr. Smithy backs away from the door and nods his head as she walks in with the child. She picks up the toddler so he doesn't step into the muck and says, "There was an older lady living here. I tried to give her a hand sometimes, but it didn't help. We have the worst landlord ever. That poor woman was paying five hundred dollars a month for this dilapidated studio apartment. Every time she got one thing fixed, three more things fell apart. The landlord doesn't care, as long as he gets his rent money. Can you imagine anyone being so inhumane? I heard your cries and thought you were in trouble, but I can see why you would shed tears in this place. I can call some of the neighbors to help you clean up. We help each other out as much as we can. You might catch some disease in this squalor. We believe something in this place killed Mrs. King, the older lady who lived here. You may want to see if the landlord will rent you another unit. Well, I don't want my child to catch anything here, so I'll come back later with some of the neighbors to help you." She hurries for the door and closes it behind her.

Mr. Smithy rushes to follow her, but the door disappears just as quickly as it appeared for his neighbor. The robots in their hazmat suits reappear and resume their watch near the vanished entry.

Mr. Smithy sits back in his rickety chair and stares at the dirty, moldy walls. "Am I so terrible that I cause people to live in these conditions? I wouldn't let my dogs live in this squalor. How have I ignored my tenants' pleas for so long? I was so distant from these living conditions that I didn't give them a second thought. Someone else handled the management, and I just enjoyed the profits. I can't imagine raising children in a place like this. I am so ashamed. Every time I take a deep breath, I know that poison enters my lungs, and I've been here only a couple of days. If I get out of here, I promise that I will do better. I'll plead for mercy from the Supreme Highnesses. I'll let them know that I will become the perfect example of a socially responsible landlord. I'll personally inspect all of my properties and make sure they're clean and healthy places to live. I'll have building managers who live on-site so that people can get immediate help when they need it."

He sits back down and hears a knock on the door. Again the robots disappear as he opens it to find at least five neighbors with cleaning supplies, ready to help out. He can't control his tears as he invites them in.

Robin claps her hands as she says, "Another tough one who never saw the problems he caused as an absentee slumlord and didn't care because he had others do his dirty work for him. What a difference it makes to feel the pain, neglect, and agony of poverty and the lack of support from the powerful. I tell you what, I would hate to be a person of color, especially a Black person in the United States and on Earth, period. We have so much work to do there if that continues to be part of our mission. Fortunately, in Mr. Smithy's case, it looks like a breakthrough has happened. Trying to find this man's humanity has been challenging."

The Supreme Highnesses applaud, and Edith acknowledges Robin's efforts as she says, "Robin, you've done a great job in a very tough situation. You're right in that there's so much more to do to combat the social injustice in America and on Planet Earth. I hope you will agree to continue working there, and we'll make sure you get the necessary resources for sustained, positive results."

Then she addresses all of the hosts at once: "Felicia, April, Gail, Carmen, and Robin, you have made us so proud. You will be well rewarded for your work on this important mission. We could have taken the approach to make things happen quickly and more extensively with the use of our powers, but the impact we've seen today would not have happened. We're building the first wave of our soldiers and advocates to create just societies throughout Planet Earth, and America is our primary target. Now, let's get some rest. Tomorrow, we will begin redemption meetings for each of your charges. Well done, my sisters, well done!"

23 Redemption Meeting—Wyatt Stone

The Supreme Highnesses gather at their headquarters and prepare to hold the first of five redemption meetings for the Travelers, with Mr. Wyatt Stone. Felicia enters the conference room where Mr. Stone has watched the human trafficking of his four young daughters with anguish and horror. Felicia sees a broken man seated with his head bowed, disheveled clothing, and swollen, bloodshot eyes from the flood of tears that he's shed during his viewing experience. The Supreme Highnesses have kindly ensured that the Travelers have had no bodily excretions during the two days they've been rebuked for their transgressions and ruthlessness on Planet Earth.

Mr. Stone lifts his head when he sees Felicia walk into the room. His eyes are wide and pleading for some respite from his unceasing agony. Felicia gives a hand signal to dismiss the two robots, and they quickly exit the room. She shuts off the projector and then walks over and stands in front of Mr. Stone. For a couple of minutes, she stares down at him and says, "Mr. Stone, I'd like you to follow me into another conference room. The Supreme Highnesses are waiting there for you."

Mr. Stone looks up at Felicia and whispers weakly, "Please, I can't take any more. I just want my girls to be okay."

Felicia takes his hand and literally pulls him from the chair. "Let's not keep them waiting." He takes a deep breath and rises slowly to his feet, then stumbles along next to Felicia as they head to the other conference room.

The Supreme Highnesses, seated around the U-shaped table, take measured looks at Mr. Stone's weakened state, and their eyes lock as they exchange satisfied smirks. Felicia ushers Mr. Stone to a seat at the front of the table, but now he sits facing the Supreme Highnesses, shifting in his seat and wringing his hands.

After a moment of silence, Felicia stands near Mr. Stone and speaks to the Supreme Highnesses. "Ladies, Mr. Stone has had a very stressful and challenging two days. I think it's important for you to hear from him about this time and what it's meant for him to see firsthand the horrors of human trafficking. Mr. Stone, you have the floor."

Mr. Stone takes a deep breath and begins to stand but then puts his hand to his forehead and decides to remain seated.

"Supreme Highnesses," he says, taking a deep breath, "the past two days have been the most painful of my entire life. Watching what my daughters were going through made me think about what I've caused hundreds of young girls to endure. I'm sure in some cases they were a lot worse than my daughters' experience. I guess I never really thought about the impact of trafficking on the girls. The revenue I generated was my only focus. I was removed from the actual cruelty and dehumanizing of the victims. I would do anything to undo the damage I've caused, the young lives I've destroyed."

He shakes his head as tears begin to form and continues, "I can't imagine the pain my daughters are experiencing right now in the hands of those brutal men. If this is God's punishment for my sins, then I would rather He killed me and left my girls unharmed. I will never be able to face my wife again because of her hurt and pain from losing her daughters. She loves those girls with all of her heart and soul. This will destroy her. She'll never be the same, and it's all my fault. I'll never be the same either. Never again will I cause any human being this type of pain."

Edith stands and speaks, "Mr. Stone, you have suffered greatly for the past two days. It would be easy for me to say that we regret your pain, but that would not be truthful. You spoke about your wife's inability to recover from the loss of your daughters. Just think of the number of mothers and fathers whom your actions have led to this nightmare. Think about parents who suffer for weeks, months, and years before reconnecting with their children. And far too many of them never even see their children again. Fortunately for you, as difficult as it was for you to watch your girls being mistreated, what you saw was a virtual reality. In other words, your daughters are safe and secure at home with their mother."

Mr. Stone covers his face with his hands. The color

drains from his skin as he takes in what is probably the best news of his entire life. "How could you put me through this?" he asks, with tears rolling down his cheeks and his hands in tight fists.

Edith walks over to Mr. Stone, stands directly in front of him, and points her finger in his face as she scolds him. "Look at me! How dare you even have the gall to ask that question? I expect your response to be 'Thank you so much that my daughters are safe.' Rest assured, if you even think of engaging in human trafficking when you return to Earth, what you saw on that screen is not nearly as bad as what will happen in reality. Do I make myself clear?"

Mr. Stone lowers his eyes and stares at the floor as he responds, "Yes, ma'am, it is very clear. I didn't mean to sound ungrateful. I am truly thankful, from the bottom of my heart, that my daughters are safe. I promise you that I will never, ever engage in any form of human trafficking again."

"That's good to hear, Mr. Stone," Edith says, "but there's more that you must do. You will use your clout in the film industry to produce a movie about the horrors of human trafficking. After all, who better than you to produce such a film, since you're so knowledgeable about this topic?"

Felicia joins in: "And don't think that once you get back to Earth, you will have escaped our grasp. You will face serious consequences for any missteps on your part. Of course, we look forward to your future role in bringing international attention to human trafficking. Oh, and we thought you might like to see this." Felicia touches the panel, and Mr. Stone's four daughters appear on the screen, happily playing cards in their game room.

Mr. Stone stands and faces the Supreme Highnesses as

he declares, "You have my word: I will not waver from the assignment you've given me. It will be hard, given my past, but I will put my heart and soul into this effort. I promise you."

Felicia says, "Thank you, Mr. Stone. We'll take you at your word, but just remember that if you falter, we'll be with you all the way."

Mr. Stone nods his understanding, his eyes drooping with fatigue. Felicia notices and says, "You've had a rough two days, and I'm sure you need to get some rest. We want you to be in perfect condition for the return trip to Earth, which will take place in a few days. I'll escort you back to the hotel. One more thing: You can't share anything about your experience with your fellow Travelers. You will tell them about the great time you had learning about our planet, about your interest in how and when the Planet Eartha was formed, and about how you are now in awe of the incredible advances that women have made here, without a single male leader like the ones you have on Planet Earth."

Mr. Stone shrugs his shoulders and raises his hands as he asks, "What can I tell them? I don't know anything about Planet Eartha to share with the other Travelers in the first place. I haven't been anywhere else in the past two days but that conference room!"

Felicia smiles as she says, "Don't worry—somehow the words will come to you. Relax!"

The Supreme Highnesses applaud lightly as Felicia escorts Mr. Stone from the conference room to their waiting vehicle. Then Edith says, "Job well done, and four more to go. We will definitely have to stay on top of this one."

Lucy raises her hand and says, "I'll make sure to keep him in check."

They all respond with laughter and prepare for the next redemption meeting, which April will lead, for the Almighty Apostle Henry Bendy.

24 Redemption Meeting—the Almighty Apostle Henry Bendy

April enters the conference room where Apostle Bendy is still watching the streaming of the rally at his church. His lips quiver as tears stream down his face. The two male robots are standing in the same places on each side of him, looking straight ahead into some unknown space. Apostle Bendy glances up as April arrives and then turns his head back to the screen. The speeches have ceased at his church, and Pastor Monty is now responding to chants of "Vote him out! Vote him out!" He waves his hand to quiet the crowd as he says, "The Almighty Apostle Henry Bendy has violated God's law by failing to take care of the needs of this congregation, and he's turned a deaf ear to the poor and downtrodden, the widows, the incarcerated, and other disenfranchised members of our congregation. His primary commitment is to self-promotion and filling his own pockets. The time to end his charade of being an apostle of God is right now. It must end today!"

The congregation gets to its feet and shouts, "Amen!"

Pastor Monty says, "I've already spoken with the church trustees, and the church bylaws state that the congregation can vote, with the trustees' approval, to remove a senior pastor for failure to perform his duties according to biblical teachings. We all agree that the Almighty Apostle Henry Bendy has certainly not come close to adhering to biblical teachings. The trustees have voted unanimously to remove him from his senior pastor role and have also given me full authority to conduct the voting process with the congregation at this meeting. Are you ready to vote?"

As the congregation yells, "Yes!" Pastor Monty calls back, "All in favor of removing the Almighty Apostle Henry Bendy from his position as the senior pastor of this church, please raise your hand." When every hand in the church goes up, except for Pastor Bendy's weeping wife, he says, "All those in favor of retaining the Almighty Apostle Henry Bendy as senior pastor of this church, please raise your hand." Not one hand is raised, and Pastor Bendy's wife just sits with her head bowed.

Pastor Monty raises his own hands in praise as he shouts out, "God's people have spoken. I also want to make sure that you know that I have no selfish motive for the removal of the Almighty Apostle Henry Bendy. I love working with the youth of this church and have no desire to assume any other position. There just comes a time when someone has to step up and call out evil, especially in God's house. I feel that I've done what God has asked me to do, and the rest is now up to the trustees, who will share the news with the Apostle when he returns from Planet Eartha. God bless you all!" The people cheer for Pastor Monty as he exits the stage.

Apostle Bendy falls to his knees and weeps. April walks over to him and says softly, "Sir, I need you to come with me. The Supreme Highnesses are waiting for you in another conference room."

Apostle Bendy looks up at April and shakes his head as he whispers, "I don't have the strength to go anywhere. Please, just leave me alone."

April nods to the two robots, and they grab Apostle Bendy's arms to help him stand and then look to April for further instructions. April nods again, and as she turns to leave the room, the robots grab Apostle Bendy's arms and assist him in walking to the other conference room. They enter with April and take Apostle Bendy to a seat in front of the room that faces the U-shaped table where the Supreme Highnesses are seated. The two robots then turn around with precision and walk out of the conference room.

Apostle Bendy looks around at the Supreme Highnesses, then turns to April and asks, "What am I doing here? There's nothing that can be done to me that's worse than losing my church. Go ahead—I don't care if you kill me. It just doesn't matter to me. I always wanted to be a servant of God, and when I watched all the big-time pastors and saw what they were accumulating, I said to myself, 'Look, these guys are living the life, and I'm barely making it with crumbs.' I went to a national pastors' conference, and they exposed me to all the things that I could have as pastor of a large church, and I fell for it because it was so enticing. I got caught up in the big-time life that so many of the megachurch preachers lead. I wanted the jet, the mansion, the fine clothes, the expensive jewelry, and the global recognition. The sad part for me is that I got all of those things and then lost my connection to God and my congregation. I forgot my calling, where I came from, and the people who sacrificed so much to get me and the church on solid footing. I preached the right sermons, sang the right songs, prayed powerful prayers, and pretended to have healing powers. I lost my way, and I'm a disappointment to all the people who had faith in me as God's shepherd, especially my wife and children, who love me and hold me in the highest regard. I don't blame the congregation for voting me out as their pastor. I have prayed so hard during these past two days, asking God to forgive me, and I can only hope that the congregation can forgive me, even if I'm not their pastor. I am so ashamed of who I've become, so ashamed." He bows his head and stares into the open hands on his lap.

Edith stands and calls out to him, "Almighty Apostle Henry Bendy, please look at me!"

Apostle Bendy lifts his head and turns to where Edith is standing. She continues, "You should be ashamed of the life you've been living as a man of the God whom you proclaim to love dearly. As I've studied your Bible, something has really stood out for me, and that's the idea of a forgiving God, even though there are consequences for sinfulness. I've also learned that you have a God who gives His people not one, not two, but multiple chances. I believe it's what you call grace.

"Today, we're extending grace to you, but with significant conditions. Number one: You will no longer use the title the Almighty Apostle Henry Bendy, because that's the title of your past, sinful life. You will now assume the title Pastor Henry Bendy. Number two: You will share with your congregation and all of your followers how your trip to Planet Eartha changed your life and renewed your relationship with your God. Number three: You will no longer engage in the deceitful practice of healing people with infirmities, using your team of actors."

Apostle Bendy cries out, "Wait a minute—I don't even have a congregation anymore. You saw what the people think of me, and they don't want to hear from me."

Edith nods at April, and April explains, "Sir, what you saw was not actually happening at your church. We used our advanced technology to get your attention about what will surely happen in the future if you don't change your ways. However, the words that members of your congregation used to describe you are real and represent their true feelings about you."

Apostle Bendy's eyes widen, and his mouth opens, but at first he cannot speak. He then drops to his knees, with his hands in prayer, and says, "Thank you, Lord. Thank you."

Edith begins speaking again: "Pastor Bendy, condition number four is that you will return home a changed man who will embody love and kindness and live the words that you preach. You will clear old debts and give Mother Brown quadruple what she's owed. You can keep your mansion, but only if you use it more for community outreach and the youth and young-adult ministries. You will sell your jet and donate the proceeds to support the homeless in your community. For the next five years, you will donate your salary to organizations that support the poor and needy. We will monitor your progress on a regular basis—"

Pastor Bendy interrupts Edith: "How will you monitor my actions from another planet?"

Edith smiles as she says, "I find it hard to believe that you would even ask such a question, given your experience here."

Pastor Bendy nods in understanding as he thinks about the last couple of days. Edith continues, "We believe that you will do everything we're asking of you, and please know, not only are we watching you, but I'm sure your God is watching you as well. Do you have any questions?"

Pastor Bendy looks around the room as he speaks to the Supreme Highnesses. "Ladies, thank you for helping me to see the path of destruction that I've been traveling. I know that I don't deserve the second chance you're giving me—actually, that God is giving me. It was painful listening to what my people think about me, but I'm so glad that I now know and can go home and begin to heal those broken relationships. Shedding the mantle of pride and greed is a major change for me, but I already feel a new freedom from constantly hiding behind so many lies. I'm now anxious to go home and begin my new life as a committed pastor. Again, I thank you, more than you'll ever know."

Edith takes her seat, and April says, "Pastor Henry Bendy, it's time for you to return to the hotel. You may share with your fellow Travelers that you had a religious epiphany during our time together over the past two days and that you're now returning to an earlier title, Pastor Henry Bendy. You will also share that you are no longer comfortable with a name that you feel elevates you to an unworthy level. We will give you the words to speak about our planet at the appropriate time when you return to Earth. Everything you share with your congregation, with the media, and with your family about your visit to our planet will be carefully planned by us. Should you be tempted to reveal what actually happened during your visit, we'll be there to help you avoid that temptation, now that we have an extraordinary connection."

Edith stands and says, "We are pleased with your growth and will be there for you in your journey back to wholeness. You're not there yet, but we are confident that you will get there. We'll see you again before your return to Earth."

The Supreme Highnesses stand and applaud lightly as April beckons to Pastor Bendy to follow her to the waiting hotel transportation. After he leaves the room, Edith says to the other women, "Well, I think we made great progress with Pastor Bendy. He's returning to Earth a new man. We have three more challenging meetings ahead of us, but the results are certainly worth all of our time and effort. Rest up, my sisters, as we prepare for the next redemption meeting, with Ms. Sweetie Harris."

25 Redemption Meeting—Sweetie Harris

Gail enters the conference center where Ms. Harris is still in her glass chamber, although no crowds are watching her disfigured body. She sees Ms. Harris sitting on the floor, hugging herself, rocking back and forth, and muttering. Her clothes are disheveled, and her hair is no longer perfectly coiffed. Gail walks in front of the chamber and makes eye contact with Ms. Harris, who quickly averts her eyes. She begins mumbling aloud, for Gail's benefit, "This can't be happening to me. I'm a good person, and I never meant to hurt those girls. It's not my fault that they died. I only tried to help girls look prettier and feel good about themselves. I didn't want them to go through what I went through, being picked on from the time I arrived at grade school until the time I graduated from high school. I got tired of being called fat and ugly and having no friends. I hated my body, and I hated myself. I tried to kill myself so many times. I wish I had died! I wish I had died!"

Gail watches and listens for a while, and then she calls

out to Ms. Harris, who still hasn't made direct eye contact with her, and says, "Please, spare me the lies about your painful childhood. Do you really think I don't know the truth? You were the leader of a group of mean-spirited girls who taunted their classmates about their weight, their hair, their facial features, and their skin color. You actually enjoyed hurting others and laughed when those girls cried. Tears meant victory for you, and it only got worse as you grew older. As a matter of fact, you've never stopped causing pain and misery for others. You, Ms. Sweetie Harris, caused thousands of girls to hate their bodies and hate themselves. You caused them to resort to harmful measures to create a ridiculous figure that you thrust upon them, and when they couldn't get that contrived form, some of those girls could no longer live with themselves. You brought ugliness into the lives of young women who had once loved their bodies, bodies that were not contaminated by your harmful methods. And then, as if you couldn't get any lower in your immorality, you made millions selling pain and suffering. You should be ashamed of yourself, and what's most disgusting is the fact that you're not, so stop right now telling lies about a painful childhood as an excuse for your repulsive behavior."

Ms. Harris turns toward Gail and screams at her, "You have some nerve judging me, when you live on this planet where being a woman who's overweight or has unattractive facial features is no big deal! No one here cares that you have a wide, pug nose, hair that needs coloring, and thin lips that barely move when you talk. No one! I live on a planet where the media's definition of beauty is flaunted in my face every single day. You can't age gracefully with gray hair, crow's-feet under your eyes, or wrinkles on your forehead. And heaven forbid your breasts begin to sag or you get cellulite on your thighs and buttocks. No one cares about that on this planet, but they sure as hell do on mine. So don't you dare tell me what I should and should not do on Planet Earth. You don't have to live my life, Ms. Highness! And one more thing: I think you and your other Highnesses envy me. Come on, tell the truth—you would give anything to have the gorgeous body that I once had. Now it's becoming clear to me why you biddies changed me into this freak. You're jealous!"

Gail stares at Ms. Harris for a long minute and then begins to laugh. Her laughter starts with a chuckle and escalates to peals that bring tears to her eyes. She laughs for another couple of minutes, before she stands up straight, shoulders back, head held high, eyes blazing, and walks over next to Ms. Harris, shaking her head. "We're *jealous* of you and your counterfeit body? You can't possibly believe that. Don't you realize that we have the power to have any type of body that we want? Look at how we changed *your* fabricated body. Lady, we are so comfortable with the way our God made us that we have no desire to change our appearance. Far from feeling jealous, we're totally repulsed by someone like you, who chooses to profit off the seeds of destruction you planted in the minds of young girls. The fact that you're disfigured in a glass cage right now and still can't find it within yourself to admit, without lies and excuses, that you've done horrible things to others speaks volumes about the depth of your immorality. Why would anyone be jealous of a creature who is so evil?"

Ms. Harris doesn't say a word as she lets Gail's comments

sink in. Finally, she rises to her knees and looks around her glass chamber and then up at Gail. She slowly stands and wipes tears from her eyes as she says, "I know what you're saying is true. You don't know how hard I've tried to change. Therapy, pills, alcohol, fame . . . Nothing has worked. I've really tried, and I don't know what else to do. Maybe there's help on this planet that I can't find on mine. I don't like the person I am, but it's who I am today and who I've always been. I would love to be different, but I don't know how. So there—I hope that makes you happy." She then crumples back onto the floor.

Gail waves her hand, and the front wall of Ms. Harris's glass chamber rises to the ceiling. She grabs Ms. Harris's hands and pulls her to her feet as she says, "The Supreme Highnesses are waiting to meet with you. Please, you need to come with me."

Ms. Harris extends her arms through the open wall to make sure she's not being deceived and, thus assured, walks slowly out of the chamber with Gail. They exit the conference center and take the waiting vehicle to the Supreme Highnesses' headquarters.

Gail escorts Ms. Harris down the narrow hallway into the conference room, where the Supreme Highnesses are sitting around the U-shaped table. Ms. Harris clasps her arms around her body and walks sideways as she tries to hide her uneven breasts and buttocks. The Supreme Highnesses exchange amused glances with each other at the futility of Ms. Harris's efforts. Gail escorts Ms. Harris to the seat at the head of the table where the previous Travelers received their reckoning. Ms. Harris scans the room aimlessly, as if she's looking for some form of reassurance that's not to be found. She continues hugging herself once she's seated, bows her head, and then bursts into tears. Gail remains by her side but looks away from Ms. Harris and offers no words of comfort.

Edith stands and intentionally lets a few minutes lapse in silence. Then she says, "Ms. Harris, I understand that you endured tremendous pain, ridicule, and embarrassment while on display in the glass chamber at the conference center. What's on your mind right now?"

Ms. Harris doesn't lift her head as she absorbs Edith's request. After a moment passes, she speaks in a soft tone: "What's really on my mind is something I shared earlier with Gail. I've made a lot of mistakes in my life, and I know that I haven't been the best person on Earth, but I'm certainly not the worst. I told Gail that I've tried over and over to change my life, but nothing has worked. You have to know that I hate who I am every hour of the day and that I would give anything to get rid of this pain." Ms. Harris grabs her chair, sits back down, and hugs her uneven breasts as she rocks back and forth, staring at the floor.

Gail walks over to Ms. Harris with a glass of water and puts her arm around her shoulders. She then offers Ms. Harris the water. Ms. Harris nods her gratitude and takes a sip. Almost instantly, her body begins to transform into its original shape. Ms. Harris's eyes become wide with delight and a broad smile forms on her lips as she looks down at her now evenly matched breasts and then moves her hands down to her symmetrically rounded buttocks. She jumps to her feet and raises her hands in the air as she shouts, "Thank you! I'm whole again! Oh, this feels great. I'm no longer a freak. Thank you!"

Edith watches Ms. Harris's reaction with a mixture of curiosity and scorn and then says to her, "You're welcome, but this is not the end of this matter. Just as you have recovered your prized body, know that you can easily become again the 'freak' that you were for the past two days. We now offer you the opportunity to achieve the change you've been pursuing for the past decade, the change that therapy hasn't produced. We see in you deeply embedded heartlessness that we can't allow to continue. We can help you let go of the part of your inner self that causes you to inflict pain on others and feed your self-hatred."

Ms. Harris slowly takes her seat, looks over at Edith and begins to tear up as she responds, "I have never been surer of anything in my entire life. I've been a slave to that area for so many years. I beg you, please free me from the person it's created. I don't want to continue to be her."

Edith looks over at Brooke and Catherine and nods at them. They both rise from their chairs and walk over to Ms. Harris's seat. Brooke gently grabs hold of Ms. Harris's shoulders while Catherine places her hand over Ms. Harris's heart. Catherine looks up to the ceiling and begins speaking in a language that is unknown to Ms. Harris but familiar to the other women in the room. "Dear Merciful One, this woman has led a life that's been harmful to so many, and she has tried to change, but she can't do it on her own. She wants to change and become a beacon of light for young girls to help them have a positive self-image, instead of the destruction she's marketed and profited from in the past. You alone can purge the evil that has taken root in her heart and replace it with love, kindness, and inner peace. Dear One, thank you for the cleansing that's taking place right now as your power travels through my hand to Ms. Harris's heart."

The Supreme Highnesses immediately stand and extend their arms toward Ms. Harris, and she slumps in her chair and appears to fall asleep. Catherine's eyes are closed, and smoke arises from the area where she's touching Ms. Harris's heart. The smoke is first snow white, and as Catherine continues to speak, it thickens and turns various colors: gray, green, black, and blue. Finally, the smoke turns bright yellow and Ms. Harris's eyelids flutter and her body begins to convulse. Brooke holds her shoulders firmly and keeps her from toppling over. The thick yellow smoke rises and slowly begins to dissipate. Catherine watches the smoke carefully, and once it's completely gone, she removes her palm from over Ms. Harris's heart.

As this happens, Ms. Harris's body stops shaking and her eyelids go still. She leans back in her chair, takes a deep breath through her mouth, and blows out the remainder of the yellow smoke left in her body. She opens her eyes, looks up at Catherine, and smiles. Catherine takes Ms. Harris's hands in hers and says, "Ms. Harris, you're okay now. You see that small flurry of yellow smoke in front of you? That's the last of the embedded pain and anger that was in your body. You are now free!"

Ms. Harris looks around the room like someone who's lost something and is trying to find, then asks Catherine, "Where was the place that I just visited? At first the land was parched, with lifeless plants, and then it slowly turned into the lushest green hills, with bright yellow wildflowers growing everywhere. It was so peaceful. I really hated to leave."

Catherine smiles at her and says, "You have a new heart, my friend. That dry, parched heart of yours is now filled with love and kindness. You will do awesome things to promote healthy girls and young women when you return to the Planet Earth."

Ms. Harris reaches out to hug Catherine as she says, "I feel so much better. The heavy load is gone, and I finally feel free. Thank you so much!"

The Supreme Highnesses applaud enthusiastically as Ms. Harris, Brooke, and Catherine return to their seats.

Edith stands and reminds Ms. Harris, "Remember one key thing when you return to Earth. You have been given the gift of freedom from your demons of selfishness and greed. To maintain the sculpted body that you obviously hold dear, even with a new heart, you will make major life changes. You will shift your business strategy to one that encourages young women to love themselves, rather than peddling products and services. You will take a strong stand and become a national advocate for healthy lifestyles and self-love for young girls. You will no longer depict before-and-after photos that lead to body shaming and low self-esteem. We will monitor your progress in these areas to ensure you remain on track. Of course, you already know the consequences of your failure to comply with these requirements. Please know that you will have an incredible impact on the lives of young girls and will actually be recognized globally. Are you fully on board?"

Ms. Harris is all smiles as she shouts out, "I am fully on board! I can't wait to get back to Earth and get started. I must thank you again for helping me become the person I've strived to become for so many years."

Edith nods to Gail as she takes her seat. Gail turns to Ms. Harris and says, "You've had a rough two days, and I'm sure you need to get some rest. We want you to be in perfect condition for your return trip to Earth, which will take place in a few days. I'll escort you back to the hotel. One more thing: You can't share anything about your experience with your fellow Travelers. You will tell them about the great time you had learning about the experiences of women on our planet. You will tell them that you were introduced to so many amazing women here that you now feel compelled to be a strong advocate for young girls in America, to embody the positive self-image and self-love that you saw here on Eartha."

Ms. Harris looks at Gail and furrows her brow as she says, "That will be a tall order for me, since I've been in a glass cage for the past two days."

Gail gives Ms. Harris more of a smirk than a smile as she says, "Don't worry—somehow the words will come to you. Relax! The vehicle is waiting to take you back to the hotel, and I'm sure you'll get a good night's rest."

With that, Ms. Harris stands and walks toward the exit. She has even lost her seductive, hip-swinging walk. She waves goodbye to the women as she leaves the conference room with Gail.

The Supreme Highnesses applaud lightly as Gail escorts Ms. Harris to their waiting vehicle. Then Edith says, "Another job well done, and only two more to go. Ms. Harris was a tough one, but she'll be fine, thanks to Catherine's efforts. Come, let's show appreciation to our sister Catherine for her incredible powers."

The Supreme Highnesses all stand and give Catherine

hugs of approval, pressing their palms against hers in Earthans' sign of utmost respect. Then they prepare for the next redemption meeting, which Carmen will lead, for Judge Morcus Bottomy.

26 Redemption Meeting—Judge Morcus Bottomy

Carmen enters the conference room where Judge Bottomy is still watching the streaming of his son Jeremy's confinement and his treatment at the detention facility. His face is still covered with the foul-smelling, now hardened mucus that flew back into his face after he tried to spit on Carmen. The two male robots are still standing on each side of him, looking straight ahead into that unknown space that draws their empty eyes.

Judge Bottomy glares at Carmen as she walks over to his chair and says, "I suppose things have gotten a lot worse since I saw you two days ago. You look an absolute mess."

Judge Bottomy can't hide his rage and shouts, "You demonic witch! How can you be so cruel as to do this to my son? He's always been a good kid, never in any trouble. It's just not right." He holds his head in his hands and looks up at the screen again just as a fellow inmate kicks his son in the groin. His son cowers and tries to cover his head while simultaneously reeling from the pain of the other inmate's kick. A Hispanic guard in the background laughs as he yells to Jeremy Bottomy, "Oh, what a shame—look at how the poor little rich boy is suffering. And his daddy can't help him now; his daddy, the big-time judge who's screwed over Black and Brown kids for decades, is on another planet, where I hope he will stay. Your daddy is a wicked man, Bottomy, and you will pay the price for the pain he's caused. And you know what else? I'm going to enjoy watching you suffer. Now, get up before I kick you again myself."

The guard gives Jeremy the finger, then walks over to another part of the recreation room. Blood begins to flow from Jeremy's nostrils, but he's too weak to cry. He wobbles as he tries to stand up, and then falls to his knees. The young Black kid he met earlier in the cafeteria shouts at the other boy, "Hey, man, leave him alone. He's not responsible for what his father did to us. He seems to be a decent kid. C'mon, man, give the guy a break."

The other kid sneers and backs off as he shouts, "You make me sick. You better be glad this brother got your back."

The young man helps Jeremy to his feet, and Jeremy asks him, "Why are you helping me if my dad is as cruel as you guys say?"

The young man responds, "I don't want to be like your dad. He took away a big part of my life—my scholarship to college, my future—but I can't let hate get the best of me. I want to do my time in here and then try to put the pieces of my life back together. You stay close to me, and the guys won't bother you. I have a black belt in karate, and they've seen what happens when they mess with me."

Jeremy smiles at the young man and says, "Thank you. I didn't get your name."

The young man answers, "My name is Tyler."

They walk out of the recreation room together, and Judge Bottomy begins to weep uncontrollably. "What have I done? I messed up the life of a kid this nice?"

Carmen says, "You messed up the lives of hundreds of young men like Tyler. You, Judge Bottomy, are a heartless bigot, a monster of injustice on steroids, and you should be deeply ashamed of your wicked self, but that's impossible when you don't have a heart."

Judge Bottomy says, "Please don't judge me so harshly. You don't know how I was raised. My parents taught me to hate Black people from the time I was old enough to talk. My dad caught me talking to a Black classmate in the grocery store when I was nine years old, and I got the worst whipping of my life. I know that's not an excuse, but I want you to know how I became this way. It's clear to me that I have to change. I see what my son is experiencing, and it pains me to my core to know that I've caused this to happen to so many Black boys because of my racism. I really thought I was doing society a favor. It's hard to believe that the young Black boy my son met in the cafeteria, a child whom I unjustly sent to detention, could set aside my injustice and help protect my child. He's a bigger man at his young age than I've ever been or will be."

Carmen nods and adds, "Even more important, that young man has more integrity and grace than you have ever had or will ever have. Now, the Supreme Highnesses are waiting for you in another conference room, where we'll talk more about this topic. It's time to join them." She nods to the two robots, and they turn and walk toward the exit. Judge Bottomy's eyes widen, and his brow wrinkles with concern, but he joins Carmen as she leads him toward the conference room where the Supreme Highnesses are waiting.

Carmen escorts Judge Bottomy in, and he quickly scans the room, taking in the sight of the Supreme Highnesses sitting around the U-shaped mahogany table. Judge Bottomy's feet betray his nervousness, and he stumbles and has to hold out his hands to regain his balance. He turns toward the table and can't help but notice that the Supreme Highnesses are all looking in his direction. He tries to smile, but the dried mucus and the tension he's feeling has his jaw muscles so constricted that he winces instead as he tentatively walks in the direction that Carmen points out to him. His legs are still wobbly from too much sitting, and he grabs hold of the back of a chair as he makes his way to his designated seat.

Edith notices his fragility and says, "Welcome, Judge Bottomy. Please take your seat. I can see that you're struggling with walking this morning."

Judge Bottomy rolls his eyes and frowns at Edith as he sits down and then snaps at the women, "You know why I'm having trouble walking after sitting for two days; it's because I've been watching my son in that hellhole you put him in. If you want to punish me, then punish me, but don't take it out on my son. I'm the one who screwed over so many young people, not Jeremy. He's being brutalized in that awful place."

Edith gives Judge Bottomy a stern look as she says, "Now, you understand what you've done to hundreds of Black and Brown youth who didn't deserve detention. It feels awful, doesn't it, seeing your son as a victim of injustice? You are feeling what so many parents have felt as a result of your lack of integrity. Mothers and fathers have shed tears as their children's lives were tainted forever because of your prejudiced decisions. You were supposed to be an impartial and unbiased judge, but you were just the opposite: a robed, racist monster."

Judge Bottomy shakes his head and says, "No! I've explained to Carmen about my background and how that's what caused my prejudice and hatred. My father hated Black men."

"Oh, no," Edith responds, "don't you dare hide behind your childhood! You've had plenty of time to change your behavior, Judge Bottomy, but you chose to remain a bigot."

Judge Bottomy protests, "I didn't *choose* to remain a bigot; I just don't know any other way to be. It's all I've ever known. But that doesn't mean I'm proud of it."

Edith continues, "You've seen the faces of innocent young Black males, your primary target, but they meant nothing to you. You saw mothers' tears and children in disbelief that they would spend months in detention centers for crimes they didn't commit. Most damaging for you is that you knew they were innocent and you just didn't care."

Judge Bottomy rakes his fingers through his hair and says, "You don't know what it's like to grow up hearing almost every day that Black males are bad and deserve to be locked up. I always thought I was doing society a big favor. It's clear to me now that I need to change, but I know I can't do this alone. It's like trying to change my DNA. I welcome any help you can give me to go back to Earth and be an impartial judge. Please, I need your help."

Edith stares at Judge Bottomy for a moment and then says, "I hope you know what you're asking for, because there's no turning back once the process begins."

Edith nods at Carmen to take charge and then sits down. Carmen walks to the front of the room and speaks directly to Judge Bottomy. "Judge Morcus Bottomy, you not only need to change but *must* change your behavior, and that starts with your core, your heart. The racism and bitterness you've shown to young Black males are reprehensible. And you're right—you can't change the past, but you must have a very different future. We need to know that you're serious about the future and want our help, because we can and will help you, but only if you're sincere."

Judge Bottomy pleads with Carmen, "I'm totally sincere. I do need your help, and you have my word that I will do whatever it takes to change my heart."

Carmen looks over at Catherine and says, "Catherine, we need your powers; please come and do what only you can do."

Catherine gets up and walks over to where Judge Bottomy is sitting. She looks into Judge Bottomy's eyes and says to Carmen, "Please take his hands in yours and hold them firmly." Carmen does as Catherine asks, and Judge Bottomy closes his eyes, as if on cue. Catherine takes her right hand, places it over Judge Bottomy's heart, looks toward the ceiling, and again begins speaking to an unknown being. "Dear Merciful One, this man has led a life that's been harmful to so many, and his hatred and bigotry run deeply within his heart. He wants to change and become the honorable judge that his legal system requires, one who makes decisions rooted in integrity, respect, and fairness for all who come before him. He's unable to make the needed changes on his own, so we now ask for your help in cleansing his heart. Dear One, please purge his bitterness, anger, hatred, and bigotry right now as your power travels through my hand to his heart."

Judge Bottomy's head jerks, his shoulders stiffen, and his eyes snap open as he looks to the ceiling, where Catherine's eyes are focused. Suddenly, white smoke emerges from under Catherine's hands and then changes to yellow and blue as it climbs and dissipates into the air. Judge Bottomy's eyes close again, and his shoulders slowly relax as he breathes deeply and expels a whiff of blue smoke. The hardened mucus that formed a mask on his face suddenly disappears. Carmen is still holding his hands when Catherine whispers, "Please release his hands."

When Carmen does so, Judge Bottomy opens his eyes and looks around the room, as Ms. Harris did before him, as if he's trying to locate something he's lost. Then he smiles at Catherine as he says, "Where was the place that I just visited? At first the land was dry and scorched, with lifeless plants, and then it turned into the lushest green hills, with bright yellow wildflowers growing everywhere. It was so peaceful. I really hated to leave."

Catherine smiles at him and says, "You have a new heart, my friend. That dry, scorched heart of yours is now filled with new peace and goodness. You will do awesome things when you return to Planet Earth."

Judge Bottomy grasps Catherine's hands as he says, "Thank you so much. I feel renewed, and I'm anxious to go home and do the right things—things that I should have done for decades. I can't thank you enough."

Catherine nods to him and then walks back to her seat, while Edith stands and speaks sternly to Judge Bottomy. "Now that you have a new heart, we expect great things from you, and we will hold you accountable as we monitor your actions. Initially, we had thoughts of removing you as a judge, but we need you there now more than ever with your new heart. There are two actions that you will immediately undertake upon your return to Earth. First, you will work for the release of the young men unjustly detained because of your biased decisions."

Judge Bottomy frowns and says, "Wait a minute—that will be hard for me to do."

Edith responds, "No, it won't—not with our assistance. We've already taken steps to make it happen, and you'll be a hero for such a bold reversal. Second, you will champion an initiative to create diversion programs and mentoring for young men of color who are brought into the pipeline of incarceration, with a focus on Black males. Of course, people will wonder what happened to the racist judge. You will share that this journey has given you time to think about the juvenile-court system and how it's part of the pipeline to mass incarceration for men of color. You will spend the rest of your life working to change the juvenile-court system, ensuring fairness and alternatives to detention. Are you comfortable with this request?"

Judge Bottomy nods his head and says, "I wholeheartedly commit to doing the things you've asked of me."

Edith looks around the room as she takes her seat and nods at Carmen, who has walked back to the panel that controls the projection screen. Edith adds, "Judge Bottomy, you're on the right path, and I'm pleased to tell you that your son Jeremy was never in detention. As you can see on the screen, he's happily swimming in your backyard pool."

Judge Bottomy looks at the screen in disbelief as tears of joy and anger stream down his face and he shouts at the women, "You made me experience this pain for no reason? How could you do that?"

Carmen responds, "But you *did* need to experience that pain—the same pain you've caused so many young people and their parents. Without that experience, you wouldn't have felt the need to change. Now, you will be a person who is a champion for justice, and you'll experience the reward of helping young people become their best selves. The joy this will bring to your new heart and your life is indescribable. We look forward to the great things that you're going to accomplish."

Judge Bottomy looks down at his hands, which are now shaking, and clasps them together to calm them. He looks up at Carmen and says, "May God forgive me for what I've done. Thank you for opening my eyes, but most of all, thank you for healing my heart."

Carmen stops for a moment to grasp the sincerity of Judge Bottomy's words, and when their eyes meet, she sees the eyes of a changed man, eyes that show humility, instead of the arrogance he's always displayed in the past. She says to him in a more pleasant tone than she's used before, "Sir, you've had a rough two days, and I'm sure you need to get some rest. We want you to be in perfect condition for your return trip to Earth, which will take place in a few days. I'll escort you back to the hotel. One more thing: You can't share anything about your experience with your fellow Travelers. You will tell them how beneficial it was for you to learn about the judicial system on Planet Eartha, and how you learned the importance of alternatives to incarceration for young people. You will explain that you now realize you need to make some significant changes in how you administer justice when you return home."

Judge Bottomy asks Carmen, "What if they ask for details that I can't give them?"

Carmen smiles as she says, "Don't worry—somehow the words will come to you. Now, relax! The vehicle is waiting to take you back to the hotel so you can get a good night's rest."

Judge Bottomy stands and bows to the women as he leaves the conference room, walking with stronger legs and a new heart.

The Supreme Highnesses applaud lightly as Carmen escorts Judge Bottomy to their waiting vehicle. Then Edith says, "Well, my sisters, another opportunity to send humanity to Planet Earth. Judge Bottomy will use that new heart for much good, thanks to Catherine's incredible powers. Catherine, we so appreciate you."

The Supreme Highnesses all stand to give Catherine hugs of approval and press their palms against hers. Then they prepare for the last redemption meeting, which Robin will lead, for Jorrome Smithy.

27 Redemption Meeting—Jorrome Smithy

The morning of his second day of reckoning in his filthy surroundings, Mr. Smithy loses his battle with sleep. He has been trying to stay awake amid the squalor, for fear of what one of the many roaches and rodents in the room might do to his body, but eventually he can't resist the urge to succumb to slumber. But no sooner has he drifted off than he jerks awake, as he feels something against his face and comes eye to eye with the biggest rat he's ever seen. They scare each other; Mr. Smithy screams and jumps out of his chair, and the rat scampers down the length of his body. Mr. Smithy grabs his face, and his entire body begins shaking. He yells to the room, "I've got to get out of this hellhole. No human being deserves to live like this. Help me, somebody! Please help me!"

As if on cue, Robin knocks on the disappearing door. Mr. Smithy yells, "Who is it? Please come in and get me out of here."

As Robin enters the room, she covers her face with a black mask with gold trim. The mask is engraved with gold capital letters "SH," for "Supreme Highnesses."

"My God," she says. "You look an absolute mess, and you stink something awful."

Mr. Smithy snarls at her, "You would too if you had to stay in this place. No one should have to live like this."

Robin smiles and says, "Why, Mr. Smithy, I'm surprised to hear you say that, because it's exactly what so many of your tenants have to experience when you refuse to maintain or make repairs to your buildings. Please don't expect me to feel one bit of sympathy for what you've experienced. Anyway, it's time for you to leave here, because the Supreme Highnesses are waiting for you."

Mr. Smithy yells again, "I can't meet anyone in this condition! I smell awful, and I need a shower."

Robin smirks at him as she says, "You will leave now, or you can stay here forever."

At that, he quickly walks to the door, and as he steps out of the room, he stops in his tracks as he realizes that he's still in the Supreme Highnesses' headquarters.

Robin walks him down the narrow hallway to the conference room where the Supreme Highnesses are waiting for his arrival. As he enters, the foul smell of his body is so overwhelming that the women around the table all put on engraved face masks that are identical to Robin's.

Robin ushers Mr. Smithy to the front of the room and motions for him to sit in a chair facing the center of the U-shaped table where the women are seated. She then joins the other women around the table. Edith stands as Robin sits, and says, "Mr. Smithy, it's good to see you again. We can see that you've had to deal with some significant challenges over the past two days. How are you today?"

Mr. Smithy can't hide his anger as he yells, "You have the audacity to ask me how I'm feeling? You have to wear masks because of my smell, and look at my clothes. I can't tell you how many rats probably peed and crapped on me. So don't ask me how I feel. You already know!"

Edith lowers her voice to just above a whisper, but still loud enough for Mr. Smithy to hear, and says, "Mr. Smithy, we *do* know how you feel, and we also know how hundreds of your tenants feel. Tell us, what have you learned from the past two days?"

Mr. Smithy looks around the room to try to read the Supreme Highnesses' faces and then smiles slyly before saying, "Hmm, what have I learned? That's a good question, and I'll do my best to answer it." Finally, he stands up and speaks with a strong voice: "I have lived a life of luxury, and as a clever businessman, I have acquired a tremendous amount of property and wealth. In fact, in some of the poorer neighborhoods, I was almost given property so that the local government wouldn't have to deal with it. I hired property managers and gave them orders to squeeze as much money as possible from tenants but to make sure they kept the maintenance costs low so my profits would continue to soar. I never went to check on the property in poor neighborhoods where mostly minorities lived. Frankly, I didn't see myself going into those dilapidated neighborhoods because I don't feel comfortable being around those people. I'm always seeing negative things about them in the news. So when I received letters from tenants about their horrific living conditions, I ignored them and gave orders to evict those tenants who were frequent complainers. It wasn't a typical eviction, but eviction by raising the rent. The tenants often complained to local housing authorities, but that didn't work out for them, because my brother-in-law was in control and most of the housing authority staff were in my back pocket. In all honesty, I'm all the bad things you said two days ago. And now, after experiencing living conditions not fit for human habitation for two days, I can only imagine what my tenants have been suffering for months and years. . . . No, let me change that: I now know firsthand what they've experienced and are still experiencing. I know that I have to do better: I know that I have to improve my tenants' housing. When I return to Earth, that will be my mission. I will make sure that my team gets to work right away on this project and helps those people." He looks around the room to gauge the women's reactions and then takes his seat when he sees only expressionless faces.

Robin walks in front of the room and claps her hands in taunting applause as she begins speaking. "Bravo, Mr. Smithy! What a great speech, and you delivered it with such passion. However, we don't believe a word you said, because your grandiose monologue totally lacked sincerity. Given what you just experienced, we expected you to say that you want to change when you get back to Earth. However, you never said how sorry you are for the way you've mistreated your tenants. You talked about what you will have your team do, but you never said what *you* will do. It would have been nice to hear that you would personally go to those buildings and see for yourself what needs to be improved, and not leave it to your team and paid officials to make the improvements. You know and we know that they would make only halfhearted, superficial efforts, and not the required, major adjustments. We're still very concerned that you haven't fully embraced the changes you need to make to address your personal greed and self-centeredness."

"Wait a minute!" Mr. Smithy shouts, as he jumps from his chair. "How can you know what's in my heart? Do you have some kind of special powers?"

Robin smiles at Mr. Smithy as she says, "My goodness, you're not as smart as you think you are. Haven't you learned anything over the past two days? Who do you think created the dilapidated living quarters you just left? You didn't come to Eartha because you won a lottery. You came because we selected you to come here, and you will leave here to execute the mission that we've planned for you."

Mr. Smithy slowly takes his seat and lowers his head with a look of humility no one has seen since his arrival. As Robin walks back to her chair, Edith stands to speak. "Mr. Smithy, we had hoped that you would have a change of heart, based on a sincere desire to right your past wrongs. We heard your words of regret while you were experiencing those horrific living conditions. We do believe that a part of you wants to do the right thing; however, you need help to do so, and we're going to provide it. Now, please listen carefully, because we have a very specific plan for what you will do when you return to Earth. First, you will share with the world how this trip to Eartha changed your life and how you had previously allowed personal greed to impact your sense of humanity. You have so many things to make right, but an immediate priority is to begin addressing property that you own that doesn't comply with safe and livable housing requirements. In fact, you will go above and beyond those requirements and will completely remodel your dilapidated properties. You will allow tenants to live rent free for one year, to compensate for all the time you've deprived them of safe, decent housing."

Mr. Smithy jumps up from his chair and shouts, "No way! That will cost a fortune."

Edith says, "Sit down! You have the fortune and will do as we say. Trust me, if you thought the past two days were horrendous, you don't even want to experience the consequences of not complying with our mission for you. Understood?"

Mr. Smithy sits back down and nods his head affirmatively. Edith continues, "You will hire people from those neighborhoods to work on remodeling those properties and will pay them a living wage. You will become a nationally recognized champion for safe and livable housing for underserved communities. Most importantly, you will begin to experience the reward of doing good for others, as opposed to your current, self-centered lifestyle. That's when the change within your heart will become a reality. We will monitor your actions every step of the way. In fact, we will provide guidance where it's needed."

The room becomes very quiet as Edith's message concludes, and all eyes are on Mr. Smithy. His head is bowed, and he says nothing for a while as he looks down at his hands. After a few minutes of allowing Edith's message to sink in, he says, "Okay, I will do everything you ask, but how are you going to help me from here?"

Edith responds, "I'll ask Robin to answer that for you."

Robin stands and says, "Mr. Smithy, we will stay closely

connected with you once you return to Earth. You won't know who we are or where we are, but you will always feel our presence. One more thing: The only thing you can share with your fellow Travelers is how much you learned about safe and livable housing on Eartha and its positive economic and social impact."

"Are you serious?" Mr. Smithy asks. "I've been held captive in the most horrific environment while on Eartha, so how in the world can I share anything about safe and livable housing?"

"Good question," Robin says. "Don't worry—we will provide all the answers you need, whenever you need them. They'll come to you with absolute clarity. Have we made everything clear for you today?"

Mr. Smithy nods again and says, this time with genuine humility, "Yes, ma'am, you have. Thank you."

"Great," Robin says, "I'll escort you back to the hotel so you can get a good night's sleep. Our vehicle is waiting out front. You will travel back to Earth in a few days, and you'll need your rest."

"Ladies, I need a favor before I leave," Mr. Smithy says. "I smell awful and look an absolute mess. I can't go back to the hotel in this condition."

Robin smiles as she says, "You're absolutely right, and we don't intend for you to return to the hotel in this condition. May I please have your hands?"

Mr. Smithy's face becomes a huge question mark. At first he clasps his hands together, as if he's afraid to extend them to Robin, but then he reluctantly grasps her outstretched palms. She stares at him without blinking, and suddenly his smell disappears as white smoke arises and floats to the ceiling. She continues her stare, and his clothes return to the freshness of the tan khakis and pink-and-white, button-down oxford shirt that he arrived wearing two days ago. Mr. Smithy's face turns pale, his eyes widen, and he begins trembling with fear from what just happened to him. Robin releases his now moist hands and says nonchalantly, "Well, you're good to go now." Mr. Smithy can only stand rigidly before her as he fully comprehends the extent of Robin's power and what it means for his future.

Edith stands and says, "Mr. Smithy, we wish you well, and we're so excited about the great things you'll do when you return to Earth. We'll see you again before your departure, but for now, please get some rest."

Mr. Smithy simply gapes at the Supreme Highnesses, his face flushed, until Robin motions for him to leave the room.

The Supreme Highnesses applaud lightly as Robin escorts Mr. Smithy from the conference room to their waiting vehicle. Then Edith says, "Another job well done, my sisters. Our days of reckoning and redemption have now come to an end and gone exactly as planned. Mr. Smithy is one whom we will watch closely. He's a smooth talker, but his words are hollow."

Lucy raises her hand and says, "I'll gladly add him to the list of Travelers I need to keep in check." They all laugh as they leave the conference room.

28 The Travelers' Reunion

The Travelers gather for breakfast in a private hotel dining room that the Supreme Highnesses reserved for them. As soon as they enter the magnificent space, they gape at the decor, which makes the room feel like a garden of exotic succulents, with two large tables carved out of dark brown teak wood into mushroom forms with flat tops, instead of typical umbrella shapes. Each table has five place settings. In the center of the room is a huge plant that resembles the snake plant on Earth and that is at least twenty feet tall. Diners walk through a row of bright red crowns of thorns to enter the lavish buffet serving area. There, they discover an assortment of delicacies that include unfamiliar fruit, like purple pineapples, pink bananas, and bright orange grapes, along with the usual apples, peaches, and yellow bananas.

What astound the Travelers most are the robotic dispensers serving made-to-order hot dishes. Mr. Smithy walks up to the meat dispenser and steps back in surprise as a voice says, "Good morning, sir. Would you like sausage, bacon, or ostrich?"

Mr. Smithy reluctantly responds to the dispenser, as if he's not sure what to say, "I'll . . . I'll have bacon, thank you. Yes, bacon slices!"

The dispenser says, "Thank you! Bacon it is. Please place your plate in the marked area to receive your order."

Mr. Smithy smiles for the first time this morning as the dispenser places four slices of nice, crisp bacon perfectly on his plate.

Meanwhile, the other Travelers serve themselves fruit and walk over to the talking dispensers to order their hot food items. Some step back when they hear the dispenser voices, and Pastor Bendy speaks in a loud, staccato tone to his dispenser: "I-will-have-sausage-please. Thank-you!" The machine responds in the same voice, "Sausage-it-is! Thank-you-sir!"

After getting their food, the Travelers walk to one of the tables and take their seats. For the first time, no one seems concerned about who's sitting next to them.

Although they've spent a restful night following their grueling two days of reckoning and redemption, there is an unusual quietness in the air. A more humble and subdued presence has replaced the Travelers' previous squabbling, arrogance, self-righteousness, and moments of internal strife. Each is lost in their private thoughts as they devour the delicacies from the lavish breakfast buffet. Other than saying cordial hellos or nods once they're seated, they eat in silence without making eye contact and appear to be lost in their thoughts.

Not long after they're seated, the Travelers hear lively chatter and laughter outside the dining room entrance. A familiar voice can be heard singing a well-known song that

Pharrell Williams made a big hit on Planet Earth, "Happy." Cristina comes into the dining room singing, clapping her hands, and moving her shoulders to the rhythm of the up-beat tune. The other astronauts laugh at Cristina, and then Lillian joins in and claps her hands to the beat. The energy in the room surges as the astronauts liven up the quiet dining room environment.

They are wearing stylish, navy reflective leggings and matching hooded jackets engraved with the Eartha Space Center logo. The Travelers overhear Vivian saying, "You know traveling through the galaxy can never be replaced as the number one experience in my lifetime, but the visit to the wildlife park yesterday comes in at number three or four, at least. Those animals were truly out of this world.

Beki chuckles as she says, "You know that's true, since you really *are* in another world."

Vivian continues, "Could you ever have imagined a red-and-white-striped zebra? Totally amazing!"

Lillian high-fives Vivian and says, "Girl, you said it. I loved the three-legged peacock with purple and white feathers and the green polar bears. I'll never forget it. I just wish they had let us take pictures, but it was made clear to us during our first trip that cameras are not allowed. Brooke reminded me that our cameras wouldn't work on this planet anyway, even if we had brought them."

Gwen joins in the chatter, saying, "People will think I'm smoking something when I tell them about those animals. You had to see it to believe it. Who knew such creatures existed? I mean, it's absolutely crazy!"

The astronauts wave at the Travelers and shout greetings before walking over to the breakfast buffet and filling their plates with the delicious fruits and hot food. The astronauts must have had previous exposure to the talking, made-to-order dispensers, because they move down the line of robots without any fanfare. In fact, Gwen says to the meat dispenser, "What's up, my brother? Do you remember me? What you got for me today?"

The meat dispenser answers, "Hello, my sister who likes sausage. Please place your plate in the marked area. Four sausages coming up."

Gwen laughs and says, "Thank you so much," and then blows the dispenser a kiss.

Cristina watches her and shakes her head as she says, "You know, the air here may be affecting your brain waves, because something is definitely off center." They both become bug-eyed and almost drop their plates when the meat dispenser starts laughing.

The astronauts walk past the huge dragon plant and seat themselves at the table next to the Travelers. After eating a few mouthfuls of food, Beki says to the Travelers, "I hope you guys have had the same kinds of awesome experiences that we've had over these past few days. We knew from our previous visit that Eartha is an amazingly beautiful planet with lush terrain and the most breathtaking sunsets and night skies in the galaxy, but we've been blown away by its museums, its botanical gardens with plants beyond earthly description, meeting the most amazing female scientists, who can design and build incredible structures, and seeing its airborne vehicles that travel on invisible freeways."

The other astronauts nod their agreement and smile broadly.

Beki continues, "But enough about our exciting adventures—we want to hear about your time on Planet Eartha."

"Yes, yes!" Lillian adds. "We can't wait to hear about your experiences. I can only imagine the surprises that were in store for each of you. Do tell!"

The Travelers merely look at each other like stunned animals, as if asking one another who will have the courage to speak first. When no one responds, Vivian says, "Aw, come on, I know at least Ms. Harris must have lots to share."

Although Ms. Harris has been silent, her face suddenly lights up and she begins speaking. "The most wonderful thing happened to me during my visit here. I was introduced to so many amazing women that I realized young girls today need to feel more positive about who they are in their own skin. On Earth, there's too much emphasis on weight, facial features, and other physical characteristics. I've certainly not done a good job of promoting positive self-image through my extensive media platforms. Now I feel compelled to be a strong advocate for young girls to embody the self-esteem and self-love that I've seen here on Eartha. I can't wait to get home and begin this work."

Ms. Harris has a puzzled look on her face as she ponders the words that have just flowed so freely from her mouth—words that were not her own. She picks up her fork and begins eating again, as she recalls the Supreme Highnesses' assurances that they would make sure she had the right words when she needed them. This was obviously one of those times.

The astronauts exchange knowing glances about the Supreme Highnesses' special powers as they observe the change in Ms. Harris. Finally, Vivian says, "Wow, that's awesome, and I wish you the best. Young girls need that message. Good for you!"

Mr. Stone is wide-eyed and can only mutter under his breath, "Is this the same woman who was so full of herself? I wonder what her experience was like with the ladies."

Pastor Bendy sees Mr. Stone's lips moving and says, "Come on, Mr. Stone, speak up so we can hear you."

Mr. Stone shakes his head and says, "Oh, it's nothing. I really like what Ms. Harris shared about her experience." He picks up his glass of orange juice and takes a long sip.

Beki eyes the other Travelers and says, "How about the rest of you? What happened during your visit?"

Pastor Bendy is the next to speak, and his words, too, begin to flow beyond his control. "Ladies, I've had a religious epiphany during my time on Eartha. I realize that I've elevated myself to a level that goes far beyond who I am as a man of God. The title of the Almighty Apostle Henry Bendy has seen its sunset on this planet, and I'm now returning to an earlier, more appropriate moniker: Pastor Henry Bendy. I am no longer comfortable with a title that misleadingly elevates me to an unworthy level. This trip has enabled me to get in touch with myself in a way that never would have happened on Earth, and I'm so grateful for this change in my life. I will focus my ministry on spreading the good news about Jesus Christ and on being a servant-leader to the members of my congregation. I look forward to being the shepherd that God has called me to be, and to lead and love His people in a manner that I've gotten away from, for multiple selfish reasons. I feel joy and a peace that

I haven't felt in years. I want to thank each of you ladies for your work in bringing me and my fellow Travelers to this amazing planet."

As the astronauts eye each other in disbelief, given the number of times that Beki has had to rebuke the Travelers for their behavior, Ms. Harris claps her hands together and says, "That's impressive, Pastor Bendy. I know you're going to do great things back on Earth."

Judge Bottomy says, "Pastor Bendy, I agree with Ms. Harris; it's good to hear about the changes in your ministry. Most of all, I think everyone will love that you have a shorter title."

Pastor Bendy breaks out laughing, and the other Travelers and astronauts join him.

Cristina raises her glass of water and says, "I'll drink to that!"

Without Beki's prompting, Mr. Stone wipes his mouth with his napkin and begins to speak about his experience. "I can't even begin to find the right words to express the great time I've had learning about this planet. I have to admit, as a male chauvinist, I couldn't believe that the women on Eartha could be so advanced without male guidance. Was I in for an awakening. I am so in awe of the incredible advances that women have made on this planet; there's simply no possible comparison on Planet Earth, with our dominant male leadership. We need more men to visit here and see what Earth, especially the United States, has missed by not fully leveraging the talent of our women. You bet I'm going to share what I've learned and seen firsthand. And, ladies, let me apologize to each of you amazing astronauts, because I didn't give you proper recognition for your tremendous accomplishments and for bringing the five of us on this voyage. From the bottom of my heart, I thank each of you!"

Beki shakes her head and says, "My goodness. You're welcome. It has been our honor to bring you to Eartha."

Vivian starts coughing and has to get a drink of water in reaction to Beki's words. Beki recognizes what caused the coughing and rolls her eyes at Vivian. Mr. Stone squares his shoulders with pride, especially given the kudos he just gave to the women on Planet Eartha. *Some things don't change, even on Eartha,* he thinks, as he smiles at the eloquence of his words, his chin held high.

Not to be outdone, and before anyone can react to Mr. Stone's comments, Mr. Smithy clears his throat and says, "I'll go next. Man—I mean, "woman" or "people"—I don't even know where to start. I'm ashamed to admit that I came here as a very rich and content slumlord who didn't care one bit how the tenants in my lower-income buildings lived. I never visited them, and I didn't think much of the people who lived there. They were mostly people of color, and they were invisible to me. Here on Eartha, I was privileged to see the importance of safe and livable housing and its positive economic and social impact. I mean, people here aren't treated badly because of their economic status. They are treated with dignity, and I could see the pride in their faces as they allowed me to see the quality of their living conditions. I can't imagine what they would have thought of me if they had known the truth about my being a slumlord. I can assure you that I have lots of work to do when I get back home and that I will work my tail off to try and make amends for the many, many things I've done wrong. That's all I have to say. Thank you for enabling me to make this journey." Mr. Smithy picks up his napkin and dabs his eyes to wipe away tears that have begun to form.

During the awkward silence that ensues, the other Travelers look down at their hands or into the distance as Mr. Smithy fights to control his emotions. Finally, Pastor Bendy reaches across the table and presses Mr. Smithy's hand in his, saying, "Proud of you, man. I believe you're going to improve the lives of a lot of people."

Mr. Smithy nods and says, "Thank you, Pastor Bendy. I'm determined to make a real difference."

Despite the seeming authenticity of the exchange, Lillian can't help but wonder, *Is this guy for real, or is this an act? I hope it's genuine, but I'm sure he, like the others, is getting much help from our friends. . . . Shoot, forgive me—I didn't really mean that, in case you're reading my mind, Supreme Highnesses.*

After another pause, Judge Bottomy clears his throat and begins, "Well, last but not least, I, too, have something to say about my experience. It looks like each of us has learned something important on Eartha about our character and our humanity and that we're leaving with a commitment to do better when we get back home. I had the opportunity to learn about the judicial system on Planet Eartha. I learned the importance and value of alternatives to incarceration for young people, especially young men of color. It would be great if I could tell you that I've been a fair, just, and honorable judge, but I've been just the opposite in a juvenile-court system where I had the opportunity to change young lives and to administer justice as the law requires. That didn't happen, and my heart is heavy because of it. The good thing is that I will return to Earth committed to be an advocate for justice and a role model for how juvenile-court judges can make a positive difference in the lives of young people. I haven't felt this good about a personal decision in decades. I, too, thank you astronauts for bringing me to this amazing planet. You will always have a special place in my heart."

Judge Bottomy picks up his cup of coffee, takes a sip, and frowns because it's now cold. He smiles internally as a thought crosses his mind: *I wonder if the other Travelers' experience was similar to mine. They're all so different from the way they were a few days ago. The women said I didn't have to worry about what to say when asked about my experience, and the words that I just spoke came as a complete surprise. I can truly say that there's a warm place in my heart that wasn't there a few days ago, and I'm glad. I feel so much better.*

Beki, Cristina, Lillian, Gwen, and Vivian are all staring at the Travelers. Yet another cloud of silence hovers over the group until Beki says, "I can't begin to say how much I've enjoyed hearing from each of you. Your experiences have definitely been life-changing, and I know that so many people will benefit from your actions when you return home."

Gwen nods and comments, "We had a great time exploring new areas of Planet Eartha, but nothing we've done compares to what you've shared this morning. I tell you, it's truly heartwarming."

Lillian looks over at the Travelers and smiles as she thinks, *These folks have changed, all right, but I can only imagine what had to happen to clean up this motley crew. Of course, if anyone can do it, the Supreme Highnesses can.*

Beki glances around the room and says, "Well, folks, before you know it, we'll be on our way back home. It's hard to believe that we've been here for almost two weeks. It seems like just two days."

It's now Mr. Smithy's turn to mutter under his breath as he says, "Speak for yourself, sister. It's been more like two years for me."

Beki doesn't notice Mr. Smithy and continues, "I suggest touring the wildlife park before our departure. It takes a couple of days to see everything, but it's worth the trip. In fact, I might join you, since there are a couple of areas we didn't have time to see."

Vivian adds, "Hey, I'll come too." Lillian, Gwen, and Cristina all raise their hands in agreement.

As the astronauts and Travelers prepare to leave the dining room, Vivian asks the group, "Should we set a time to go to the wildlife park? This afternoon might be best, since we have work to do for the next couple of days to get ready for the trip home."

Beki says, "Sounds good to me. We're perfectly dressed for it."

Mr. Stone looks at the other Travelers and says, "We don't have any plans, so this afternoon sounds good to me," as his companions nod.

Lillian raises her hand and says, "I'll check with the front desk for transportation."

Ms. Harris looks at the astronauts and then looks down at her stiletto heels and form-fitting knit dress and asks, "Do you mind if I change into something more comfortable? These shoes are already killing my feet. I believe I saw a nice pants outfit in my closet."

Mr. Stone shakes his head and says, "I need to change as well."

Beki looks at her watch and says, "Okay, let's meet in the front lobby at noon. That will give you an hour to change clothes while Lillian arranges transportation." Pats on the back and laughter ensue as the astronauts and Travelers leave the dining room with uplifted spirits.

29 The Supreme Highnesses' Mission in Motion

The Supreme Highnesses gather at their headquarters as the day finally arrives for the astronauts and Travelers' return voyage to Earth. The ten women have several conversations going on as they sit around the U-shaped mahogany table in the large conference room where the reckoning and redemption meetings were held.

Edith stands, and the other women cease their conversations to hear from their supreme leader. Edith begins speaking: "Ladies, what a time we've had with the Travelers from Earth. They are quite a group, and our most challenging guests to date. I don't mean challenging in regard to our power over them; I mean it from the perspective that their hearts were impure and their profound selfishness was apparent from the minute we selected them as our first test group from America. We'll have to monitor them carefully and make sure they don't return to their areas of weakness.

"Our work in America is just beginning. We must continue to focus on all the issues there that need our attention and intervention. It warms my heart to know that the five Travelers, who came here as deeply egotistical, selfish, and devious individuals, are leaving as changed individuals who will do great work for their fellow citizens. The next mission group we send to the United States must conduct significant research and study into why their human population has so many character flaws. One can't ignore the prevalence of racism, sexism, anti-Semitism, homophobia, economic disparities, wars, oppression . . . and the list goes on."

April raises her hand, and Edith nods for her to speak. "I feel compelled to add, based on my lengthy visit to America, that there are some amazing people there whom we also need to acknowledge in the midst of the evil ones. It's unfortunate that America has a culture of using its public media to highlight what's wrong with the nation, instead of balancing those stories with the many things that are right. American media cause so much of the strife when they create negative images of certain groups, especially Black Americans. They incite a lot of the fear and anxiety about race. The wealthy whites own the media, and they ensure that news stories are told as they see most profitable. Thank you for the opportunity to share another point of view."

Edith says, "Thank you, April; it's good to have a balanced perspective. Perhaps some of those media tycoons should be among our next group of visitors from America. At any rate, I salute our sisters, Carmen, April, Felicia, Gail, and Robin, who have done amazing work selecting the Travelers from America and then shepherding them during their visit. This mission could not have been successful without your great deeds. Catherine, your powers have worked wonders and truly caused a breakthrough with a couple of the Travelers. We also greatly appreciate the work of April, Laura and Lucy, as they spent a couple of years studying the United States during their time on Planet Earth. The mission itself could not have been accomplished without their work. They embody the courage, strength, and giving of oneself that are at the heart of our sisterhood."

Edith begins applauding, and all of the Supreme Highnesses join her. Then Brooke stands and announces, "Our astronauts should be arriving shortly so we can make sure they have their final orders. They still have work to do."

Just then, the conference door opens and the five astronauts walk into the room, led by Beki, followed by Gwen, Lillian, Cristina, and Vivian. Lucy gets up and directs them to their assigned seating. Edith stands again as the astronauts take their seats and welcomes the group. "Ladies, it's so good to see you again. We hope you had time to really get to know Eartha during this visit. I hope your tour guides helped you get acquainted with what we know is one of the most beautiful and advanced planets in the galaxy."

Beki says, "We've had an incredible time and thank you for your wonderful hospitality." It's been a very full, informative, and most enjoyable week. Each day was filled with experiences that we never imagined possible. The ride in one of your spacecrafts was an opportunity to see the magnitude of your technological advances. You would never have convinced me that someone could walk in outer space and not be tethered to a spaceship. It's something that we were too afraid to try when given the opportunity by your talented space team, but seeing it was believing it."

Vivian says, "The trip to the Blue Sea was off the chain. The water was so blue that it looked like a sea of sapphires. Most of all, I loved wearing the shoes that enabled me to walk on water. As a person of faith, I knew that only my Lord and Savior could make that happen, and I admit I was scared to death to try it. I give Cristina credit because she was brave enough to try it first, and then we all followed suit."

Gwen laughs as she jokes, "I can now say that I walk on water unassisted. Seriously, the day we met your all-female military was a big highlight for me. I didn't think you needed that kind of protection on your planet, but I understand it's for visitors from other planets. Those women have it totally together. The technology still blows me away, and the fact that you have weapons that make people disappear . . . Well, I don't ever want to get on anyone's bad side here." Edith laughs and says, "We believe in peaceful coexistence and would never use weapons of mass destruction unless our people were threatened with harm. No one on Eartha has personal weapons. The ones that you saw are under very tight control and used only for the defense of our planet—never, ever against our citizens or peaceful visitors."

Beki comments, "A few days ago, we joined the Travelers on their visit to the wildlife park. It was the second visit for us, but it was truly worth the repeat trip. We were just as excited the second time as the first. What an incredible place. The animals we saw were beyond our wildest imagination. We wish the Travelers had gotten a chance to see some of the other sights and to spend time with the talented women who are the brain trust of this planet. It was humbling for us all to meet such talented individuals. Oh, and thank you for the wardrobe that you generously provided for us. As you can see, we love our outfits from the Eartha Space Center. It's the first time Lillian has worn the same outfit twice."

Lillian scowls at Beki, then turns it into a smile as she says, "Hey, let's not get personal!"

Gwen laughs as she agrees, "Come to think of it, you're right. This *is* a first for Lillian." Even the Supreme Highnesses have to chuckle at that.

Cristina chimes in again: "I love the wardrobe, but most of all, thank you for the amazing food. I hope I can fit back into my space suit."

The other astronauts laugh, and Edith reassures them, "Don't worry, your space suits will fit perfectly. And now we'd like to provide some final instructions for the return voyage to Earth and the final stage of your support of our mission. We can't thank you enough for bringing the Travelers to Eartha. I will now turn things over to Laura, the architect of our mission on Planet Earth."

As Edith takes her seat, Laura stands and says, "Ladies, you have played a key role in our mission on Planet Earth, and, as Edith said, we thank you for your support. I can hear your thoughts that you had no choice, and you're right—you really didn't have a choice—but you still performed in a manner worthy of our praise. Your last contribution to the mission is to get the Travelers back to Earth. As you know, we will make sure the trip is successful. Your communication will be slightly different this time when your spacecraft lands and you're welcomed home. You will speak about what you've learned from this journey with the Travelers, about their transformation and the joy of spending time with such amazing people. Of course, we will help you with this communication, as we did after your previous visit."

Lillian shifts forward in her seat as she says, "We'll definitely need your words for that bunch. They've been one royal pain in the neck—although, I have to admit, they were very different when we had breakfast together a week ago."

Laura smiles as she says, "We're glad you noticed a difference in the Travelers, because we've taken great pains to ensure they leave as changed individuals. And that's a good thing for them and your nation. After about two interviews with the media, your work will be done. You will remember only certain aspects of your visits to Eartha, and we will no longer control your minds and words. You will have the power, however, to reach out telepathically if you need our help. Any questions?"

Cristina asks, "How will you select the next team of astronauts for future visits? Do we have to help with that?"

Laura says, "Good question, Cristina. No, we have already begun the process of selecting the next team of astronauts. As a matter of fact, they're currently in training. Of course, if you'd like to make another visit—"

Cristina quickly interrupts Laura, saying, "No, no, no, I was just asking out of curiosity. Other astronauts should have the privilege of visiting this awesome planet."

Laura winks at Edith and says, "Yes, they should and they will. Any other questions?"

Vivian asks, "When you purge information from our minds, what will we retain in our memory?"

Laura answers, "Another good question. You will retain only what you'll need to respond to questions about this planet."

Gwen leans forward and asks, "Will you still have some control of our minds and feed us those answers, as you've been doing, or will we use our own words again?"

Laura answers, "Wow, another excellent question. As I said earlier, we will no longer control your minds and words, but you'll be able to reactivate our telepathic relationship whenever you see the need. We promised you that when you accepted the mission, and we always keep our promises."

Lillian perks up and says, "Thank you for that—although I'll miss being super smart."

Edith comments, "Lillian, you're already super smart. That's why we chose you and your sister astronauts for this mission."

Gwen raises her hand and rather shyly says, "I have one question that's been gnawing at me ever since our first visit. How do you have so many children on this planet, when the men are all robots?"

Edith smiles and says, "Robin, you're probably the best person to answer that."

Robin stands and says, "Many visitors to our planet have asked this question. As the chief scientists of our Reproductive Research Center, we have mastered the process of in vitro fertilization and artificial insemination. We harvest the eggs of our women and use sperm specimens that we've replicated in our labs, after years of research and analysis of male sperm we collected from willing male donors who visited our planet. Therefore, the absence of men has no impact on procreation on Eartha, where the population is ninety-eight percent female."

Gwen has a puzzled look on her face as she says, "Wow. Now, that's deep."

Cristina adds, "Well, since Gwen asked her provocative question, I'd like to know where the planet's two percent men are. I haven't seen a male yet who wasn't a robot."

Robin looks around the room at the other Supreme Highnesses as they exchange chuckles, then answers Cristina's question. "The male population *are* the robots. We have both male and female robots, and we've perfected the technology so perfectly that they live productive, programmed lives. That said, our population of female robots is very small—less than half of a percent of the female population, to be exact. The male robots do most of the service jobs, while the female robots are superior beings who perform complex atomic assignments using their extraordinary brilliance."

Cristina gives Robin two thumbs up as she says, "Now, that's what I'm talking about! Supreme women rulers running the planet, and superior women robots created by superior women? I think I could get used to Eartha really quickly . . . but nah, I have to go back to Earth. I have this thing for real, live men."

Robin rolls her eyes and says to Cristina, "As I've heard on your planet, 'whatever floats your boat.'"

The Supreme Highnesses break into laughter, and the astronauts join in. Then Laura stands again to speak to the astronauts. "Ladies, I believe you have all of your instructions for tomorrow's journey back to Earth, and we have your vehicle ready for launch. You will find the Travelers much more manageable on the return trip. Again, please acknowledge and encourage them, for they have tremendous work ahead. I wish each of you well in your chosen future. If you have no further questions, I'll turn the meeting back over to our supreme leader."

Laura takes her seat as Edith says, "Thank you, Laura. I, too, wish each of you well. And now Brooke has some final comments to share."

Brooke goes to the front of the room and pulls up a photo on the screen, of four of the astronauts receiving medals of honor from the first elected female president of the United States of America. Brooke then says, "Ladies, this is your future, so treasure it."

Lillian calls out, "That's amazing, but where's Beki?"

Beki looks confused and annoyed as she says, "Yes, why aren't I in the photo?"

Brooke smiles at her and says, "Beki, your life takes another turn; however, don't be dismayed, because you have great things in store for you as well."

Beki frowns and says, "I can't imagine what's greater than the first female president of the United States of America giving you a medal of honor."

Brooke shrugs her shoulders and says, "I understand, but, as I said, your future is equally bright. Now, ladies, we want you to get your rest so you'll be ready for tomorrow's voyage. Your transportation is waiting to take you back to the hotel."

Beki raises her hand and adds, "There's a question I'd like to discuss with Laura about some of the spacecraft changes that will need additional explanation, but I don't want to take away precious rest time from my colleagues." She turns to Lillian, Gwen, Cristina, and Vivian and says, "If you don't mind, I'll meet you back at the hotel."

The other astronauts nod their heads in agreement, and as they stand, the Supreme Highnesses make the same hand gestures they did on the astronauts' previous voyage. Their palms are facedown, just above their waists, and they lift both hands up and down four times. They turn their palms over and extend them to the astronauts, and then wave their right hands in a circle two times. But this time, they surprise the astronauts by giving each of them a nice, warm hug after their signature hand gesture. The astronauts leave the conference room, waving goodbye to Beki on their way out.

The Supreme Highnesses remain seated around the U-shaped mahogany table as Beki stands in front of the group. Edith rises and says, "Our sister, you've done us proud. We know it hasn't been easy assuming the role of an earthling. We had a rather awkward moment when you didn't appear in the medal-of-honor photo that Brooke showed to the astronauts, but she did a great job with her response to Lillian's question. And you played your role to perfection. Your sacrifice has been tremendous, and we couldn't have accomplished this mission without you. When you return to Eartha after tomorrow's voyage, you will join the sisters in training to be a future Supreme Highness. You will also join the master trainers at Eartha's Galaxy Epicenter. We used the term 'Space Center' for the American visitors' convenience."

Beki curtsies to the Supreme Highnesses and says,

"Thank you for the opportunity to lead the mission to Planet Earth. It has been one of the greatest experiences of my life, even the crazy moments when I had to pretend to learn some of their primitive methods. Can you believe they cook with an appliance they call a microwave, which is technology we phased out about a century ago? They even still use cell phones to talk to each other when they're apart. I mean, I had to act excited when a new one was launched, even though I wanted to yell out that we discarded the use of such silly devices over a century ago as well. It was laughable."

Edith smiles and takes her seat as Brooke stands and walks over to the panel that controls the projection screen. A live video appears on the screen, and it's none other than Ms. Donna Watters, the head of the National Space Center in America. The women wave to Donna, as she's known on her native planet, Eartha, and she waves back and says, "Hello, my sisters. It brings me much joy to see all of you. I know this is an opportunity to congratulate Beki on a great job as captain of a very important part of our mission on Earth and in America. She has done us proud. You'll be happy to know that the next team of astronauts, only four this time, is fully prepared for the next voyage to Eartha. They are super excited and, thanks to Beki and the other four members of her crew, eagerly awaiting their launch in about three months. Our young sister Ferol is the captain of this voyage, and she's a worthy replacement for our Beki. Ferol and Beki will spend some quality time together when Beki returns to Earth. I salute you, Beki, on behalf of our Eartha sisters across the continents on Earth. I look forward to seeing you in a few hours. Goodbye, my sisters. I can't wait come home in the not-too-distant future." The women in the room wave goodbye to Donna, and Beki yells out before she disappears from the screen, "Thank you for all your support, Donna! See you soon!"

Laura stands and tells Beki, "My sister, you still have more to accomplish in America, and we've already planned your future departure from Planet Earth. You can expect to return home within the next two months. As Donna shared, the next team of women astronauts from America is in the final stages of training, and we need your assistance in keeping them excited about Eartha and eager to make the journey here. As always, we will be with you every step of the way. Now, you'll go back to the hotel, join the others, and pretend to get some rest, which, of course, your body doesn't need. I will probably say this a dozen times and more, but thank you, Sister Beki, for your tremendous sacrifice in allowing yourself to become an emotional, less intelligent being to support our mission in America!"

Beki clasps her hands and bows to the Supreme Highnesses as she declares, "Thanks to all of you, my dear Supreme Highnesses. To serve you in this mission is an honor that I'll cherish forever. If I were on Planet Earth, I'd be in tears by now from all of your acknowledgments. You'd be surprised at how easily people there cry when they're overjoyed. I can't deny that I've really enjoyed working with the four astronauts. Fame is fleeting on Planet Earth, and I hope the visits to Eartha enable them to get some of the positions that are routinely given to males. There were a few times I wanted to zap some guys into eternal sleep, but that wasn't part of the mission."

The Supreme Highnesses laugh, and Edith says, "Sorry, Beki, no zapping guys on Earth."

Edith then announces, "Okay, ladies, tomorrow is the big day, so let's adjourn. We'll meet in the morning to send Sister Beki and our visitors back to Planet Earth."

30 The Return Voyage to Earth

The five Travelers meet in the hotel lobby early the next morning. They refrain from their usual sarcasm and cutting remarks as they mentally prepare themselves for the journey back to Earth. Mr. Smithy, ever focused on being the star of the group, finally breaks the uneasy silence by saying calmly, "Well, my fellow Travelers, looks like we're headed home today, and I can't wait to see my family. We had a rough start, but it's been my pleasure to make this trip with each of you."

Before anyone can respond, Lucy walks into the lobby and greets the Travelers. "Good morning. I hope you all rested well last night, because you have a very full day ahead of you."

The Travelers say, "Good morning" in unison, and Lucy continues, "The astronauts are already at the space center, doing all the last-minute checks on the spaceship. We'll head there now so that you can get suited up in your space gear and settled into the ship for liftoff. Your transportation is waiting out front, and I'll accompany you there. The rest of the Supreme Highnesses will be there to give you a nice send-off." Lucy turns and heads toward the front entrance, and the Travelers follow her lead.

When they arrive at the space center, the Supreme Highnesses are lined up at the terminal for the Travelers' farewell, similar to the way they greeted the Travelers when they arrived on Eartha. They wave to the Travelers as their vehicle lands. Mr. Smithy is the last person to exit and can't help himself as he says to the robot chauffeur, "Well, sir, it's been nice to see a male figure, even if you are a doggone robot."

The robot chauffeur responds in his programmed voice, "Thank you, sir. It's nice to see a human male, even if you are a doggone fool." He then closes the vehicle door and drives away.

Mr. Smithy's mouth opens wide, and his head jerks around to see if anyone else heard the conversation. While his fellow Travelers are busily receiving instructions, he can't miss the looks of utter satisfaction on the Supreme Highnesses' faces as they smile his way, raising their eyebrows.

Lucy then extends a snarky greeting: "Welcome, Mr. Smithy. It's so good to see you this morning. Thank you for your kind words to the chauffeur."

Mr. Smithy's face turns bright red as he rushes over to join the other Travelers.

As the Travelers follow the Galaxy Epicenter team to their dressing quarters, they get their first glimpse of the astronauts, already in their space suits, as they pass by on their way to a final briefing. They wave at each other, and Judge Bottomy gives the astronauts two thumbs up.

The male Travelers are directed to their dressing room,

and Ms. Harris is sent to another room. The men look around with upturned noses; even Mr. Smithy pinches his nostrils in disgust at the cramped space, which lacks the privacy that the National Space Center afforded them in America and contains only one shower. Mr. Smithy makes his usual comments about the lack of male presence as he says, "You see, guys, this wouldn't have happened if men had a more dominant presence on Eartha. We'd have a much larger dressing area, with all the amenities we'd ever need. I bet you Ms. Harris has the total opposite of this tiny space."

Judge Bottomy shakes his head and gives Mr. Smithy a look that speaks volumes about his fear of being heard by the Supreme Highnesses. Mr. Smithy gets the message and quickly says, "Of course, this space is adequate for us to change into our space suits. I really don't have any complaints; I was just wondering what might be in the space for women. I'm just saying."

Finally, Mr. Stone says, "Sometimes it's better just to be quiet."

Mr. Smithy shuts his mouth and turns his full attention to getting dressed.

On the contrary, Ms. Harris is simply amazed at the elegance of her dressing area, which contains seven rooms equipped for all of her personal needs. She could use one of seven showers if she wanted to bathe before heading to the spaceship. Instead, she quickly changes into her space suit, not wanting to miss any information or activities that her fellow Travelers might receive or experience.

After dressing, the five Travelers meet in the center lobby, where they are met by the Supreme Highnesses and escorted to one of the Galaxy Epicenter conference rooms.

As always, Edith stands and speaks to the group, which now includes the astronauts. "To our wonderful Travelers from Planet Earth, we hope you have enjoyed your visit to our planet. You are leaving something special behind with us, and we hope you're taking something special from us with you. We are truly grateful to your astronauts for their willingness to make another trip to our planet and for bringing the five of you with them. As you would say in America, we've been so blessed by your presence. We wish each of you the very best and know that you will always have a special place in our hearts. Each of you will begin amazing new chapters, and some old chapters will come to an end. The most important thing is that each of you will experience a new joy in your life from having been here. Well, I know that you're ready to make the trip back home, so we won't delay you any further."

Pastor Bendy raises his hand to speak. "Ladies, I can't leave without thanking you for your kindness and for my unique experience, which I will treasure for a lifetime. If I ever have an opportunity to return to Eartha, I will gladly make the trip. A special thank-you to April, my wonderful host. God bless you all!" He folds his hands in a prayer gesture beneath his chin and bows to the Supreme Highnesses, as they nod their acknowledgment.

Judge Bottomy quickly raises his hand and adds, "Please, I can't leave without expressing my appreciation for my life-changing experience, and, like Pastor Bendy, I would gladly accept a return visit. Thank you so much!"

Not to be outdone, Mr. Smithy raises both hands to share his parting thoughts. "I'm not good at goodbyes, but I want you ladies to know that I appreciate the hospitality you've shown to us Travelers. I will take such fond memories back to Earth with me. Thank you, thank you!"

Ms. Harris steps out from behind the male Travelers and says, "Ladies, you bring a whole new meaning to 'woman power,' and I love it! Thank you for being the most talented, powerful, and caring beings in the galaxy. I can't wait for Earth to meet you, and I hope that happens one day soon. I also thank Gail for being a fantastic host." Gail gives Ms. Harris a nod.

Before Mr. Stone can speak, the Galaxy Epicenter team enters the room to escort the astronauts and Travelers to their spaceship for the journey back to Earth and America. The Supreme Highnesses applaud as the visitors leave the conference room. At one point, Mr. Stone stops and looks back at the Supreme Highnesses, bowing to them and throwing them a kiss as he whispers, "Thank you!"

The Supreme Highnesses watch in silence as the spaceship departs with its precious cargo, heading to Planet Earth. Shortly after liftoff, another spaceship from Planet Earth makes a hard landing. Just as its occupants are suiting up to exit the spacecraft and explore the terrain, they detect a barely audible but hypnotic sound: *thump, thump-thump, thump-thump-thump.* It grows louder, until it's like iron fists banging against empty metal pots: *clang, clang-clang, CLANG-CLANG-CLANG.* The noise becomes even louder, until it sounds like a thousand sledgehammers hitting metal walls again and again: *BANG, BANG-BANG, BANG-BANG-BANG, BANG, BANG-BANG, BANG-BANG-BANG.*

The banging sounds are so loud that pressure builds up in the ears of the cabin's occupants, two astronauts and one special visitor, and the astronauts begin to feel faint, as the five female astronauts did when they first landed on Eartha. However, even as these two astronauts begin losing consciousness, the special visitor remains unaffected by the noise and mocks the plight of his companions. He curls his lip and taunts, "Wake up, you weaklings. Look at me—I'm the best space traveler in the history of space travel. You're supposed to be superior physical beings, but, just as I thought, I'm much better than you guys. And I don't believe the fake news about a Planet Eartha, because I know we've landed somewhere in New Mexico. People are always trying to trick me, especially those idiot scientists. Being a genius myself, I know that Eartha stuff is just another left-wing hoax."

The Supreme Highnesses rush to their headquarters, and Catherine is immediately appointed to lead the mission, since her special powers will be needed more than ever before to handle this incoming special visitor. Edith says to her sisters, "It was our intent not to have Earth visitors until the four astronauts had completed their training with Donna. However, we received an urgent request for help from our sources in America. We wanted a challenge from Planet Earth, my sisters, and everything we've seen and heard tells us this one will be *huge*!"

Acknowledgments

For some time, my husband, Fred, has encouraged me to write a book based on a humorous speech I gave more than three decades ago about a planet called Eartha that was ruled by women. I represented the state of Hawaii in a national Toastmasters humorous-speech contest that was held in Southern California, and my speech was titled "Heaven on Eartha." I was the only woman and the only person of color in the finals. I was also the only speaker to receive a standing ovation after my speech, but, in spite of that, came in second. The judges weren't ready to give this sister first place in a contest that white men had traditionally dominated. I thank my husband for continuously nudging me to write a book about that speech because, in his words, "Honey, I know you won that contest, and everybody else in the room knew it. Don't let them have the last word!"

As I began to write this book, I just couldn't get past the first chapter, because something was gnawing at my soul. I kept thinking about the plight of women today, especially women of color, and my heart led me away from humor. I couldn't embrace humor when we live in a world where leaders with misogynistic behavior can malign and humiliate women on a national stage, with no accountability. Young girls, more than 40 percent Black, are trafficked for the sexual pleasure of perverse individuals, with little to no accountability. The number goes as high as 90 percent in places like Los Angeles County. Black women, like Breonna Taylor and Atatiana Jefferson, are murdered in their homes and dehumanized in their nakedness, like Anjanette Young, as police invade the wrong houses, with no accountability. Former First Lady of the United States Michelle Obama was called an ape and other dehumanizing terms solely because of her Blackness, with no accountability.

It's because of the plight of women in our nation and globally that *Heaven on Eartha* is not a humorous novel but one that speaks strongly about accountability. This novel provides a reckoning for a group of individuals from Planet Earth who inflict pain and suffering on other human beings through unjust courts of law, inadequate housing, negative female imagery, human trafficking, and even the Church. The strong women who lead Planet Eartha represent women globally who fight unapologetically for equality, justice, and respect. I thank these women for their courage and for being the motivation for this work.

Thank you to the women who refuse to sell their souls for a corporate title or position, women who stand tall under attack and give voice to racial indignities, like Patrisse Cullors, Alicia Garza, and Opal Tometi, who founded the Black Lives Matter movement.

Thank you to the women of faith who not only pray for their sisters but lend a shoulder to cry on and offer encouragement and support during times of distress.

Thank you to women like Stacey Abrams, from the

state of Georgia, who took personal defeat and turned it into a battle cry for voting rights, and achieved the impossible by successfully turning a long-standing conservative red state blue.

Thank you to my diverse network of dynamic women who make the world a better place just by existing.

Special thanks to my publisher, Wheatmark, for its support in getting my third book published.

I thank my awesome editor, Annie Tucker, who has been a guiding light for this book. I could not have done this work without her support.

Most of all, I thank God for His goodness and grace and for gifting me with the will and ability to write truth in the midst of life's storms. He is the center of my joy and the source of my strength.

About the Author

Daisy M. Jenkins, Esq., is president of Daisy Jenkins and Associates and a retired human resources executive with more than forty years of experience in the defense and health care industries. She has written two previous novels, *Within the Walls: A Journey Through Sexism and Racism in Corporate America* and *The Green Machine,* which captures the devastation of the mass imprisonment of Black males. Jenkins has also published several articles in *The Root,* Ebony.com, and the *Huffington Post,* including "Pro Athletes, Big Winners and Losers When the Career Clock Goes to Zero"; "The Roberts Court Gave Affirmative Action Its Last Rites, It's Up to Us to Revive It"; "Justice Department's Anti-Smoking Efforts Exclude Black Media"; and "Teaching Black Girls to Be Beautiful." She is a woman of faith and a staunch education advocate, and she mentors diverse professionals across the country. Jenkins and her adorable husband, Fred, have been married for fifty-four years and have two sons and ten amazing grandchildren.

Made in the USA
Las Vegas, NV
16 February 2022